ANYANG FOR YOU

A SMALL TOWN ROMANCE

CLAIRE CAIN

Cover design by Jess Mastorakos - Jess@jessmastorakos.com

PRINT ISBN: 978-1-954005-72-3

EBOOK ISBN: 978-1-954005-71-6

CONTENT WARNING

Dear reader,

Anything For You is a fade-to-black small town romance. It's generally lighthearted, and includes implied intimacy, frank discussions about sex, purity culture, celibacy.

Other material covered includes main characters recalling membership in a cult, experiencing battlefield trauma and PTSD, severe depression and suicidal ideation, abuse by parents, verbal abuse by a sibling. The story also depicts kidnapping and insinuates human-trafficking.

I hope readers who find this content to be particularly sensitive can make the best decision for their health and happiness. I want you to walk away with only happy, lovely feelings, and I hope you'll feel safe proceeding with this information in mind. If you have questions or need more information, contact me at claire@clairecainwriter.com.

My very best to you,
Claire

CHAPTER ONE

Dove

Growing up in a cult masquerading as a commune teaches you things. Namely, lock picking.

Happily, I didn't have to do a whole lot to jiggle the door open. Didn't even need to enlist the bobby pin holding back the hair straggling out of my ponytail. The deadbolt hadn't been engaged, only a button-style lock that popped open with a little elbow grease and positivity.

Or maybe I'd developed Hulk-style strength and didn't realize it. Possible. I was tired enough that maybe the pure exhaustion becoming a living being in me could've been gamma radiation for all I knew.

Actually, no. I knew why I could barely keep my eyes open to drive here, and why I felt the clock ticking on my ability to stay conscious and upright. _Ten... Nine... Eight...._

I'd worked my usual shifts, picked up two at the clinic, and been the on-call nurse at Silverton Springs four nights out of the last ten. I'd slept a full six hours... last... Saturday? Maybe? Couldn't recall for sure. The one day I'd planned to take a nap in a naïve attempt to apologize to my body and give it a moment's reprieve, I'd gotten a call from the facility where my nan had recently moved asking a simple question about her medical paperwork, and my brain had latched on and spiraled into worry so effectively, I'd been wired until long after the nap window was over.

And so it goes. It happened. But right now, I needed a bed and I needed sleep, or I'd probably end up endangering myself or someone else. I'd been a good nurse for a lot of years and, if I didn't mind being a bit cocky while loopy from lack of sleep, a great one for at least the last few. Even that wouldn't keep me safe from myself right now.

Was I annoyed my key didn't work? Yes. Did I want to take time to call the landlord and meet him for keys or go figure all that out? No. Maybe a well-rested version of myself would take issue with the corner-cutting, but the absolutely spent woman stumbling toward bed in her new home embraced the logic.

With one last vestige of determination and energy, I hauled my giant Mary Poppins-style bag over my shoulder and stumbled into the home that would be my new place. I'd take time to check out the furnishings and, well, every-thing else soon.

For now, I stumbled down one hallway, spotted another, and continued my path, losing the bag from my shoulders somewhere just before I nudged open a door with light streaming in from the windows. Probably a nice view, but I only had eyes for the cozy-looking cobalt blue duvet covering at least a king-sized bed. *Hallelujah.*

I stumbled out of my shoes and socks, but abandoned any effort to change out of my scrubs. I should've. *Please forgive me, new room. I'll do better*, I promised, and collapsed onto the bed. In seconds, I found blissful, peaceful sleep.

Something tickly and... wet?... brushed across my arm and roused me from the deepest depths of sleep. I slowly came back to consciousness, feeling the heaviness in my body sinking deliciously into the mattress beneath me. Oh, and the comforter, because I hadn't even bothered to crawl underneath it. No way I'd slept all night, but maybe a few hours. I could get up, get some food, and ideally slide right back here into this pine- and laundry-scented heaven. Maybe I wasn't actually even awake—maybe this was an odd little interlude between dreams.

My ears perked when I heard the tinkling of something... a small bell?

Wait. What?

My eyes popped open and gazed up at the ceiling fan, then I scrubbed at the tiredness sinking a ten-pound weight on each orbital socket. Woof, I really should've taken out my contacts, but I'd do that in a minute.

Speaking of, I needed to move, or I'd sleep through dinner and wake up at a weird time and that wouldn't help things. I shifted, sitting up and swinging my legs over the edge of the bed.

My head snapped up when I felt more than saw a shadowy figure just feet away from me.

An absolutely huge man stood in the darkness and next to him, some kind of attack dog.

Finally, *finally*, my brain kicked in and registered this wasn't a dream, I didn't know this person, and I was in danger.

So naturally, instead of bolting from the room and booking it to my car, or grabbing my phone and dialing the police as I karate-kicked the stranger, I froze and just screamed.

As someone who loved singing and had the lungs for it, I screamed *loudly*.

Like, blood-curdling, break-the-windows screamed.

But instead of rushing me with a machete, the man in the corner crouched low and clutched his dog to him close, almost like he was restraining the beast from attacking me.

Run! Flee! Goooo!

No luck. My body was utterly failing the stress test of stranger danger in real time.

I scrambled back to the corner of the bed, effectively placing myself in the location farthest from the exit—*well done, Dove, as if you've never watched any horror movies*—and I couldn't seem to find my phone through the adrenaline-fueled panic screeching.

Now I knew very clearly the impulse was *flight* and not *fight*. Cool, but not a surprise, really.

The person was still just... there. Why wasn't he leaving? Why was he in my bedroom?

Who—

My screams cut off right in time for me to hear his words and register he wasn't restraining the dog... he was clinging to it!

"Who are you? What are you doing here?" I demanded, my pulse thready and my breaths uneven.

He released the dog, who stepped forward but sat, blue

eyes pinning me and sending a shudder of recognition through me.

Oh.

It hit right as he said it.

"I'm Dorian Forrester. I own this house. And I believe I'm your new landlord."

My mouth dropped open because *how* had I not realized *he'd* be my landlord? I mean, I knew, but I'd been led to believe I'd never see the man. I hadn't at any point in the rental process—we'd done everything over email via a rental agency and I'd picked up the keys at the Saint Security front desk. In my brain-melt of exhaustion and stress, I'd completely neglected to think about him being in my space because why would he be?

But also... how did I not recognize him? To be fair, it'd been a few months since I'd last seen him.

Still... now that he'd stepped into the light spilling in from the hallway and my contacts weren't glued to my corneas, it was clearly him.

He was tall—like, he probably had a foot on me, not that I was towering at five foot four, but he was a massive person. Probably clocked in just shy of Jude Rawlins's size. Broad shoulders and a dark beard bushy around his face and neck with longish hair under a hat on top. He wore a plaid shirt and dark utility pants like so many of the Saint Security guys... Honestly, even in the dimly lit room, I should've recognized him sooner.

But wait, that still didn't explain this. "Why are you in my bedroom?"

He exhaled, dropping his head and then finally meeting my eyes for the first time.

"Well, Ms. Jensen, this is *my* bedroom."

CHAPTER TWO

Dove

No. *No no no no no.*

This couldn't be happening.

"Your bedroom? Like, um, like the one I'm renting from you and therefore it *is* yours but it has very recently, upon the signing of the lease I emailed you yesterday, become mine, you mean?"

He grimaced, and my eyes snagged on a chest of drawers in the corner with a photo on top, one drawer slightly ajar with what looked like a single sock peeking out.

So. Yeah. Not the appearance of a furnished rental so much as a person's actual home I'd apparently invaded. Which was totally fine and not horrifying to recognize at all.

He stepped forward, over Bear's dog bed which I clearly hadn't noticed earlier either, and held out a hand to me.

And yes. I knew his dog's name. I was mildly obsessed

with his dog now that I could see him in the light and recognized his Alaskan Malamute beauty and that he was not, in fact, a vicious killer beast.

My new landlord's earnest gaze peeked out from under the brim of a well-worn hat fraying at the front edge. I'd never seen him up close enough to know what color eyes he had, but this was Dorian, or Stone, as the Saint Security team called him.

One of funny, adorable Kenny Carmichael's best friends. One of charming, gorgeous, gentle Luc's best friends. One of steady, medically brilliant Adam's best friends. I could keep going...

His beard was long and scraggly with what I'd guess was a mix of colors, looking incredibly unkempt and every bit the wild man I'd imagined him to be the few times I'd gotten a glimpse. His expression was serious, though he could've been beaming under all that facial hair for all I knew.

"I'm sorry for frightening you," he said, his voice low, even, and calm, and his hand still outstretched.

Just as I reached toward him, I saw a brief tremor before he clasped my hand in his.

"No, *I'm* sorry. I—" Horror dawned fully when I remembered the lock. "I may have broken in here."

His brows raised, though he didn't appear to be all that surprised. Clearly, he'd noticed his door was unlocked because no doubt I'd forgotten to lock it behind me.

Dangerous and *rude. What a fun combo, Dove!*

I climbed to my feet, releasing his hand like I was dropping a burning coal and standing next to him for the first time ever and feeling a shiver of... something run through me.

He wasn't just tall. He was big. I was sturdy and on the shorter end of the spectrum, but I'd been around people of all sizes. Heck, my dear friend Jess was married to a man who was six-six, and Jo had a stepbrother who was a former NFL player and similarly giant-sized.

This guy wasn't quite *that* big, but he was still the kind of tall and broad that made my heartbeat quicken.

Run away, little rabbit, before the wolf gets you.

We may say we don't judge books by covers, but it happens all the time. Before I'd had to sell them, I'd had whole shelves of books I'd bought purely based on their covers. And even though I was a trained healthcare professional with well over a decade in service to my fellow Silvertonians, I judged. It was part of the job.

Perhaps a more palatable term would be *assessed*. Especially in the ER when triaging was imperative to taking care of patients, we judged and assessed. Was he hiding something under that hat, or was it simply what he'd been wearing when he came inside to find a zonked out, misguided Goldilocks holding his bed hostage?

Couldn't get a look at his eyes, but at work, I'd look for clarity, responsive pupils if the light was right, maybe redness or focus dropping. I'd check hair for cleanliness, check skin for complexion, check the hands, fingernails, and so on.

Much of this I couldn't make out in the dim light, or maybe it was just me being unable to function in the context of such a horribly awkward moment. Also cue scratchy eyeballs and dried-out contacts.

But also, yeah, I was trespassing.

"I'm really so sorry about this. I'm so embarrassed," I admitted as heat burned into my cheeks and caused a flush, maybe even full idiopathic craniofacial erythema. Hadn't had that in a long time, but my face sure felt on fire as he stepped out of the room and picked up my bag while I slipped my feet back into my shoes.

"Bear, come." He pressed a palm over the dark green pants covering the side of his thigh. "I'll show you to your place, if you like," he said from outside the bedroom door, shifting from one foot to the other.

I was the biggest jerk on the planet, and thanks to the combination of my aforementioned exhaustion, the blush burning my face into a twin sun, and the realization that I'd just broken into my brand-new landlord's house and slept in his bed, my eyes watered.

How could he be so gracious to me right now? I'd not only broken into his home, I'd slept on his bed. Was there a place more personal in a home? No. And yet here he was, speaking with such gentleness and offering me kindness I surely didn't deserve.

Keeping my eyes down, I sniffed back the tears and grabbed my bag.

"I'm truly so sorry. I don't know how I'll make this up to you, but I'd be happy to wash your bedding or make you dinner sometime once I get groceries, or, um, brush your dog?"

I stepped out of his bedroom, but since his feet were still glued to the same place they had been seconds ago, I glanced up to see him watching me.

As soon as he saw my face, his gaze narrowed. "Are you crying?"

"No," I said, *clearly* sounding all watery and upset.

Ugh! Why did I have to cry when I was upset? Why couldn't I be like Liz and go stone-faced or pull a Jess and light up with the fiery indignation of a thousand stars?

"You are." His brow furrowed even more, amazingly,

and his words weren't exactly accusatory, maybe, but they felt that way.

"I don't mean to. But honestly, it's a weird situation, and I appreciate it's weird for you, too, but—" I swiped angrily at the tears for showing up and shoving their way into this conversation and continued. "I need to not be crying right now."

That somber face stared back at me full of what I would swear was concern if I knew the guy, but maybe it was for my mental state. Perhaps he was considering calling the police and reporting the incident, or maybe he already had?

"You don't have to apologize for crying. Your feelings are valid."

I froze, and the amazement and confusion etched into the lines of my face could've been carved into stone, they were so distinct. Oddly, my pulse ticked up, up, as my words tumbled out. "My... feelings are valid?"

He nodded slowly, just once.

"Yes."

Those eyes, still undiscernibly colored, held mine for another few seconds, and then he turned and plodded down the hallway.

Just like that, huh? This giant man validated my feelings like it's a thing people just do willy-nilly and then just... wandered off?

Was I maybe in a *Twilight Zone* version of life right now?

Bear nosed my hand as though to cue me to walk and I jumped, then relaxed into petting his head once.

"Sorry, sweet boy," I whispered, embarrassed I was still so twitchy after being the one to cause all this mess.

The dog followed his owner, and finally, my feet got the message to do the same.

Meanwhile, my heart was still standing in that hallway listening to a man I'd never spoken to before tell me my feelings were valid and marveling at how effectively he'd squelched the tears with something I'd hardly ever experienced with a man.

Acceptance.

CHAPTER THREE

Stone

She hadn't stopped talking since we'd made it into the living room, though she'd slowed down when we passed through the kitchen and she saw the two pies on the counter.

Did she like pie? It wasn't necessarily the landlord's job to know what kind of sweet tooth his tenant had. Shouldn't be thinking about that because she would live her life and I'd live mine and we wouldn't be interacting. I never would've gone ahead with this if we would.

Dr. Corrigan had encouraged me. My friends had, too. It'd made sense to rent the space once I'd redone it. I'd get a neighbor, and the person Kenny had suggested needed a good place to land. So why not my place?

Especially if we both kept to ourselves, which I'd assumed we'd do. Then I wouldn't be thinking about asinine things like what I should and shouldn't know about her.

But pie preference couldn't hurt.

"So I thought the directions were to go to the left, but honestly, I see now how wrong that was," she said at a clip I was only barely understanding, it was so fast. "Like, *obviously* that's the main house and that's my little cabin. Right? I mean, how? Except, I know how."

I didn't comment because she wasn't leaving me any time to, not that I would've.

"I've been so tired. That's the only reason this happened, and I promise you it'll never happen again. On a normal day, I would've realized it was your house."

I stopped at the top of the small set of four stairs leading to her cabin's front door.

"Perhaps when your key didn't work?" I suggested, intrigued beyond measure how the lock hadn't stopped her from coming inside.

By all accounts, this woman was a little ray of sunshine wrapped in a too-pretty bow. She was a nurse and friends with many of my friends. I'd accepted her application because this was a test for me and she needed the place, but I hadn't accepted *because* it was her.

Well, it wasn't the only reason.

"Oh, right. Yeah. Let me just..." She dug into her truly gargantuan purse, her arm disappearing completely before she held up a ring of at least a dozen keys triumphantly. "Ta-da!"

I held out a hand, welcoming her to try the lock. She fiddled with the crush of metal for a moment before finding the one she'd picked up from the front desk at Saint Security when she'd signed her lease, and sure enough, it worked.

"Ah, see! There it is," she said, flashing me a grin and then winking like we were in on the joke together. Her bright smile made creases in her cheeks and tiny lines around her eyes, though she still had a hollow look that spoke to her persisting exhaustion.

My chest seized. Bear's head slipped under my hand, and he sat. *Whoops.* Apparently, he could sense my stress. "It's alright, bud."

"Oh, this is cute."

Dove's voice came from inside, so I followed after asking Bear to wait on the porch for now. She wasn't a threat to me, and Bear was really only here to help when I was a threat to myself, anyway.

In the small living room, Dove perused the bookshelves on either side of a built-in TV nook housing a decent-sized screen.

"I can remove those if you prefer," I offered, wondering if she was irritated I'd left the books. The cabin was furnished, which she'd apparently wanted, though she did have some belongings to move in based on the stuff crammed into every nook and cranny of her small sedan where it sat in the driveway like it'd screeched to a halt about ten feet before actually parking.

Sadness peeked out those bright eyes before she tucked it away and smiled yet again. "No, that's fine. I'll enjoy being surrounded by your books."

Hmm. What an odd thing to say.

Why did I like it?

Instead of saying so, I simply nodded and showed her the kitchen. "Electric cooktop here—not glamorous, but there are no gas lines to this cabin yet."

"That's fine. I've used gas, but our old house just had electric coil burners. It was fine. I'm okay with cooking, but not gourmet or anything, so as long as I can figure out low, medium, and high on there, I'll be fine."

She ran a finger along the edge of the windowsill, then touched the light-colored drapes I'd hung.

Internally, a clock started ticking. The stress from earlier, the unexpected interaction, even though she was no threat and I even kind of liked her, sent a tightness winding around me. I'd need my own space soon.

I moved down the short hallway. "Bedroom's there. Bathroom there. That room can be used however—couch folds out into a decent bed."

I'd imagined it as an office, but more than one person had suggested the couch, and based on her response, it had been the right move.

She grinned. "That's amazing. I could have someone come stay! Thank you so much."

She clasped her hands together, and I couldn't tell whether she was about to jump or beg or pray, and I didn't want any part of any one of them, so I turned toward the front door.

"AC unit's there on the wall. Heat if you're still here in the fall, same place. You can light a fire but not in the summer, and—"

"I'm planning to be here. Should I not be? I thought this was a six-month lease to start. Is it not?" The words tumbled out at a panic-level pace.

"Right. Yes. Just meant if it's not working out, I'll let you out of the lease. But yes. You've got until December first." It had been a leap to commit to having someone else so close for that long, but Dr. Corrigan agreed I was ready.

I am ready.

I just need to go home now.

She sagged with relief and pressed a hand to her heart.

"Okay, good. I'm not moving furniture, but... I definitely need a few months before I have to do this all over again." She sniffed and swiped a finger under one eye.

I didn't know the full story there, but Kenny and Luc had made it clear she needed a break. I wasn't an altruist or a saint, but I could offer that. As long as she didn't break into my house a second time...

"I'll go. You have the number on the lease if you have issues. Just make sure you keep the lids on your trash cans and all that—the usual." Pulling the door open, I halted at the threshold, a low-level headache starting at the base of my skull, when she spoke again.

"Is it dangerous here? I know we're a ways out of town, but I didn't actually think it through, maybe? Kenny and Luc and Adam all said it was safe, and I even saw Bruce the other day and he said it was a great spot, so..." Her brows pinched in the center, and she worried her lip.

"No. Sometimes wildlife, but nothing too bad since they scent Bear and he has a mean bark. I don't leash him when he's outside, but I can if—"

"No, don't leash him on my account. I'm not scared of him."

I nodded. "Okay. Shouldn't be anyone unknown around. If you do see people, it's farmhands, but they don't usually come over this way. All vetted. All good people." And they knew to stay away from here because of me.

"Great. Awesome. Yes. Cool. Super." She pushed some stray hair behind her ears and cleared her throat. "Thank you, Dorian."

No cheery smile, no lilting laugh, no attempt to hide the exhaustion, sadness lingering at her edges, and her gratitude. Cerulean blue eyes with what might be tears gathering before she blinked them away pinned me in place, a tack through the shirt on my chest pricking at parts of me no one had touched in years.

I nodded. Exited. Closed the door behind me. Bear nosed into my side, tail wagging as he followed me down the stairs and back to the house.

Away from her. To give her space. To take my own.

To keep her safe.

CHAPTER FOUR

Dove

One week later

The professional nurse in me ran five minutes early. The slug who took over her body at the stroke of the end of my shift ran ten minutes late.

I hoped someday I could find a partner who wouldn't mind my perpetual personal tardiness. I wouldn't mind someone like the men who worked at Saint Security—strapping lads who'd served their country, then come to *my* small town to find a home and the love of their lives—particularly since all of my friends had found their own Saint man, but if I did, I'd need him to allow me the grace to run late.

Prompt in the streets, late in the sheets? Hmm, no. Not quite right. I needed a pithy slogan to sell my penchant for lateness and then maybe it'd seem cute and fun and not irritating. My nan had accepted it with as much grace as she could, though I suspected this was primarily rooted in the fact that she wasn't normally waiting on me on a schedule. I never ran late to take her to doctors' appointments or the beauty parlor, as she called it, and I tried not to tell her what time I'd come visit every few days so she wouldn't become agitated if I missed the chance.

But tonight? Yet again, my habitual lateness had me hustling into a room full of people who'd already been there long enough to circle into natural conversational groups so I had the delight and awkwardness foisted upon me to insert myself into a given bunch.

"Dove! You're here!"

Elise hugged me, and Liz, Nikki, Winnie, and Jo smiled. Catherine was notably absent tonight, her job running over again. Jess arrived with a glass of champagne she handed me, and something colorful with a little umbrella for her.

"Glad you made it. Drink up and toast to Saint!" she said, raising her drink. "And don't worry, this is a mocktail Jude made me." Her smile brightened just saying his name.

Ugh. Those two were adorable. And perfect together. I could honestly say the same for each of them.

I raised my glass, grateful to be surrounded by people I loved and celebrating a company that'd brought so many wonderful, gorgeous people into my life. "To the babes of Saint Security!"

They all laughed but followed suit, clinking glasses and taking sips.

"Looks like a full house," I said, marveling at the chockfull event space. The old mill building had been converted into one of Silver Ridge Brewery's properties and it was gorgeous. I could remember a few years back when it was only this and the restaurant a pipe dream John Wallace and Liam Morrison shared, and now look.

"So many people from town are here, plus I guess some of the overseas staff came. And hey! Jenna Halter and Jack McKean are here, too." Elise nodded toward the two A-lister stars.

"A few of our people couldn't come, but quite a few did. I haven't seen Hijack in a while, and the Washingtons are back for a minute, too," Jess said with a big smile.

"Hijack. That's intense," I said, looking around for someone who matched the name. "Though I guess Jaws isn't exactly chill," I said, winking at Nikki.

"I mean, neither is Beast," Elise said, eying Jess.

She rolled her eyes in fake exasperation. "Right? But as I've been delighted to find out, he's all bark. Well, and a little bite." She waggled her brows, then gently patted her growing belly.

Gag. But also, sigh. If someone had told me she and Beast would not only get married but get pregnant before the year was out this time last year, I would've called them absolutely insane.

Still, seeing my friend so well-loved by a man who had apparently loved her for years was a treat.

"Doc's pretty straightforward. And I love Oak—it matches Tristan perfectly," I said, nodding toward Adam, Jo's fiancé and one of the medical guys on the staff? I honestly wasn't clear what his nickname had to do with how he functioned *now*, but he'd been a medic while in the military, and I enjoyed chatting medical stuff with him. Plus, he was a wonderful partner for Jo. And Oak was Winnie's quiet, steady husband. Just thinking of how those two got together brought a smile to my face.

Well. Not so much the coercion or threats or kidnapping, but definitely the end result.

"I'm partial to a man with a sweet tooth, so I'm pretty pleased with Cookie," Elise said, eyes pinned on her boyfriend, who looked ridiculously handsome as he listened to Kenny telling a story.

Our beloved donut shop owner had absolutely ended up with the man for her, even if it'd looked a little messy getting there.

Liz started laughing, her long hair free around her shoulders and her demeanor so much lighter than I would've imagined it could be just months ago.

"I can definitely say I never imagined falling for a guy nicknamed *Barbie*, but I'm not mad about it."

Gosh, no she wasn't, and the hearts in her eyes were proof. Any day now, they'd be engaged if the way they were looking at each other was any indication.

"I like Pop the best," I said, gently nudging Jess with an elbow. Since she, too, was a Saint employee and came from the same fancy Army unit the other guys had, so she also had a nickname. "Pop" nodded to her maiden name and also her love of champagne—and thus our abiding friendship.

"There are more, right? Wilder's Saint, which is a bit obvious for my taste, and then..."

"Stone."

The named slipped out in a whisper before I knew I'd opened my mouth right as my gaze landed on the tall, dark figure settled against a wall not far from Kenny and Luc. He stood alone, beard somehow bushier than it had been a week ago, arms crossed right against his chest. The parts of his face I could see were somber, maybe even angry. He looked a little bit like a nightmare and yet...

I shucked the light jacket I'd thrown on. The sun had just started to set in the west, and I'd tossed it on because it always got a little chilly this time of night outside the cabin. Tall trees created shade in the latter half of the day and, well, I didn't need it now because all of these people had been breathing out their hot air and had effectively set me on fire.

As I struggled against the disturbingly tight cuff of my denim jacket, Elise set a hand on my wrist and helped me escape.

"You okay? I know you said you like your place but..." She trailed off, gaze following mine to the man across the room.

I shivered, then shook off the odd tractor beam pulling me toward him. This wasn't helped by the fact that my friends knew all about my first meeting with him, B&E and all.

"Yes. It's great. Maybe a touch far from town, but in some ways, that's helpful."

It forced me to stay home and rest instead of running out to the store or to pick up a coffee or pop over and see Nan an extra time or two. We'd lived ten minutes from downtown and the clinic where I'd worked most of the last ten years, and now I lived closer to twenty. Nothing tragic, but it was a change.

"I'm glad."

"I'm happy to see him here," Jess said, clearly following the path of my attention.

Nikki, Winnie, and Jo all agreed.

"He keeps to himself, right? I thought I might see him around here and there, but so far, nothing. I haven't even seen him walk his dog or... anything."

It'd been wildly lonely. Granted, that statement could apply to my entire life, but I hadn't realized how much smiling at my old neighbors on the way to the mailbox had meant to me. This probably signaled just how pathetic my life was, but to say I'd noticed the absence of any contact with neighbors since he was my only one would be putting it mildly.

"You should go say hi. Be neighborly," Jo urged.

My heart rate ticked up. "Um, yeah. You know what?" Having recently broken into the man's house, I needed to show him I was not, in fact, a nightmare.

I knocked back the rest of my champagne, sputtered a bit because it was a touch more than I'd realized, and handed it off to someone, probably Elise, who took the empty glass.

A small chorus of "go get him" and "go girl" sounded as I headed toward my new landlord. Why? Why would I approach a man who clearly did not want to interact with me since I hadn't even spied his dog since I'd moved in, let alone him?

Too late—here he was, already ahead of me.

"Hey there, neighbor," I said, slowing up as I approached.

His eyes snapped to mine, and he dipped his chin. "Hi."

"I just thought I should stop by and say hey. You know. Since I live in your cabin now."

Smooth, Dove. Super smooth.

He nodded again. "Going okay?"

I perked up. "Yeah. It's great, actually. I mean, there's this weird thing happening with the shower? When I turn on the water? But otherwise—"

"I'll come by. Let me know when."

"Oh, yeah. Okay. Thanks. Cool. Yeah." *Stop the madness!* "Thank you. I have the day off tomorrow so I'm around in the afternoon after I run some errands, if that works?"

The dip of his chin was the only answer I got. He then glanced down at his watch. "I need to go. I'll be there at noon."

He notched his chin at someone behind me and then he just... left.

Turned and walked out.

It was only after he'd walked away that I registered a few things. He'd worn subtle earplugs. He'd had his arms crossed tight over his chest—not because he was grumpy or mean, but because, if I was remembering right, he was creating pressure against himself.

It dawned on me, finally, like a cardioversion shock straight to the chest.

Stone wasn't a grumpy recluse who showed up and segregated himself just to be rude. Not that I'd ever *really* thought this, but he'd always seemed a bit off to me. The only way I'd agreed to stay living at his house was how kind he was to me after I'd screamed at him, and after I'd screamed at my friends who hadn't made it clear he was the landlord. But they'd reassured me, and their partners had all sworn on their lives he was safe.

And now, I knew he wasn't grumpy so much as he was anxious. He'd been working some serious social anxiety coping mechanisms, and yet, he'd showed up. He'd been brave in the face of a challenge that left him vulnerable. He was doing the work.

Oh, no.

No, no, no, no, no.

I didn't need this tiny little leaf unfurling like a bud opening in the spring sunshine, but there it was. The first tiny inkling of a crush.

My squishy little heart was all keyed up from seeing my friends and their partners making eyes at each other, that was all.

You wish, dreamer.

I sighed and wandered back to the table, afraid of what I might've felt as I put the pieces together.

He wasn't mean; he was overwhelmed. He wasn't taciturn so much as he was naturally quiet. And, ugh, this was the one that got me, arrowed straight to the tenderest parts of me.

He had been trying so hard to stay here in this room and support his friends, and I'd ruined it.

CHAPTER FIVE

Stone

Hands on hips, I glared at the gigantic pile of black trash bags bursting and spilling over with garbage onto the edge of my property.

"Yo, this is nasty, man. What is this?" Connor asked, cringing away from the pile we stood a full twenty feet from.

"Communes don't do this crap," Pedro said, angry with the knowledge we'd likely be the ones to have to clean this up.

"I called the sheriff out. Said he'd be here soon." I didn't want to have to involve law enforcement, but these folks were pushing me.

The northeastern line of my property abutted a commune, which had supposedly caused zero issues for the Templetons in all their years owning the place. Apparently, something changed with the commune's leadership right about the time I bought this place two and a half years ago.

Richard Templeton, the former owner, had mentioned they were peaceful and sometimes visited the farm for their homeschool's fieldtrips, which wasn't uncommon in the area, and they always brought him baked goods on their holidays. Nothing like what I'd enjoyed, especially in recent months.

It started with hearing shooting of not just a rifle for hunting, but an assault weapon. Naturally, this alarmed me since I had people working all over the property and at Christmas, I had families. When I saw someone setting up a series of targets right up against my property with no back-stop clearance, I approached and told them I didn't give my consent for them to use my land for target practice. After a bit of back and forth, they moved their setup, and I assumed the issue was handled.

Pedro reported finding what he thought were small deposits of trash here and there, but we chalked it up to teens sneaking in and leaving picnic refuse or whatever. I didn't mind people wandering around enjoying the trees as long as they were respectful. A section of fence brought down and a few trees chopped at the northeastern edge—these weren't enough to get hostile about, but it merited a conversation. And now, trash. This was the second trash dump, and about three times as much—probably a whole neighborhood's trash for a week right here in the back pasture that nestled right up to the property line we shared with Sego Lily Commune.

Connor hopped in a Gator and rumbled away to go grab some of our industrial trash containers and a few other supplies. I'd thrown a few shovels and such in the back of the farm truck but hadn't expected it to be this bad.

"I just want to get this cleaned up. It's foul," Pedro said, upper lip rightfully curling in disgust.

"Yep. Can't touch it until the sheriff comes." He'd need to see the full scope of this mess, maybe take some photos. I already had, and I'd add them to the file I kept on issues we'd had with these folks, but who knew if it'd stop them.

The sheriff's truck rumbled up the lane we used for skirting around the farm and came to a halt. He nodded at me, then grabbed his hat and slipped out, shaking his head at the pile as he settled the hat in place and approached me.

"Not great."

"Nope," I agreed.

"I'll have a talk with them, get 'em to come clean it up. If it's like last time, they won't own up to it so we won't be able to issue official warnings, but let me see what I can do."

"I appreciate it. Figure we'll go ahead and get it cleaned up, otherwise we'll be waiting days, though I'd love to offer it right back to them over the line." I tended toward the opposite of vengeance, and I could be very slow to anger or impatience, but this had frustration stirring in me. Mostly because it'd mean Pedro, Connor, and I would spend all day cleaning up this mess and we'd lose the progress we'd planned on making elsewhere on the property.

"I'd rather you not, if you can help it," Sheriff Ryan said, lips twitching to indicate he'd rather I not but he couldn't blame me if I did.

"Thanks for coming out so fast. I called it in to Whitacker, as well, but this whole section is technically yours, so you get the gig, I guess."

Since Forrester Tree Farm sat on a large swath of land that extended out from Silverton and into what was unincorporated Juniper View, the law enforcement's lines weren't entirely clear. So far, Ryan had the pleasure.

"Lucky me." He notched his chin up and stepped away to make a call, likely reporting into his station and soliciting whatever he needed.

Connor rumbled back up right as the sheriff got off the phone.

"Give me an hour before you start on this. I'll see what I can do about taking it off your list."

He held out a hand to me, and I took it. We shook hands briefly and then he moved to Pedro, then Connor.

Small gesture, but shaking my men's hands, and especially my obviously teenaged farmhand? I liked that. Every interaction with the sheriff had been like this—one in which he presented as capable, to the point, and respectful of everyone, not just the person in charge. We were in good hands.

And for now, we'd do something else until we got word on whether the Sego Lily Commune would be helping in their trash removal.

After hours of hauling and shoveling garbage into a truck, then driving it to the county dump, I tossed my gloves on the dash and got out, taking a moment to stand in the driveway and feel the soft summer breeze blow through the damp hair at my temples and neck.

In the madness of being overheated from the bright midday sun on my back while working, the truck's broken AC, the long-sleeved button-up I'd torn open and no doubt destroyed once back in my vehicle, and the frustration at how the neighbor relationship was rapidly deteriorating, I'd considered taking the pruning shears to my overgrown beard to free myself from the heat-trapping monstrosity.

But back here in this little slice of perfection where the trees provided shade and the scent of pine needles lilted on the breeze, I inhaled peace and exhaled frustration. Inhaled calm and exhaled anxiety. Inhaled safety and exhaled instability.

"Hey, uh... are you okay?"

Dove's voice startled me, and I glanced to the left, finding her where she stood on the cabin porch.

"Odd day." Not much of an explanation, but I didn't want her to think I was out here having a meltdown. Just taking a moment.

If she was going to be alarmed by me standing out here breathing for a few minutes, this setup wouldn't work.

"Sorry. Looks like you were, uh, w—" Her eyes widened, gaze dropping to my torso as I turned toward her.

I waited. Her gaze stayed glued to me for another beat, then jumped up to meet my eyes.

"Um, sorry. You're— It's just that you— You look like you were working hard today, is all. And it's hot. So you look hot. From the working. You look like you got hot working. The work is what made you hot. Well, and the air. Because it's desert, and even though we're in the mountains, it gets really hot, so you did, too, and now—"

Her hand smacked over her mouth, and she turned away for a moment.

I kept my face neutral, not wanting to betray how easily I could see she was flustered. Damn, she was cute when she started babbling. I couldn't recall anyone who did that like she did, not even Kenny. I'd rather listen to her rattle on about how hot I got working than listen to... anything Kenny had to say.

Okay, not true, but right about now, I didn't need to be thinking about anyone but her, especially since I just remembered I was supposed to help her with her shower.

"I'll run inside for a minute. Get cleaned up. I'll be over in a few."

She turned back slowly, nodding, but hand still covering her mouth.

She shouldn't feel bad. I had gotten hot. I had been working hard.

And I took a very cold shower.

CHAPTER SIX

Dove

The ways I had been awkward so far in my tenant-landlord relationship were numbering in the dozens and I hadn't even lived here for two weeks. I wondered what new embarrassment I might cause myself when he came into the house any minute now.

I scrubbed the sink in the bathroom and checked the shower. If the man was about to enter my bathroom, I wasn't about to have toothpaste remnants or a tumbleweed of hair haunting the place. I'd done enough damage with my borderline drooling.

Though honestly, could I blame me? No. No, I could not.

The thing about Dorian Forrester was, he could be a little... off. Odd, at least. Mysterious and cagey and unknowable. That was how he'd seemed to me until I'd moved in.

He was this large, imposing figure with an unruly beard and eyes I'd figured out were a shockingly light brown.

And this afternoon, he'd gotten out of his truck in a pair of filthy jeans and muddy work boots that did remarkable things for him, no hat covering damp, wild hair, and he'd just... stood in the shade with his face to the sky.

Hat and keys in one hand, forearms bared under rolled-up sleeves, he'd just stood there. Breathing.

I couldn't have said why it was compelling to see this large man take a moment for himself, but it had nicked open something in me I'd let grow hard. How often did I stop and take a breath? When was the last time I'd let myself pause, let alone be grateful and feel the breeze on my face?

And sure, maybe he was standing there cursing his enemies or manifesting billions, but my suspicion said that wasn't the case.

I figured since I was witnessing the moment, I should break it before he heard me breathing heavily and weird as I took in his quiet reflection, so I asked if he was okay. And then my brain short-circuited as I tried to say he looked hot, like temperature hot, because he turned toward me and mountain man beard be darned, *he was so flippin' hot.*

Some of his dark hair had blown over his forehead, and I could actually see his mouth was opened softly with a hint of white teeth, and then—good with a side of ness, his plaid shirt was unbuttoned and a three-inch strip of his chest and abs were showing and yes.

I would raise my hand and admit it in the courts. I was temporarily mesmerized by the sight of golden skin and intriguing ridges and even a dusting of hair between his pecs.

I'm sorry, your honor! I didn't fully realize how ridicu-

lously hot my grizzly bear of a landlord is until he teased me with this pec and ab cleavage! I cannot be blamed for my ogling because it was due to his assault with a dead-sexy weapon!

Okay, so maybe I was being dramatic, but the utter vomitorium of word salad that spewed from my mouth in the seconds after my brain whited out from his magma-hot post-work appearance absolutely required an apology. It did. And I still needed to apologize for making him leave last night. Clearly, he'd found a way to handle the crowd or circumstances or whatever had been bothering him, and my approaching with abandon had ruined that.

When a curt double-knock came at my door, I gave myself one last look and flared my eyes, pointing my rubber-gloved finger at myself in the mirror. "Keep it together, Jensen."

Tossing the gloves at the kitchen sink, I sucked in a calming breath and centered myself.

Ha, j/k, I danced around in a panic silent-screaming at myself to calm down, then swung open the door with a clownishly large smile.

"Hi. Thanks for coming. It's just through here," I said in a pitch I wasn't certain my voice had ever reached. Vocal constriction due to nervous energy, coming in hot!

He waited, evidently willing to follow me into his own cabin as though he didn't know the way. I pivoted on a heel, not ever quite letting my eyes reach his face since the whole voice and energy situation clearly indicated I'd have a blush to light a thousand fires on my hands.

I hovered at the doorway of the bathroom and flipped on the light, turning to face him. "So, the—oh! You trimmed your beard!"

His big hand reached up and scrubbed across the facial

hair remaining. It was still a full beard covering his jaw and chin, but I could see the shape of things. And... yeah. He had a nice face.

As though I needed any more assistance noticing this man's assets.

"Yeah. Gets hot this time of year and just hadn't gotten around to it, but today was too much. Had to go." He ran his hand over his head, which still had the longish strands with a slight wave and curl at the end.

Honestly, it was gorgeous hair. I couldn't say whether I'd ever thought much about a man's hair other than appreciating when it looked nice, maybe? Or that time when Jamie Morris cut off all his hair and everyone on Earth mourned the passing of his man bun? But otherwise, I'd never looked at a man's hair and wanted to touch it.

Not like now...

"Well, looks nice. You have a nice face."

His brows jumped up, then lowered. "Thank you?"

I giggled because nerves and also, was he confused? "Is that a question?"

He blinked, shaking his head. "No. It's... no."

Without any way to read his mind or expression or anything about him because I hardly knew the man, I let it go.

"Well, so, the shower..." I slipped past him, trying not to feel the sizzle from contact with his warm skin as our arms brushed. Pulling back the curtain of the tub, I flipped the water on. "Brace yourself."

I pulled the knob to start the shower, and water sprayed everywhere. Instantly, he moved to shut the water off, his hand covering mine briefly before the flow halted and he removed it.

"Sorry about that. Shouldn't take me long to fix it. Let me grab a few things and I'll be back, if you don't mind?"

"Of course. Thanks. Just come on back in whenever, no need to knock again."

Aware enough to know I'd seem like a real creep if I hovered in the doorway and watched him work, I grabbed my e-reader and snuggled into the couch. It was way too warm to have a fire, but I could see myself sitting here reading all evening come fall, and I couldn't wait for future Dove to enjoy such a simple pleasure.

He knocked, but then the door swung open and he moved through the space on fairly light feet considering the heavy-looking work boots. These must've been a different set than he'd been wearing earlier because they looked nearly pristine whereas the others appeared to have been dipped in mud.

The water in the bathroom went on, then quickly back off. I'd have liked to see what he was doing to solve the problem, but maybe I could just ask. Eventually, I'd own a home again, and when that time came, it'd be good to know more about plumbing and such.

My childhood education focused on practical and "womanly" pursuits. Plumbing wasn't part of the course, nor was anything much outside of meal prep, child-rearing, and sewing. There was a reason I would never enjoy cross-stitch or crocheting as an adult, though fortunately my interest in medicine had been allowed.

It'd been my loophole to escape the role of nanny or preschool teacher given to all the young women as though we all loved kids equally. Don't get me wrong, I loved kids, but I didn't want to spend all day every day with them. God bless the people who did, women and men... 'twasn't me.

Still, there were times when I felt the reality of not

knowing how to do things it felt like most people knew. Not so much fixing a shower, but... other things, lock picking notwithstanding. I hadn't ever pumped gas when I moved in with Nan—hadn't ever even seen someone do it. And of course, there was a long list of other gaps I suspected most people simply didn't have.

My palm rubbed circles on my sternum in an attempt to rid myself of the dull ache there. *Focus on the fireplace. Focus on the cozy couch and the giant, nice landlord fixing the problem instead of having to call someone and pay them to fix this. Focus on knowing Nan is at Silverton Springs and this is better for her. For us.*

I ran through the practice, working with every bit of me to find gratitude for the situation and not feel the gut-level sense of loss that followed me around lately.

Loss. Failure. Change.

Rude.

Honestly, just hard and rude and not thoughts I wanted to think about, so I shoved my face back into my book and tried to focus on the grumpy yet oh-so-lonely Duke begrudgingly falling for his new bride.

Try as I might, the tinkering sounds in the bathroom kept pulling my focus. Probably time to switch genres again. I loved romance, but within that larger category, there were so many different subgenres to explore. I followed where my whims took me and usually hung out in a given subgenre until I got tired of it. Looked like the months-long reign of historicals was coming to an end.

What next?

Maybe something fantasy. Fairytale retellings, maybe? A *Beauty and the Beast* vibe could do it. Or, maybe something a little less expected, like a *Little Red Riding Hood* or a Goldilocks who stumbles into a house and sleeps in her future landlord's bed?

Granted, thinking about my more than a little sexy landlord's bed after encountering the creeping growth of a crush was far from wise. But also, I *had* been in his bed. I already had. Maybe not by invitation, but—

"All set. Shouldn't be an issue again." Dorian caught my eye and tipped his chin down, not stopping until he reached the door and pulled it open, then exited.

Meanwhile, I tossed my book aside and scrambled off the couch, jogging after him in a completely normal way and not at all like I'd been thinking about his bed.

"That's awesome, thank you." Shuffling down the stairs, the ghost of Christmas idiocy came over me, and I swung my arm like I was doing an old-timey dance and asked, "What do I owe ya?" in a terrible Southern accent.

We will never know why. We must make peace with the things we cannot change.

He turned back from the truck, mercifully having missed my odd little jig to accompany the terrible accent, and shook his head. "No charge. It's covered by your rent."

Oh. Duh. Right. *One of the bonuses of being a renter!*

My hand jutted out. "Well, thank you. I appreciate it so much."

His amber eyes shifted down, and after a second of hesitation, he took my hand.

My stomach flipped, then flipped again when he lifted our joined hands up and down. Instantly releasing me, he left me to contemplate life's cruel reality of a hand now empty that'd once been held by his.

With one last little nod, he turned and trudged up the stairs. Curious little weirdo that I was, I watched him go.

Lucky I did, or I wouldn't have caught the way he shook

out the hand that'd shaken mine, then balled it into a fist before he disappeared inside.

My heart sank with a familiar embarrassment. With a hustle in my step, I jogged back inside and buried myself in my book and tried desperately to convince myself he'd made that fist because he'd enjoyed the contact and not because having me here and touching me had made his skin crawl.

CHAPTER SEVEN

Stone

Other than a wave here and there, one stop into her place to fix a faulty outlet while she was away at work, and the occasional polite acknowledgement in town on the rare occasion we were there at the same time, I hadn't seen or interacted with my new tenant.

Dove.

I'd done my level best not to think about her or worry about her either. Most of my concerns centered around the nonsense cropping up thanks to the commune and of course the excitement now that Jo and Adam had finally set the date for their wedding. This coming December, a little over a year after they got engaged, they'd tie the knot. Everyone expected them to do it sooner, but with Elizabeth coming back, Jo insisted on waiting until her sister was settled. Now that she had wrapped up everything in DC and would be home for good, Jo had wasted no time.

I wondered how Dove would feel. She struck me as the kind of person who would delight in her friends' happiness, but I knew from experience that so often, life and emotions weren't that simple. My own response was at once delighted for my friends and tinged with something hidden and aching. Maybe not a fully formed desire for the same thing for myself, but the intrepid inhale acknowledging I wanted to be capable of it.

My thoughts about Dove counted among those complex things. And when we'd shaken hands the other day, I'd felt it in my entire body. In some way, it felt like her hand slid against mine, our palms pressed together, and the world stopped turning for a breath while my mind wrapped itself around the contact.

A faint buzz had lit under the skin where we'd touched, even after letting go. The sensation had remained even after I'd clenched my fist and released it. And it was one more thing running around in my head, bringing my thoughts back to my neighbor.

Try as I might, she was often on my mind, so finding her right in front of me after days of merely *thinking* of her sent a jarring thrill through me as I eased into my parking spot between our houses.

Since I hadn't interacted with her much, I had no idea what would cause the woman to be sitting at the base of the cabin stairs with her head tucked down into her arms, but there she sat. Was she sleeping? Resting?

Far be it from me to criticize someone for wanting to simply be outside and soak up the beauty of the surroundings. I'd found and purchased this place for the express purpose of just that.

But something about her posture had me on alert as I parked and exited my truck. After my own experience with severe depression and coming back from being suicidal, I couldn't ignore the worry in my gut. So, I rounded the vehicle and approached her slowly.

When my shoe crunched against gravel, her head popped up.

My heart seized.

"What's wrong?" I asked, the sight of her red face and swollen eyes gripping me by the throat.

She spoke as she wiped her eyes with the bottom hem of her royal blue scrub top.

"Oh, um..." Shaking her head slowly, she pressed her lips together, so much so they disappeared. After a moment, she said in a grief-roughened voice, "I'm just having myself a little meltdown. Never ye mind."

Even in crisis, she was an oddball. But it wasn't enough to convince me to leave her. Knowing all too well how hard it could be to take help and solace when we needed it, I stepped closer. "May I?"

"You don't have to." She dabbed at her eyes again.

"I know."

Slowly, she looked up. I sat down, moving with purpose and caution, not wanting to do anything that might make her doubt my desire to sit right here with her.

Her brows pinched together, her chin trembling, the tears slipped out again. "I'm just sad. And so terribly lonely. And I hate myself for that because I have so much. I still have Nan and my friends. I have this place—" she gestured to the cabin behind her. "—I have so much, but I'm so, so sad and I hurt with how lonely I am."

And then, she cried. She sobbed out a gut-level grief I didn't fully understand the details of but which I knew well, folded over on herself again, letting her hands and knees muffle the sound.

Instinct sent me toward her, my hand reaching out, but I hesitated, wondering if it was okay to touch her. Would she want that? Should I ask? But as she let out all her grief and sadness, that same gut-level knowledge of what someone might need in this moment urged me forward. I'd been there, in those same trenches, and I trusted my heart. So I settled a hand on her back, fingers splayed wide, willing her to know she wasn't truly alone. Whatever pain she was feeling, she wasn't alone in it.

At times, that'd been the most overwhelming part of my depression. I'd felt certain no one understood the depth of the problem or how impossible it was for me to climb out. I'd been terrified my mind might convince me the world was better off without me.

If it hadn't been for my friends, my brothers, I wouldn't be here. They'd sat with me. At times, they'd held me. More than once, they'd fed me by hand when I was too ravaged by grief and mental illness to lift my head.

Sometimes, those days felt like a lifetime ago, and sometimes, they felt close, like something in a rearview mirror that looked far away but was still closer than it appeared.

I would never stand by and watch someone suffer because we never knew what was going on. And if my friends hadn't stepped in, if they'd left me to battle the demons that rose up unbidden for fear of overstepping, who knew where I'd be?

So with my hand on her back, she wept with a kind of agony at first, and then eventually, it softened. She sniffled and sighed between now-silent tears, then eventually sat up and scrubbed at her eyes and nose.

"Perfect day for mascara, huh?" she asked, then huffed.

My hand fell away, not wanting to linger and overstep

now that she was talking. She wouldn't want that, and now I could show her with words I was here for her.

"I'm so sorry."

I shook my head once. "Your feelings are valid, Dove. Please don't apologize to me."

Her chin wobbled again. "Okay." And then she tipped sideways and fell over so her head settled on my shoulder. "Thank you."

I tried to stay still so she wouldn't feel the jolt of shock at the movement, the utter trust in me she'd displayed with this simple lean against me. The shock waned in an instant and determination set in—I wouldn't move or do anything to disturb what little peace she might find here with me, no matter what. The stars could fall down around us and I'd stay here on the porch with her until we crumbled into dust.

She exhaled slowly, and I could feel her letting a bit more weight lean into me. On instinct, I turned my hand so my palm faced up. She must've felt my arm move a little, because she sat up and noticed my hand sitting there atop my thigh, open.

With a slow swallow, she held my gaze with her brilliant blue eyes and slipped her small hand into mine. My fingers wrapped around hers, and we sat there, hand in hand, just breathing together and sharing the moment.

After another breath, she turned back to the view of the trees and tilted her head against my shoulder again.

My mind stilled, quieted. Something in me gave way, and I breathed in the scent of her shampoo and the summery breeze. I'd stay right here as long as she needed me.

And so we sat. Together.

CHAPTER EIGHT

Dove

A thought occurred to me the other day, and I hadn't been able to shake it.

It bounced around my head during days at work, accompanying me to my visits with Nan and even slipping into bed with me each night. It swirled around in my dreams and pressed against my temples when I woke the next day.

It whispered that my neighbor, Dorian Forrester, might be the sweetest man I'd ever met.

Trick was, once I'd had the thought, I couldn't shake it. It latched on like a burr into a hank of hair and the only way to get rid of it would be to cut it out.

I didn't want to cut it out, though. I wanted to obsess over it and gather more evidence. I'd done exactly that thus far, expertly combing through every interaction I'd had with Dorian AKA Stone Forrester and finding proof to reinforce what I knew in my gut. He'd been so gracious that first night

I'd invaded his space. He'd been kind about my oddities and awkwardness, good-natured about my panting after him that day in the sun, and completely amazing when I was breaking down over... everything.

The man was a downright sweetheart, and I was doomed.

Especially when I found a small white box sitting on my welcome mat when I got home from work. I opened it to find a tiny peach pie the size of my palm topped with a dollop of what I suspected was fresh whipped cream sitting inside.

How was my desperate little heart supposed to resist peach pie, people?

Did he know what he was doing to me? He couldn't. He probably pitied me—that was it. He felt sorry for me after I'd snotted all over his shoulder while sobbing my guts out in front of him, a veritable stranger, and he'd peach-pied me.

Except not a second of our time together that day had felt pitying. The way he'd seemed to deeply understand and genuinely want to sit with me and remind me I wasn't alone in a life raft in the middle of the ocean had been the very thing that solidified my opinion of him.

He'd offered me a shoulder. Offered me a hand.

He'd been a really, really good friend to me.

And now pie.

Had I vacillated between a wild, delighted cackle upon my first bite of said pie to an ecstatic groan that led right into a horrifying burst of tears?

Indeed. Indeed, I had.

Then I'd scarfed down the rest of the utterly transcendent miniature pie, stared out the kitchen window at the field of summer wildflowers swaying in the breeze while I chewed, and vowed I'd thank him for his gift. And maybe ask him where he'd gotten it so I could buy myself a pie every few days. I'd call it a balm for my exhaustion or spinsterhood or whatever, and I'd gobble them down thrice weekly with glee.

By the time I arrived at Romance Readers Book Club, I'd shifted from weepy and amazed to determined and... contemplative? Maybe.

Probably that.

"Earth to Dove. What's going on in your head?" Jo asked, an amused smile on her face.

"Me? Oh, I'm just reminiscing on how I live next to a burly, reclusive neighbor and how he's totally different than I thought he'd be."

I slipped two appetizers onto my plate. Jo still refused to tell us who'd started supplying our book club food once a month, but whoever it was had my undying love.

"Stone? Everything okay?" Jess asked, shifting in her seat with a grimace.

She was eight and a half months pregnant and looked visibly uncomfortable. She was bearing a man named Beast's child so she'd brought this on herself, though I couldn't really blame her. Beast he may have been, but the man loved her fiercely and if someone looked at me like he did Jess, I wouldn't be able to resist. I probably wouldn't even have to have sex to get pregnant—I'd just start ovulating instantly and the animal magnetism would—

"He's a good guy. If he's a bit gruff, it's just his way," Winnie explained.

Her comment brought me back from my very weird sidebar. Hormones were a' ragin' in me.

And this is what happens when someone gives us pie.

Liz nodded. "He is fairly resistant to conversation, so far as I've found."

Catherine likely had the least interaction with him, both because she wasn't partnered off with a Saint man, and because as her business had gotten busier and expanded over the last year, she'd been less available for social functions—not that Stone showed at many of those.

"He's been great. I mean, we obviously got off on an odd foot," I said, laughing self-deprecatingly. They joined me, all of us remembering my dramatic retelling of the event via text the very night I'd moved in, after I'd nabbed a few hours of sleep. "It's mostly that I hadn't seen much of him, and then the other day, I was..."

I swallowed down the truth. They were all in the throes of wedding planning and imminent baby-birthing bliss, and I didn't want anyone worrying about me. They didn't need to.

I waved a hand in the air like whatever I was going to say didn't matter. "It was a weird day, and he was really kind."

Jess blinked. Jo smiled. Winnie full-out grinned, and everyone else leaned in, waiting for more.

"It was unexpected, but I think I'm realizing he's just a really sweet guy." It sounded so... facile. But I didn't think I'd ever interacted with anyone quite like him.

"Aw, he really is. He's been through so much. I love that he's starting to show up to stuff more, too." Jo's happiness beamed out of her, so genuine.

He'd been through a lot? I mean, duh, of course he had. He'd sat with me like he was no stranger to grief, to tears, to the desolation I'd been feeling right then. And he hadn't looked at me with pity. He'd looked at me like he knew me —that part of me, at least.

So of course he'd been through something. But why was my heart twisting in my chest, trying to wriggle free from having to face that? The man who brought me that darling little peach pie shouldn't have had to go through anything awful, ever.

"He's a lot like the hero in Josie Wade's fourth book," Catherine offered.

Liz snapped and pointed at her. "Yes. Totally. I see that."

Jo squinted. "Hmm. I can see that. I mean, I do."

From there, the conversation shifted back to our latest club selection, and soon, the dream of sitting and chatting about books with my closest friends for the evening had come to an end. We helped clean up, but eventually, Jo and Liz shooed the rest of us away, and Elise and I made up the caboose of the exiting train.

"So what really happened?" she asked, voice low enough Catherine, Nikki, and Winnie wouldn't hear. Jude had already picked Jess up at the curb minutes ago, the doll. He doted on Jess to the point he drove her a little crazy, but she deserved someone completely wrapped up in her.

"I had a bit of a spiral." She looked at me, waiting for more, and after avoiding it all evening, I let her in. "I've been lonely lately. And even though I really like the cabin, I'm kind of out there on my own. Other than occasionally seeing him and waving, I haven't interacted with Dorian much at all. We don't talk. And you know I tend to be a talker. And I've been so tired. Plus seeing Nan is stupidly bittersweet," I admitted, wiping at a tear sneaking from my eye without permission.

"I'm sorry," Elise said, and held out her arms. I walked into them, desperate for the contact and comfort. "It's a lot right now. You're handling it so well."

She squeezed me tight, then released, and I pressed my face into the sleeve of my dress in a futile attempt to stay the tears. Sometimes, I wished I could be harder, less prone to tears. But this was just me, a little watering pot.

"What can I do?" she asked, sincerity in every word.

I sniffled and then laughed. "I don't think there is anything. I've felt a little better since I had my total emotional breakdown in a stranger's arms," I said, another chagrined laugh slipping out.

"*In a stranger's arms?!* Okay, I think I need more information on that part of the event, please and thank you."

I toed the pavement with my platform sandal. "So, yeah. He came home and I was already a wreck sitting on my steps, and he just came and sat by me, and then I literally ended up crying on his shoulder." A buzz of warmth grew in my palms when I remembered. "He held my hand."

Elise blinked back at me, processing. "Luc loves him. I know he's a good man. I just... I don't even know what to say."

I shrugged a shoulder. "I don't either. It was absolutely disarming, and since then, we've not spoken. Then today, I came home to a tiny, perfect peach pie on my doorstep that had to be from him because there's no one else around. And Elise, when I say this pie was perfect..." I shook my head like I couldn't find words because I couldn't.

"Whoa. Dangerous man."

I nodded, feeling that deeply. He'd come out of nowhere with his gentleness and rampant displays of decency and then polished it off with pie. What the heck was I supposed to do with all that?

"Do you like him? Is that what this is, or...?"

Did he make me all fluttery and empty-headed half the time? Yes. Did he weirdly make me feel safe? Yes. Did he support me like we'd been friends for years, not neighbors for months?

I didn't say any of that, though. "Great question. I don't know him enough to say. But I like what I've seen. I'd like to see more. I think I'd like to be his friend. He's already been a good friend to me."

Not that my friends here weren't checking in and keeping our group chat thread going day in and day out. And Elise knew the depths of things with Nan and our sale of the house, but they all understood this was a huge change and I'd had to work more to make ends meet the Silverton Springs bill.

But Dorian had been in the middle of it with me, emotionally. He easily could've seen me crying and gone inside. Instead, he'd chosen to sit down and be there.

In my experience, this was very much not what men did. Growing up, I didn't see any man in my life over the age of about twelve cry. I was never consoled by my father, nor was my mother. In retrospect, it was cultural. Vulnerability and especially crying were deeply taboo for the men in the camp. I'd chalked it up to *emotions* being off-limits to them at one point, but in truth, it wasn't all emotions. Men could display happiness, joy, and especially anger. That was the manly one where they funneled all their discomfort or sadness or angst.

Why cry or hold someone who's grieving when you could fight someone or go boss someone around? *Or worse.*

None of the men I'd met here in Silverton were like that, thankfully, but Dorian's behavior was so foreign to me, it'd made understanding him actively challenging.

"Friends sounds nice," Elise mused aloud.

"It does. Especially since he's my only neighbor." We chuckled at the truth. "Question is, how? How do you repay someone for letting you literally cry on their shoulder?"

She tsked. "You don't repay, for one. But two... maybe

you come up with something to give him—a little token like the pie."

I hummed in response, liking the idea. I could leave him something on his doorstep and that way, he wouldn't have to see me if he didn't want to. The last thing I wanted was to invade his space.

"I think you're onto something there. Know where a gal can get a decent donut?"

CHAPTER NINE

Stone

Monday morning, I came back from making rounds on the farm to find a small, bright pink box containing two donuts inside a paper shopping bag. Next to it sat another box, this one white, holding a collection of dog biscuits I recognized as the ones Ethan Carter sold at Joe.

Unfamiliar but not unwelcome, a little laugh of wonder jumped out before I could stop it. I glanced around like I might catch her spying on me as I retrieved the items, but no sign of honey-blonde hair or glacier-blue eyes.

Pity.

Bear's collar tags clinked behind the door.

"I'm coming, buddy. Be right there," I said, pushing it open and edging past him. He must've smelled the treats or maybe he'd even caught a whiff of evidence Dove had been here, because he pranced around in a swirl like an untrained puppy.

"Simmer down, man. She brought you something, too." Granted, he might've even recognized the small white box since I'd brought them home often enough after forays into town. "Let's see what flavors Ethan has for you."

I opened the box and held it out for Bear. "Just one, okay?"

Mournful eyes ticked up to mine, then back down to the box. Up again, then back down. Ever so carefully, he dipped his muzzle into the box and edged out a single treat between his teeth. He watched me, waiting, old enough not to shake with energy but anticipation clearly buzzing around him.

I dipped my chin, and in half a heartbeat, he'd swallowed the treat.

"Good work. Now how about breakfast?"

After a few minutes, I dipped out a cup of food and slid a fried egg on top. He settled into his breakfast with his bushy tail arching high with pleasure while I washed my hands and retrieved a plate. My chest fluttered as I lifted the lid, choosing a plain glazed donut and setting it on the plate. After a prayer of thanks, I took a big bite, and while I chewed, I did what I'd wanted to do since I saw the envelope under the boxes.

The back flap hadn't been secured with adhesive, so I lifted it and slipped the small card out. A charming swirl of feminine letters spelled out thank you in bright yellow with a little blue bird perched atop the k. And inside...

Dear Mr. Forrester,

Well, that got off to a weird start, didn't it? Would I call you Mr. Forrester when I suspect, despite your substantial beard's best efforts to conceal your face, we are peers? I think I'll call you Dorian, if you don't mind. Though if you do, it'd probably be awkward to tell me so, in which case, maybe I'll just say "hey, you!" next time I see you and we'll go from there.

Anyway, this is a small note of appreciation. Thank you for your kind support the other day and for being an excellent landlord thus far. And thank you for the adorable peach pie. It was orgasmic.

And, well, I regret the word choice there, but here we are, this far into a letter and I've got to get to work, so I can't start over. Let's just call it delicious and leave it at that.

But mostly, I wanted to say if you ever need anything, I'm right next door. You know where to find me. (And I wish you would.)

Sincerely,

Dove L. Jensen, Esquire

PS. I am not actually an esquire but once I tossed in the middle initial it just felt weird, so let's pretend you didn't see that, or chalk it up to my recent mood-reading stint with historical romances.

By the time I'd read the letter a third time, Bear had curled up on his bed in the living room and I'd been smiling consistently enough to make my cheeks a little sore.

Dove's writing read just like she spoke—stream of consciousness and with a funny lilt to her words that felt both bolder than I ever expected and completely endearing. She was smart and funny and self-deprecating in the most charming way I'd ever experienced.

I didn't often instantly like people I hardly knew, but I liked her. I enjoyed being around her, and that was a supremely odd thing to think considering our longest interaction had been when she was grieving and I sat silently by.

And yet.

Her presence next door felt like the difference between coming back to a darkened home and coming back to a porch with the light left on. Even if no one was there, it felt good knowing someone had thought of it.

It was one of many reasons Dr. Corrigan was supportive of the move to become a landlord. No more being an island on my own. I could still seek solace in the farm and in my house, but I wasn't isolated. There was value in that.

And it was a small step toward... more.

Dove and I didn't interact, and yet here we were... doing just that.

I'd had an extra pie after Kenny, Cookie, and Beast came over for tea the other day, and I'd thought she could use a little something. She hadn't given me much to go on in terms of understanding why she was so upset, but everyone could use pie, right? A little something sweet didn't make anything materially better, but it didn't usually make anything worse.

And now, she'd brought me donuts. She would've had to drive to town, get them, and then bring them back. *And* she'd thought of Bear.

The letter was easily the best part. And though it'd been years since I'd handwritten much of anything except notes on recipes, later while taking Bear out and adjusting a sprinkler in the apple orchard and checking the eastern field for something Connor had mentioned, I thought about what I might say.

Then I worked on something to give her since she'd mentioned she'd be at work. I wasn't certain what time she got home, but usually by six, her little sedan rolled up to the side of the cabin. I could make something for dinner and dessert, but that might be overstepping.

Would she want a meal? Not tonight, but sometime?

Maybe I could ask her.

Probably way too much, though.

Once the hand pies were in the oven, I sat down to pen a response.

CHAPTER TEN

Dove

Nan grinned from behind her wine glass, crow's feet winging from the corners of her eyes like fireworks shooting into her hairline.

"You seem to be doing well, little Dove."

Her hand was steady as she set the glass down. Her eyes were clear, skin seemed fairly well hydrated, and even her strength had improved in the months since she'd moved in.

"I am. I like my new place, and I've been able to take a few days off lately, which has helped."

She didn't need to know I'd quit one of the jobs now that the house was sold and I could use some of the money from the sale to help pay for her housing. I didn't want to dip too far in, but my friends had sat me down a few weeks ago and begged me to ease up on myself. They'd seen the signs of burnout.

I'd made the move last week after my crying jag on the

porch steps to quit one of my part-time jobs that typically had me working nights or weekends, or both. Now I primarily worked in the clinic and occasionally took shifts at the hospital ER. I'd done a stint in palliative care and home health last year, mostly to develop my skills in those areas with an eye toward helping Nan if we never got a spot at Silverton Springs or ended up needing to turn it down due to finances.

Thankfully, here we sat with her looking healthy and eyes bright, assessing me with her sharp gaze.

"Good. You were working yourself too hard. And I'm sorry I let you." Her brow furrowed, and her lips pursed in that way that told me she was unhappy.

"It's not about permission, Nan. I'm thirty years old. I loved living with you, and I miss you a ton, but I'm so happy you're happy here." My eyes got a little glassy as I reached for her hand, which she readily took. "You are happy here, right?"

She covered my hand with both of hers. They were warm and so soft. The skin at her wrists was paper-thin and showcased the amazing collection of veins and blood vessels that kept her system going. With knobby knuckles on each finger, thumbs bent from age and arthritis, and nails painted bright magenta, these precious hands held mine, and I couldn't keep the tears at bay.

We'd had enough check-ins like this, I didn't doubt. But hearing the words again, having the reassurance that all the stress had been worth it, and everything was really as good as we'd anticipated... it eased some of the merciless ache that caught me off-guard a few times each day. The reminder I didn't have the one person who'd been my safe place when no one else was, and that someday, I wouldn't even be able to visit her, stung.

"I am so happy, little Dove. And I am so grateful to you." Tears lined her eyes, and she smiled, her face so loving and soft. "Thank you."

With a quick flick of my napkin under each eye, I beamed at her and told her what was most true. "I'm grateful to you, too, Nan."

I drove home in silence. No audiobook, no music, just the sound of the road lulling me along. If I hadn't been so sad, I might've fallen asleep. But my heart felt like it was breaking and as exhausting as it was, it kept me focused on getting home.

Once inside, I could huddle up on the couch and let it out. I could cry for what I'd lost and what I'd gained. I could cry for missing Nan and missing the rest of my family who hadn't been safe but had still been mine. I could cry because I loved my job but wanted to take a week off, and I could cry because what I wanted most in this life felt so far away right now.

The lights burned in the windows of Dorian's home. A wild thought flitted across my mind and said, "*Just go knock on his door.*" Thank goodness I had enough wherewithal not to or I'd end up crying into his shirt again.

But after trudging up the small staircase, I found another small box tucked behind the storm door. This time with a folded piece of notebook paper taped to the top.

My heart leaped as I quickly unlocked the door and hustled inside. After washing my hands, I opened the box and sighed at the delicious little creation. I didn't even need to know what was in it—I'd eat it. I didn't know where he was getting these, but I needed the name.

Flakey crust with a cinnamon-sugar dusting and what tasted like peaches again, and maybe blackberries, on the inside. *Delicious.*

I consumed the little delight in a matter of seconds and then unfolded the note with a wild little flip in my chest.

Dear Ms. Dove L. Jensen, Esq.,

I'll call you Dove if you call me Dorian.

I appreciate your note and the donuts. That is one delicacy I can't seem to replicate to my satisfaction. You've earned Bear's unending gratitude as well, though it's worth noting he's easily bought.

It's important you know you don't need to thank me for anything. You're a person. You're a paying tenant. Sometimes we all need pie.

Please enjoy this peach and blackberry hand pie. If you ever want me to show you the berry bushes, let me know.

I hope work was good and you rest well.

Sincerely,

Dorian M. Forrester

PS. Bear would like to request a visit at your earliest convenience.

I grinned to myself so hard, I nearly pulled a muscle.

He wrote back!

And he didn't seem put off by my weirdness. If anything, this felt like an open letter, one I could possibly reply again to. Why did I feel so completely charmed by his offer to show me the berry bushes?

First, obviously yes. Second, had this man picked fresh berries and then baked the little delight I'd just hoovered up in seconds by hand?

A swoon forced me to rest my elbows on the counter—or maybe that was the general exhaustion and emotions piling up again. I'd come home with every intention of sobbing into my pillow after a bowl of cereal, but here I was, smiling and glowing.

In the scheme of things, this meant nothing. Dorian—and yes, I officially had the green light for first-name basis—couldn't change my exhaustion or the bittersweet feelings churning around in me about living apart from Nan. He couldn't affect anything about how all of my friends' lives were moving on in these beautiful ways and I felt stuck.

But the man was proving to be an unanticipated bright spot. A gift.

And so, without anything to give him except my enthusiasm and friendship, I pulled out another card and set to writing.

CHAPTER ELEVEN

Stone

My heart felt so full and light, I didn't know what to do with it.

"Thanks, guys. I'm so happy, I hardly know what to do with myself. Obviously, she has to say yes, but... yeah. It'll be good." Kenny wiped his hands down his quads, then knocked back the last bit of tea in his cup. "Right?"

His gaze moved from Luc's to mine.

I nodded. "It will. She loves you."

I'd never had much experience with love until moving here and watching every one of my friends find their person. I'd seen it happen over and over again now, and so I said it with certainty.

"And she told you she was ready. She wouldn't have said it if she didn't mean it," Luc affirmed.

Kenny chuckled lightly, then let out a gusty exhale.

"Yeah. I know. Logically, I know that, but then another part of my brain is like, 'dude, she's way too good for you and this is going to crash and burn.'"

"No. Don't think like that." We'd all been in enough therapy to know focusing on the negative rarely helped.

"She'll say yes. But if you're going to do it this weekend, you better get everyone on board." Luc's admonition was wise.

Kenny had big plans for an engagement *and* impromptu wedding for him and Liz, and he'd need major reinforcements. Plus, he only had about seventy-two hours before his go time.

"You're right." His head perked up at the sound of a car out front. "Is that by any chance Dove?"

The sound of her name made a ball of warmth burst in my chest. "Likely, yes. Not many other people come out here except you guys." Occasionally Adam and every so often Beast, but he'd been doting on Jess and more anxious to be even five minutes from her now that she was in her last few weeks before the baby came.

"I'm going to go catch her and check her off my list if that's okay?" he asked me as though I was his keeper.

I shrugged. "Might as well."

We worked together to clear the low coffee table where we'd set up the plates and tea service. They always insisted on helping clean up even though I assured them I didn't mind. I looked forward to our afternoon teas, and it'd become oddly soothing not only to prepare for them, but to clean up after them.

Dr. Corrigan would say this was one of my healthy routines.

"Go on before she gets busy with something and you

interrupt her," I said, a fingernail of irritation nudging me at the thought of him getting to talk to Dove.

Not that I couldn't. Not that it was even a thing. I just... didn't want him to upset her. This was all good news, but I wondered if she'd have any complex feelings.

Maybe we could talk about that.

Or just... sit next to each other.

I'd planned to bake something particularly good on Saturday, just in case she needed to decompress. That way, she'd have something sweet to cheer her up, and I'd have the pleasure of giving her something, which would do the same for me.

"Everything okay?" Luc asked, sliding the last plate into the dishwasher as I hand-washed the bone china teapot.

"Yes. All good."

His hand on my shoulder made me freeze, then turn to find concerned gray-green eyes looking back at me.

"Really?"

My stomach clenched, bracing. I didn't begrudge him the concern or the insistence on a real answer from me. I'd relied on him and the others to force me to be honest in the past, and sometimes, I still required a bit of a push.

"I'm just thinking about how good this is. All of it. You with Elise and Kenny getting married. Adam and Jo setting a date. Jess and Beast about to have their first kid... everyone has found their person. It's good."

His furrowed brow told me what was coming before he ever said it.

"But?"

I loosed a small sigh. "Not really a but. Because it is purely good. *And* I..." What was the word? "*Je ne sais pas?*"

He huffed a laugh. "*Non. Essaie encore une fois.*"

Try again.

Wasn't that the challenge for so many parts of life?

"I started to say I'm envious, but that's such a hard, ugly term, and it doesn't mean I want any of you to give me what you have. I want you to have it. And I wonder what it would be like if I did, too. If I even can."

A sound came from the doorway, a muffled, almost agonized sound. We turned to see Kenny listening.

He rushed to me, hauling me into his arms as though he was the larger of the two of us.

"You can have whatever you want, okay?" He pulled back, his blue eyes so full of sincerity and urgency, my heart clutched. "You can find someone. I know it. And I can guarantee that person will be incredibly lucky to have you."

He cupped my face and shook, giving me a hard look until I rolled my eyes and gave him an unwilling smile.

"Thanks."

"Don't thank me. It's true. And I know that's going to be a process for you. A lot is changing and thankfully not all of us move at lightning speed like me, but it *is* a lot if we think about where we were a few years ago."

His eyes held the memories we all shared. The deployment gone wrong. Getting out of the military. Them carrying me through the darkest days of my life. Starting over here. Even the first year in Silverton when I still struggled fairly regularly. And for them? They'd struggled, too—adjusting to civilian life, making all the decisions we'd handed control over to the military for ourselves. Even being fully open to a relationship, at least for them.

I'd never been closed to it. I'd always just known it wasn't an option. At least after the deployment that literally changed my brain and ability to function.

"I know. It's a process." I patted his shoulder, and he nodded as though satisfied.

"*À demain, okay?*" Luc asked, brows raised.

"Yeah. See you tomorrow."

They left, each giving Bear his due as they walked out. From the front door, I glanced at the cabin next door, and my pulse did something weird I ignored. After Luc's and Kenny's cars were out of sight, I stood on the threshold of my home and wondered.

Would it be out of place for me to go check on Dove? Would she want that? Was it weird I was considering it given that we'd received happy news?

The questions slipped through my mind, but my feet were already moving toward her porch. I didn't know her all that well and yet I knew with certainty we didn't rely on pretense. After a knock on the door and no answer, I tried once more, and then left. Her car wasn't there, but she occasionally parked in the small garage on the far side of the cabin, so I hadn't wanted to assume.

She'd probably gone straight into town to talk with Jo and Elise or whoever else about the upcoming engagement and wedding. She had people. And... maybe she even had a person. She'd seemed so lonely, like she didn't have a partner, but maybe I'd read it wrong.

I swallowed hard at the thought.

I'd hardly interacted with her, so how could I know? It would make sense someone as sweet and lovely as she was would have a partner. She couldn't be married, and one might wonder why she was living out here with me—well, next to me—if she was in a serious relationship because if I had a woman like Dove, I'd do anything for her, including ask her to move in.

No matter. I'd see her again. I'd still make something

tasty on Saturday, and maybe she'd drop another letter by. Not that I was waiting for one or anything.

"Bear," I said, hand at my side. He trotted over and stayed in step with me.

We had things to do, and worrying about Dove Jensen's feelings about our friends' engagement wasn't one of them.

CHAPTER TWELVE

Dove

My face hurt from smiling, and my feet killed me thanks to my choice of heels for the wedding.

Liz and Kenny's wedding. _Wow._ When the man went for it, he _went for it._ I loved it for both of them. The more I got to know Liz, the more I liked her. She belonged here with us in Silverton, and she belonged with Kenny.

Also, I hadn't attended a wedding since Winnie's last year, and oh, man. To no one's surprise, I tended to be a crier at weddings. It was all just so beautiful. And of course, the best possible thing on earth was looking at the groom when everyone else looked at the bride.

Kenny had tears in his eyes, the sweet softy, and his face was basically an explosion of happiness. If a confetti cannon could be packaged into an expression, that was his face when he saw Liz at the end of the little white chapel's aisle on her dad's arm.

Their sweetness? *Ugh.* Their handwritten vows? *Ugghgh.*

That little ache in my chest I kept at bay so it wouldn't turn into a full-on blackout chasm?

All the *ughs.*

Being one of the only single people left in a group of friends who started out as all single was pretty brutal. Catherine and I were the only holdouts, and she was so consumed with building her empire, if she felt the pinch of not having someone, she didn't let on.

One of the most delightful realizations of the day was Dorian's presence. He'd stood at Kenny's side and he looked like such a proud friend. His posture had been stiff, but his eyes had been glued to his friend and though I'd only caught the tail end of it, I saw a brilliant smile on his face when Kenny scooped Liz up and jogged back down the aisle like he was stealing her away. Everyone had laughed and he had, too.

Dorian Forrester had grinned full out and it was nothing short of mortally wounding.

Shot straight to the heart.

All the ways he stayed tucked neatly into himself behind his beard and hats and brown eyes, right then it was like a spotlight shone down from heaven and the scales fell from my eyes.

No. No no no no. Not good.

Because along with the other discoveries I'd made about Dorian? This one proved deeply inconvenient.

The man was totally and completely gorgeous, and that smile drilled the truth straight into my brain.

"Having fun?"

The deep voice startled me, and I dropped a small lemon tart, mercifully catching it on the plate I held with my other hand. And because I was calm, cool, and completely collected, I turned slowly with a pleasant look on my face and not one that screamed, *Did you know you're super hot when you smile?* and said, "Hello, neighbor."

His eyes smiled this time, but the straight white teeth and general splendor stayed tucked away, thank goodness. I didn't have much of a face for lying so he'd probably see the thirst plain as day if he dared do it again.

"Did you enjoy the ceremony?" he asked, taking a plate of his own.

The small reception was being held on the cobblestone patio outside the chapel, the bulk of Silver Ridge Resort just far enough to make it feel like a cozy, sweet world of its own. With the mountains towering in the background and the late summer day glittering like it'd decided to show off just for Kenny and Liz, everything was perfect.

"Loved it." I smiled at him, then focused on the task of taking one of each of the little confections at the all-dessert spread. "I don't think I've ever disliked a wedding where both people were willingly pledging their lives to one another."

His brow dipped. "Have you attended a wedding where someone was *not* willingly taking the step?"

I froze, but restarted normal movement once my brain sent the *don't be weird!* signal. I didn't want to go there—not now. Not in the midst of this joy.

"No! No. Of course not, no. I just... It was really special and sweet. I loved it." I glanced at him sideways and he'd taken one small tart and nothing else. "You?"

He nodded but kept his eyes on the table, now serving himself some coffee. "It was great. I didn't get to stand up with Oak, so..." He swallowed, his throat bobbing. "I'm glad I could today."

A flood of epic proportions crashed down on me as I remembered him haunting the edges of Winnie and Tristan's wedding last summer. I'd wondered about him then, but I'd been paired with the charismatic super soldier Ryan West, and I hadn't given it too much more thought since he always seemed to be on the fringes.

My heart squeezed at how he'd said it—that he *didn't get to* with Oak, with Tristan, and now he did. I wanted to understand what he meant so badly, my toes curled in the evil pointy death traps that were my shoes.

"I'm glad you did, too. I know Kenny was so happy to have you with him."

I didn't even have to guess because, though it wasn't a traditional wedding or reception, Kenny had insisted on making a speech in which he thanked every single person in attendance with personal details and compliments and managed to do so in under ten minutes. Honestly, it was impressive, and hilarious and charming, just like the man himself.

Dorian had gone quiet on me, each of us moving down the table in silence. My friends were all here, everyone laughing and chatting and so happy. But I felt the pull toward this man—this giant, curious man.

"So, um, you mentioned blackberries?" I asked, squirming internally but determined to coax him out of his shell a little bit more before we parted ways. Who knew when we'd talk again after this?

"Yes. They're in the northeast corner of..." He stood there, staring at the coffee cup he'd turned over almost like he'd lost his train of thought.

I waited a few seconds, then asked, "Where are they?" as gently as I could. I didn't care about the berries so much as I wanted to urge him to talk to me.

He seemed to be struggling internally over something I couldn't figure out, but that made sense when I remembered I didn't know this man. I wanted to, that much was clear thanks to the way my mind couldn't stay away from him and I was drawn to him every time I saw him whether at our houses or out in town, but I didn't know what demons he might be wrestling as I foisted small talk on him.

"You know? Don't worry about it. I didn't mean to—"

"I'll show you. I'm sorry. Sometimes..." He exhaled, bringing his eyes up to meet mine. "Sometimes, being in groups is still pretty hard. And I think I've about hit my limit."

A vine of tenderness wrapped around my ribcage and tightened. "Understandable. This is a lot."

I glanced around, spotting Kenny and Liz on the small dance floor with Elise and Luc, Bruce and Nikki, and a handful of others while the rest of those in attendance laughed and talked. Even in the outdoor setting, the volume from the DJ and the din of conversation was actually quite loud, now that I noticed.

"You've done amazing. Go whenever you need. You know Kenny understands." I didn't know the man all that well, but I knew he cared about his friends and would never want Dorian to stay if he wasn't enjoying himself anymore.

He turned and looked toward the raucous dance floor, brow furrowed, empty coffee cup in his hand.

"Can I take this for you?" I asked, gripping the edge of the saucer and then daring to gently rest a hand on his wrist over the cuff of his shirtsleeve. He wore a pair of gray slacks and a white shirt with suspenders and a deep blue tie. He and the other groomsmen had shed their suit jackets after the ceremony.

I'd never seen him dressed like this, but he looked

dapper and yet increasingly like he was crawling out of his skin.

His gaze shifted to where my hand rested and I removed it, slow to realize the contact might've been unwelcome or could be adding to his sensory overload.

"Go ahead, Dorian. Take care of yourself."

His attention shifted back to Kenny and Liz, his expression almost barren in its dread. He'd seemed so unreadable to me in the past when I'd seen him at a distance, but right now, it was like I had some sort of inside track to his thoughts. I could swear I knew exactly what he was thinking.

"How about I let them know you're leaving?"

He swallowed hard and gave me his stunning eyes.

"Thank you, Dove." He searched my face for a beat, then released the coffee cup and saucer and stepped back. "Thank you."

I watched him walk away for a few seconds before I realized that might make this worse and instead shifted gears, burying the flutter in my belly. An unbearable affection for the man bloomed in my chest. Little vines shot up and twined around my ribs, tethering me to yet another moment when the twin desires to protect him and swoon over him took root.

But those thoughts shouldn't be my focus now, even if they kept creeping in unannounced, so I focused on the here and now. After delivering my plate of desserts and coffee to a table where I'd left my purse, I slid into the fray of dancers and shimmied up to Kenny and Liz.

"Dorian sends his love."

Kenny's eyes softened. "I'm so glad he could come today." He glanced around like he might be able to see his friend and give him a final wave, but Dorian was long gone. "I'll text him."

Relief punched through me, and my esteem of Kenny Carmichael rose another notch. "Good."

His eyes narrowed for a flash, then widened when the song switched to one he apparently loved.

"Have fun! I have some lemon tartlets waiting for me."

Kenny beamed then. "Yes! They're so good! Too bad he didn't get to see you enjoy them, but make sure to tell him you loved them, okay? Swing by tomorrow or something?"

I blinked back at the man who'd pulled Liz in for a twirl and then dipped her. My friend was giggling—yes, ex-spy and total badass woman was *giggling* with happiness as her new husband showed her his moves.

That was my cue. "Of course! Have fun!"

Back at my table, I sat down to the plate of small bites and allowed myself to fully absorb Kenny's words. It was entirely possible he meant the chef at Silver Ridge Resort. But I had the distinct feeling Kenny meant Dorian had made these desserts.

And I had the wildest burst of anticipation when I decided I would absolutely be giving my compliments to the chef before the weekend was over.

CHAPTER THIRTEEN

Dorian

The knock came early Sunday morning.

When Bear let out a cheery woof and jumped in a circle, I knew to expect someone he liked. Opening the door to find Dove standing there in an oversized T-shirt with a giant Dolly Parton face winking back at me and shorts slightly longer than the hem of the T, my heart rate picked up to a jog.

"Hey, good morning. I'm sorry to bother you, but I thought you might be an early riser, and I wanted to check in and see how you are. Not that there's anything wrong with you, you know, but just because yesterday was a lot, and I know—" A wide, pained smile stretched across her face. "Sorry. I tend to babble when I'm nervous."

I waited, not sure what to do. Invite her in? There wasn't quite a question in her speech, and suddenly, I couldn't remember what on earth to say.

She pressed her hands together and laughed, head dropping in a show of chagrin before turning those bright blue eyes of hers back on me.

"Can I start over?"

Still wordless but interested, I notched my chin down.

She bit her bottom lip lightly, then smiled genuinely before straightening her shoulders, dropping her hands to her sides, and pushing out her chest a little as she lengthened her spine, and raising her chin. "Good morning, Dorian. How are you today?"

This, I could do. "Good. You?"

She grinned. "I'm good, too." Her faced dropped, smile easing into something more thoughtful. "A little bruised up, I think."

"Are you hurt?" I asked, right as Bear finally lost his self-control and slipped past me to greet her.

She instantly dropped down to one knee to pet my giant dog.

"Oh, hello, Sir Bear. You are looking so handsome today. Have you been keeping your dad company?" She spoke so sweetly to him while her hands stroked over his head and back.

"That's what he gets paid for," I said, sounding oddly irritable.

Her face tilted up to mine with one raised brow. "And is the pay fair?"

God, she was cute. That thought wasn't helpful, and I hadn't moved past her earlier mention of pain. "Are you hurt? You said you're bruised?"

She tsked. "Well, my feet are not happy with my shoe selection from last night. But otherwise, I'm fine. I more meant..." She whispered something like "good boy" to Bear, then stood and gave me her eyes. "Emotionally bruised?"

The way she said it sounded like a question, but I understood what she meant. At least I thought I did. And though I'd never have a conversation like this with someone I didn't know out of the blue, Dove and I had shared some oddly vulnerable moments in the last few months, so this didn't seem outside of that pattern.

Stepping out onto the porch, I gestured to the swing and two large chairs. She almost skipped toward the swing.

Knew it. Don't ask me how, but I knew she'd choose the swing.

I took one of the other seats. "It's bittersweet, to say the least."

This time, her smile was more subdued. Almost pensive, she pushed back with her toes and let the swing rock her back and forth.

"I'm so happy for them. Truly just... heart bursting with joy for these dear friends."

I nodded, hearing the "but" without her having to speak it. "All that brightness can end up casting a shadow on the places that feel most tender."

Like she said, that bruised feeling.

She blinked back at me. "I thought you might get it."

I dipped my chin. I did. More and more, the strange combination of happiness for my friends and wistful longing for myself tangled inside me. I'd done a lot of work on allowing for two emotions to exist in me at the same time, and I accepted the duality applied to this situation.

"One thing my therapist talks about all the time is how we can feel more than one feeling about something. I have a personality that wants to figure out how I feel about something, address it in some way, and move on. But these last few years, I've been learning how complex and messy a lot of life is."

She continued pushing herself back and forth on the swing, still anchored by her toes, eventually finding my eyes and sending a dropping sensation straight to my gut when she held my gaze.

"What kinds of things?"

I shifted, patting Bear's head where he sat by my legs. He might like Dove, but he could tell my energy was off in some way, so he wouldn't sink down into full repose just yet.

"Biggest one is probably my time in service and something that happened there. I was in for fifteen years so it's not easy to sum up anyway, but I wanted to compartmentalize it. For some people, that means taking whatever experience or expertise or trauma or whatever you have and tucking it away into a different room or a closet where the door can close and lock. You only address those things when you choose to open the door again—if it works right. For me, the way I thought about it was like a labeling system. I could endure anything as long as I could process it and give it a label. Good. Bad. Evil. Worthy. Painful... whatever. I could make sense of whatever I needed to if I could slap a label on it and move on."

She waited, not interrupting or asking questions. Just leaving me space to talk. As chatty as she tended to be, she could be so quiet and present.

I shrugged, not embarrassed to have talked too much, but not wanting to drag this out. "Long story short, it's not that simple. And I've found I agree with the idea. Still challenging to not get frustrated when things feel conflicting, but I think it's wise to... allow it, if that even makes sense."

"It does. I mean, rude, because that's hard, but it does." She offered me a small wink, and we both chuckled.

"I think you're doing a good job," I said, wanting to give

her something. Needing to, since I could feel the way she ached, even from here.

Her lips pressed together, and she grimaced. "I don't know about that."

"You are. I don't see everything, but I saw you yesterday. You were present. You were celebrating. Having other emotions but not letting them ruin your ability to be in a moment like that? You're nailing it, Jensen."

She laughed, a genuine smile spreading wide and creasing her cheeks. "Nailing it, huh? Well, you are, too. Kenny was so happy to have you there."

I nodded. He'd sent me a text last night to say as much and I had no doubt he'd be reiterating that for a while. "Thanks for understanding when I left."

But what I really should've said was, *Thanks for knowing what I needed without me saying it. Thanks for being so observant. Thanks for being gentle with me, not making the moment harder than it already was. Thanks for taking a little of my load and telling my best friend I had to leave his wedding reception because I couldn't tolerate so much input for so long. Just... thank you.*

"Don't mention it. No big thing," she said, waving it away.

The impulse to argue and say it had been a big deal to me rose up, but I resisted. Part of accepting where I was now and where I'd come from was trying not to apologize for asking for what I needed or doing the things that allowed me to function.

Dr. Corrigan would be so proud. I'd likely tell her about this at our next session.

Wanting to get far away from my social limitations, I shifted forward and fiddled with Bear's collar so I could ask as casually as possible, "Are you free today?"

Her movements on the swing halted. "I am. What do you have in mind?"

What did I have in mind?

Strangely, my heart thudded, almost dragged in my chest. An image of my hand on her face, my thumb taking her chin and tilting her just right, just how I wanted her, then dipping to capture her mouth flashed through me.

Shock followed instantly, and I cleared my throat, scrambling for something other than relaying exactly what I'd just had in mind. "Want to pick some blackberries?"

CHAPTER FOURTEEN

Dove

A dark, purply-black berry burst on my tongue, and the sweet, woodsy flavor made me sigh and give Dorian a dreamy look.

"How do you not just stand here and eat berries all day?" I asked, plucking a few more and watching them tumble into the small container he had given me before we walked to the edge of his property where the bushes grew with abandon.

"I've spent hours picking, for sure. I'm in more danger with the nectarine trees than the berry bushes, though." He kept his focus on the dark green leaves and thorny branches of the bush in front of him.

It must've been because the veil had been torn from my face last night, but every time I glanced at him or even got very near him, my heart rate picked up. The conversation on his porch hadn't helped any.

"You have nectarines? What else do you grow? And why did I think this was only a tree farm?" I glanced around as though I'd be able to see everything he grew on the acres of land.

"Mainly trees, but Templeton had a small grove of fruit trees, a moderate apple orchard, and then I've done some planting for other things I enjoy. Mostly vegetables. I'd like—"

He cut himself off and frowned down at the berries in front of him.

"You'd like what?"

"I'd like to build a hothouse so I can grow during winter, too. Just haven't had the bandwidth so far. Maybe next summer."

I couldn't quite read his expression. He had what I thought might be embarrassment for some reason, and a fair amount of surrender that this hothouse couldn't come to be before next year.

"Is it a complex thing to build? Luis, the owner of Guac, has one in town for his avocadoes, so they must work okay around here. I have no other knowledge. But I did grow up with one near where I lived." That sounded innocuous enough, right? "It was always my favorite place to go in the winter."

"Where are you from?" he asked, reaching for a cluster of berries and pressing against a line of thorns.

"Idaho, mostly. We lived in New Mexico for a bit, but, yeah." Without explaining more about my life, which I wasn't about to do, there was nothing else to say. I liked that we were getting to know each other, but coming out of the gate with *I was raised in a cult and after it was raided in New Mexico we had to move north* just didn't suit the mood. "What about you?"

"Virginia."

"Ooh, 'Virginia is for lovers,' isn't that the state motto? I've always wanted to go there." I popped another sun-warmed berry into my mouth. *Goodness.* I'd eaten berries from the bush before, but these tasted spectacularly good.

"Never visited DC?" he asked.

"Nah. I haven't traveled much. I'm sure that seems weird for someone who I assume has been a lot of places."

My cheeks pinked. I didn't often feel like a bumpkin anymore. I'd lived some life. Heck, I had a college degree now. But I'd only taken a few trips in my life, and compared to the places this man had been, my life felt so small.

"I went a lot of places on road trips as a kid. Saw Gettysburg and the Liberty Bell. Lots of Civil War battlefields because my dad was a history buff. Basic training in Missouri, stationed in a few places before North Carolina for quite a while. And then deployments." He exhaled, shoulders rising and falling. "It's not all that glamorous."

I chuckled. "Deployments aren't glamorous? You don't say."

He slid his eyes to mine, but right as he opened his mouth, a loud buzzing sound startled us both. We turned toward the now obnoxiously loud whir of an engine, and through the trees past the berry brambles, I saw the culprits.

Dorian muttered something under his breath, eyes glued on the space where people on dirt bikes whooped and hollered as they rode what must've been a track.

"I'm guessing that's not your property?"

He shook his head, clearly annoyed.

Our peaceful chat and the pleasant morning evaporated like so much smoke thanks to the idiots on crotch rockets. *Thanks, dummies.*

"I think I've got enough berries," I said, holding my full bowl.

He scowled toward the trees, then nodded. "Let's go."

Once we walked a few minutes down the path that brought us to the berries, the engine sounds of the bikes dissipated, and his mood eased a touch.

"Did you grow up on a farm? Is that how you ended up here?" I wondered out loud, a breeze rustling through the scrub oak on either side of the trail. Every part of this place was beautiful. It had manicured and neat sections like the rows of pines that made up the Christmas tree farm part, and then there were these wild parts that felt a little closer to their owner.

"No. Average suburbia for me. But after I got out and planned to move here, I read about this place. It was for sale, and I became a little obsessed with it."

A chuckle tripped out of me. "Really? Obsessed with a tree farm?"

He let out a little huff. "Pretty weird, right?"

Why did his response make me borderline giddy? "I mean, so far, all I've seen points to total weirdo."

He gave me a side-eye, and I burst out laughing, pressing my free hand to my heart. "Said with love because you're standing next to a someone who embraces she is also a total weirdo. So hey, we make a good pair."

I bit my lip, a sense of shyness nudging my shoulders and heating my cheeks. He was quiet, not surprisingly, until we emerged from the little trail and out into the driveway our houses shared.

Or, his house, and my rented cabin.

"You think we're a good pair?" he asked, a little low and like he'd swallowed a handful of gravel before speaking.

"Of course I do. That's why I'm here," I said, cheery and bright and not letting on all the ways I thought that might be the case. Signature weirdo move, and he wasn't ready for it.

A soft, shy smile tugged at his eyes and lips, and I wished his beard were a touch shorter so I could enjoy the expression on his face. But then, that wouldn't help with the buzzing sensation that'd been twirling around like a drunken bee in my belly the entire time we'd been together this morning.

"Thanks for showing me the blackberry patch. They're delicious." I popped one more into my mouth for emphasis.

"Thanks for letting me."

Our eyes met, and the chirp of crickets and low hum from an engine somewhere out there dimmed. The rustle in the trees, the slow movement of lazy butterflies... they all stopped.

His gaze traced my face with what my brain read as tenderness. My heart flipped.

And then I panicked and stuck out my hand and said, "Put 'er there, partner."

His gaze didn't waver. He closed his hand around mine, our second-ever handshake, and I waggled our hands together like a maniac until he cracked a smile, and in an effort to pretend I didn't feel all kinds of things winging through me, I did, too.

He didn't snatch his hand away. Instead, he held tight, shaking right back, until one of those blazing smiles broke free, and my breath caught in my throat while we just kept pumping our hands up and down like absolute fools.

Finally, I started cackling and laughed, backing away as a trill of wild butterflies exploded in my chest.

"Okay. Well…" I bowed low, continuing my mind-blowing awkwardness. "Thank you for the berries. And. The, uh, handshake."

We both grinned.

My heart did something real dramatic.

And then, I turned and beelined to my cabin door.

CHAPTER FIFTEEN

Dove

Baby Jude William Rawlins was born ten days ago, and I had never felt love at first sight was real until I set my eyes on his scrunched-up face and chubby cheeks.

It didn't help that I wanted kids. I wanted several. Growing up, it'd been me and my brother against the world. At least until the influence of the elders in our small community took root.

Baby Will—as he was being called because apparently Southerners had some weird thing where they went by their middle name—was precious, and Jess was a superhero. She delivered the nine-pound-eight-ounce giant of a baby naturally with her former nemesis-turned-husband by her side.

Heroic. Truly. He was eating and sleeping and voiding as he should, and I couldn't have been a prouder adoptive auntie. I'd gone on a grocery run to get more diapers and more food in general because Jess's appetite was endless as she breastfed the little monster, and Beast was dead set on supplying her with every possible option at all meals. He was doting and obsessed with his baby and his wife and it was pure magic.

It gave me this sweet ache in my chest that was pain and pleasure at once. I'd been working to let myself enjoy both sensations. Or, if not enjoy them, then at least acknowledge and accept them.

I was deliriously happy for my dear friend who had both a devoted and wonderful husband and a precious, healthy child. I already loved her baby boy so much.

And I longed, with a ravenous kind of wanting, for the same for myself.

And that was okay.

I could want love and children for myself, want it with borderline desperation, and feel utter joy for my friends. It hurt sometimes, but I could.

When I pulled up to the Rawlins residence, a familiar truck sat in the driveway, and my pulse notched up. *Speaking of the man himself.* I wouldn't say devil because thus far, I wasn't sure I'd ever met a less devilish person than Dorian who insisted on being straightforward and kind. Yes, he was quiet and kept things close, but he was just so... him.

I knocked gently, then let myself in the front door since Jude had instructed me to do so. He could still be bossy, for which Jess apologized, but I saw it for what it was. He wanted to make sure Jess wasn't bothered and baby Will wasn't disturbed, so no doorbell and no incessant knocking.

Slipping off my shoes, I padded quietly into the house and set the bags on the counter. After washing my hands, I put away the groceries, then washed them again before entering the living room about to greet my friend, but the sight I beheld stopped me short.

Dorian sat on the ottoman of the chair where Jess had set up camp and in his arms was a snoozing baby Will. Jude sat on the coffee table nearby and spoke quietly—so much so, I couldn't quite hear it. Dorian nodded, then glanced at his friend and smiled softly before returning his gaze to the infant.

I'd seen burly men hold babies before. Around here, it was nearly impossible to avoid, especially when Wilder Saint and his brothers kept cranking out babies like they were paid bounties to do so and then all the Saint Security staff liked to parade around as if they had no clue they should be slapped on a monthly calendar as they did.

But this? This giant, rough and tumble on the outside man holding that sweet little bundle and just... looking at him?

Oh, my heart.

Jess's attention snagged on me, and she smiled.

"Hey. Thank you so much," she said, and gratefully accepted the items I passed to her, including a fresh glass of ice water and a croissant from Rise and Shine. "Stone got to see him milk-drunk," she added, grinning.

She was such a proud mama, and I couldn't help but delight in it.

"Never understood the expression until today," Dorian said, glancing up at me with the most peaceful expression I'd ever seen on his face. Almost like holding that tiny person in his arms set him at ease.

So often, men could be a little squirmy or anxious around babies. I'd seen it plenty of times in the medical setting, even with dads who'd had kids a while. If their family dynamic meant the mother did most things for the little ones, dads could find themselves easily overwhelmed. I hated to see it, but I had. And I'd grown up in a circle where that was exactly how things went. There, men had little to do with children before about five when they could help with small tasks. Even then, any actual parenting was the on the mother unless it came to discipline.

But here, men were only men if they were good to each other, to women, and to children. And being good meant being involved, understanding them, helping them, raising them, loving them no matter what.

Dorian had those qualities in spades. I honestly wouldn't have been surprised if he'd come to visit and dropped off some food since that seemed to be his mode of caring for others, and left without touching the babe. But here he was, lovingly cradling baby Will.

"Uncle Stone has a nice ring to it," Jude said, patting his friend's shoulder.

Dorian looked up, and his eyes locked with Jude's. Something weighty passed between them, and Dorian's face, completely somber and so full of significance, struck me so I looked away. It was a private moment, almost like they were reliving something in the exchange.

I wanted desperately to ask about it, and yet I held my tongue. *Maybe later*, I promised myself, and then eased into a seat on the couch.

"Your turn?" Dorian asked.

"Not unless you're ready." No part of me wanted to take baby snuggles from the man.

We sat and chatted quietly for another few minutes until a low rumble sounded and Jude beamed. "Pipes are working like a charm, and now my next mission begins."

Dorian gently handed Jude his son, then stood when Jude did and followed him out.

Jess looked starry-eyed after her husband and baby, then turned to me and sighed. "I am so tired, I can hardly think."

I patted her knee. "I can only imagine."

We talked for a few more minutes, and Jude returned with the baby, who miraculously still slept after a diaper change.

"Did Stone leave?" Jess asked, settling back into her chair with Will, then tilting up her face just in time for Jude to press a kiss to her forehead, then mouth.

"He did," he said, eyes glued to Jess's for another minute before he shifted to look at me. "Want to stay for dinner?"

My brain had caught on the fact that Dorian had left without so much as a chin nod in my direction. It felt surprisingly bad, and yet... should it? We weren't exactly best friends or anything. He was my landlord. We'd picked blackberries and exchanged a few pleasantries.

And you opened up your heart and soul to him.

Why did it bother me he hadn't said goodbye? I was probably too tender about everything these days. And maybe reading into our interactions in a way that was bound to catch up with me.

Shaking off those thoughts, I answered Jude. "No, you don't need me mooching off of you. I'll get out of your hair, but promise you'll call me if you need anything?"

"Bruce and Nikki are coming tomorrow morning with breakfast, so we won't be left solo for long," Jess said, running a hand over the downy-soft hair on Will's still-sleeping head.

"Perfect." I blew Jess and Will a kiss, then waved at Jude where he stood in the kitchen, gathering ingredients for dinner. He dipped his chin, and I slipped out the way I'd come in.

Restless, I thought about ways to approach Dorian when I got home. Should I knock on his door? Should I...

The idea clicked, and I began composing the letter in my head. Sadly, before I had the chance to deliver it, I got called into work, the group chat kept on exploding with all of us taking turns to check on our new nesting family, and thus began another gauntlet of days that quickly blurred together until I caught my first glimpse of Dorian again more than week later.

CHAPTER SIXTEEN

Dorian

I heard Kenny's voice again right as he opened my front door on his way out.

"Oh, hello there, Dove Jensen."

My insides dropped, and I hustled to the door. Who knew what else Kenny would say to the woman, and since I hadn't seen her in days, I wanted to set eyes on her.

Some part of me needed it, strangely.

"Hello to you, Kenny Carmichael and Luc... what should we call you?" Since Luc had readopted his last name once his identity came out, the question made sense. Luc murmured his response and Dove's tired eyes blinked at Luc standing next to Kenny, then shifted to meet mine. "Hi, Dorian."

A sweet, sharp jab pinched my ribs. "Did you need something?"

Kenny scowled over at me, and Luc shifted around. *Okay, so the tone wasn't right. Noted.*

Her cheeks flushed. "No. I was actually just dropping this off. Didn't mean to interrupt." She held out an envelope.

My pulse ticked up with anticipation, and I wanted Kenny and Luc to leave this instant so I could sit and read whatever it contained.

We hadn't exchanged letters since before we picked blackberries. Before I'd seen her with baby Will. Before...

Just, before.

And now, I wanted whatever words she'd give me. I'd started to crave them.

"Not interrupting. We were just on our way out! We had a *lovely* tea time, and if you haven't yet, you've gotta get Stone and Bear to have you over for tea. These boys know how to do it up right," Kenny said with a wink at Dove.

Why would he be winking at her? It was a weird impulse for a man who had a wife. I didn't like it.

I also had no plans to say anything, but I stood taller and might've been scowling now.

"Tea?" Her bright gaze landed on me right as my face was verging toward downright bothered, and she stepped back. "Sorry. I really didn't mean to pester you. Just hadn't had a chance to pop this over. And now I'm finally off work for more than twenty-four hours, so I'm going to go... not be at work." She chuckled at herself with a twinge of what sounded like embarrassment.

She turned and bounded down the stairs as Kenny and Luc both bid her adieu, then disappeared inside her house before I'd even opened my mouth. I tended to be a little slow to speak in situations like this when things were moving quickly, but I hadn't meant to be unfriendly.

Kenny folded his arms and turned to glare at me. "You have so much to work on. Like, I'm super proud of the ways you've grown the last few years, but that?"

"*C'etait une catastrophe*," Luc said, somber and concerned.

"You answered the door. She—she was hardly here. What should I have done?" I asked, mild panic creeping into my tone and around the edges of my vision.

Kenny settled a hand on my shoulder. "You looked furious."

"At you because you were being so... obvious."

His eyes widened and then his *Barbie takes over the world* smile bloomed on his face.

"I knew it." He clapped me on my shoulder again, then shook me. "You *do* like her!"

Inside my chest, tiny little caterpillars were dipping around, rolling up into cocoons and storing themselves up for a big reveal at a later date.

Luc simply grinned, eyes shifting between me and Kenny.

"I want to be her friend. I think I understand her." At least some things about her. And I thought maybe she might understand a bit about me, impossible as that sometimes seemed.

"I love it. I love this so much," Kenny started, but when he looked at me, he halted.

My frown was heavy on my face, pulling at me today and no doubt revealing too much.

"It's nothing, and I don't want her feeling pressured." The thought she'd somehow figure out I liked her, if that's indeed what this was, and would feel anything but happiness or freedom, was a sentence I didn't want completed.

"Please don't joke about this or speak about it. Please, Kenny, I'm beg—"

"I promise I won't say a word. I love you and I really like Dove, and I'd love for the two of you to click, but I'm sorry. I get that my reactions aren't always helpful." He gave me a wry grin. "I'll lock it up until there's actual reason to celebrate."

I nodded.

"But will you tell us? And let us know if there's any way we can help?"

I nodded again.

"And will you swear to allow yourself to have this, if she wants it, too? That you won't deny yourself?"

My teeth clenched, and I exhaled. Could I do that?

There were so many *ifs* involved, I wasn't sure I needed to think it through too closely, but I took a heartbeat. And then I nodded once more.

"Good. And will you—"

Luc covered Kenny's mouth with his hand and shoved him outside, both of them laughing as they stumbled onto the porch and into the driveway.

"Thank you," I said, hoping they knew I meant for coming for tea and... whatever else had just happened.

Kenny blew kisses as though to a crowd and Luc rolled his eyes and dropped into the driver's seat. Looked like they'd driven together today. When Kenny's door finally closed and they eased out of the driveway, I nearly tripped over myself as I shut everything down and hustled to the couch. Bear trotted along next to me, a spike of worry in his energy.

"It's alright, bud. I'm being an idiot." But damn if I could help the surge of excitement sending me to my favorite spot in the living room and sliding a finger under the edge of the envelope. She'd sealed it down this time.

Had she licked it?

Shut up, weirdo.

I was grinning by the time I unfolded the card.

Dear Dorian,

I'm writing this in a somewhat perturbed state. See, I saw you holding Jess's baby (adorable, btw) and we chatted a bit. And then you disappeared.

Dorian Q. Forrester, why'd you do that? Aren't we friends? Don't we say hello and goodbye?

But then, I've ended up working for seven and a half of the last eight days and I haven't seen you. And I guess I'm writing to say I'd like to, because I had a great time picking blackberries and hearing about your life and the farm. I'd like to do that again, especially if my dear neighbor covertly slides me a blackberry cobbler the next day and said cobbler sustains me for the next three days because I can look forward to it during my long shifts at a job I'm losing my passion for.

(Thank you for that, by the way. As with everything you've given me, I've never had a more delicious blackberry cobbler. I'm sorry my gratitude is coming woefully late. Also, are we going to finally acknowledge that you are the artisan of all these delicious delights? It's obvious to me now, even as much as it seems unlikely or maybe even impossible one human man could make so many things so completely perfect.)

Can we do that again? The berry adventure? I mean, no pressure, right? I don't want you to think you have to haul me around with you, but it was good for me to get out and be reminded of things other than the antiseptic world that is nursing care.

So that's all.

Have a good week.

With aspirations of friendship,

Dove L. Jensen, IV

Instantly, I wrote back.

Dear Dove,

You're a fourth now? Will you be a fifth in the next letter? I wonder. I hope I'll find out.

I'm sorry I left. I'll explain in person because it is both less compelling and more valuable to tell you face-to-face.

I'm glad you came over today, and very happy Kenny interrupted your surreptitious delivery. I'm going to invite you to tea, but I'll do that in person, too.

Do you think you'd like dinner, sometime? I could drop something by on a day when you work so you don't have to worry about cooking. I'd love to do it. It's more a favor for me than anything, should you decide to accept the offer. Just drop me a note and let me know if you have any allergies or food preferences to be aware of.

And yes, I may as well confess. I love to bake. It started as a way to learn something new at a time when I had neither appetite nor desire to learn. With growing interest came some amount of capability and now I'm a bit addicted to it, but can't eat everything I make so my newfound joy is to foist the things I make on other people.

Thanks for stopping by and for the note, and if I may be so bold, for accepting my invitation to tea.

Yours,

Dorian Q.

CHAPTER SEVENTEEN

Dove

Dorian stood on my doorstep at six o'clock that night, a few hours after I'd dropped my nerdy little letter on his doorstep just in time to be found out by his BFFs. *Rude.* But also... they'd been having tea?

Had I ever wanted something more than to have tea with Dorian and Bear? If I had, I couldn't recall what it was or when such a desire had hit me. I could practically taste it, like one of those old Listerine strips that slowly and creepily dissolved on your tongue.

"Hi."

Yes, yes, my voice had come out all breathy and high, but I'd been lounging, moving in slow motion as I'd gotten out of the shower, having dried my hair in the buff, and consequently I'd had to scramble to get clothes on before I could answer the door.

"Hi. Am I interrupting?" His gaze slid behind me.

"No. That's just an audiobook." I cringed, hoping he wouldn't hear anything too steamy because in my haste to dress, I hadn't paused it.

He did his not-quite-a-smile look and handed me an envelope.

I made no attempt to hide my pleased grin. "Why, thank you. That's quality turnaround time, there."

He dipped his head, almost like an old-timey bow.

My heart, a little Victorian-era lady complete with gown and gloved hands, swooned.

"I wanted to say I'm sorry I didn't say goodbye before I left Beast and Pop's. I struggle a bit with how long to stay and how to know when to leave. It wasn't because I didn't want to see you again..." He cleared his throat. "Anyway, I came to see if you're available tomorrow for tea. If you work, maybe another day?"

He swallowed, and I noticed he shifted his weight from one foot to the other.

Was he nervous? Was it possible I made this giant, sweet man nervous like he did me? *Cue the lady absolutely draped over a velvet settee in some ornate sitting room.*

"I'm off. *Finally.* And I would absolutely and completely and totally love to come to tea tomorrow. What time? What can I bring? What should I wear?" I held back from dancing a jig right there, though I'd never actually learned how, so probably best not to attempt and injure him or me.

"No need to bring anything or wear anything particular. Let's say three o'clock?" He stepped back, the lines around his eyes giving them a fine, soft appearance.

Good grief, he was just so... unexpected. Cute and boyish were words I never would've dreamed of associating with the man, but right now, he embodied them.

"See you then," I said, almost giggling with delight as he jogged back home, and I reluctantly turned back to my empty cabin.

Then I remembered his letter and opened it right there, gobbling down each word with a giddy feeling swooping around in my belly. He'd made everything he'd given me— of course he had, and yet knowing it for certain sent another thrill through me.

He was even a little playful. And he said he'd tell me why he disappeared, which he did before I even read the note. The man had follow-through, that was for certain!

And most of all, he'd known I'd say yes to tea… a little cocky, almost, and that shouldn't have charmed me, but it did. *"And if I may be so bold, for accepting my invitation to tea."*

Well played, Sir Dorian. Well played.

Though honestly, was there a scenario in which I didn't say yes immediately? Clearly not.

My audiobook cut off, and the too-loud ring of my phone sent me scampering for the device. Few people called me, so this had to be work or Silverton Springs.

"Unknown" flashed on the screen, and before I thought better of it and let it go to voicemail, I answered. "Hello?"

"Dove?"

I froze.

"Dove?"

My heart jumpstarted and I summoned one word. "Hawk?"

Silence practically echoed around me and I found myself leaning against the bathroom counter and staring at my own worried face in the mirror. "Hawk, is that you?"

"Yeah. It's me, Sis."

Like a shot of lightning, energy zapped through me.

"How are you? *Where* are you? Is everything okay? Did you leave—"

"I'm calling to say you need to stop acting like a slut."

A gasp caught in my throat, and I blinked like I'd been punched, my eyes watering as I whispered, "What?"

"You heard me."

And the line went dead.

I stared at the electronic block, the cold materials feeling foreign in my hand. Or maybe that was the heartbeat that'd slowly moved into my ears. Or maybe it was my brain desperately trying to process that my only living relative outside of Nan, a person I hadn't heard from in years, had just called my phone and accused me of something nonsensical, then hung up.

Sinking down to the floor with the device still in my hand, I closed my eyes and rested my forehead on my knees.

Funny how I'd thought maybe we could talk. But I wanted to talk to my brother, my friend. Yet, he'd grown into exactly the man he'd been trained to be, the way all the men from the cult came out... and certainly not someone I knew anymore. It niggled at me, this thought, but I couldn't brush away the suspicion that Hawk wasn't anything close to my beloved brother any longer.

I spent the night crying, as I tended to do when things were stressful or hard or I was exhausted, and then I made myself get up and go for a walk. It was a beautiful cool morning and the September air was lulling me into a fallish mood I couldn't help but delight in.

I was exhausted, yes. But feel that breeze!

My crap brother had proved himself to be unchanged and maybe even worse than the last time I'd heard from him? Get a load of that autumnal scent in the air.

My career felt like a dead end and I didn't know what to do about it? *I have tea with Dorian this afternoon.*

Well, okay. That last one wasn't fall's fault, but I was so grateful to have something to look forward to. Yes, we'd have book club next weekend and I'd already marked myself as completely unavailable on all of my various schedules, so I'd be there.

But tea with my mysterious and kind of cute next-door neighbor?

Why, don't mind if I do!

After my walk, I did some boring adult chores like laundry and tidying up. I'd made a habit of avoiding going into town on days off since I spent days at work in town and could easily do groceries or other errands then. The more time I spent tucked away at this little cabin in the woods, the more I wanted to be here.

Especially if I had a decent chance of running into my landlord.

By two-thirty, I was pacing around in a blue tea-length dress and flats. Wearing a dress was overkill, of course it was, but I couldn't help myself.

I tended to dress up whenever I wasn't working or truly grunge-ing at home. I loved sweatpants as much as the next girl, but I spent most of my days and sometimes my nights in scrubs, so occasionally dolling up and feeling a little more... human, or something, was key to my mental health.

My long hair was pulled back into a ponytail with a cute blue ribbon to match the dress, and I'd applied light makeup—again, just enough to make me feel like I'd done more than crawl out of bed.

Nervous energy tumbled through me as I rang his doorbell. Why did this feel like a date? It wasn't, obviously. We were becoming friends and that merited nerves, too. Totally normal to have some antsy feelings.

"Hi, welcome. Bear—" He swiped for Bear's collar, but his big beast of a dog was already out of the house and trotting around in a circle at my feet. "He loses his mind when you're here."

I bent down and told him what a good boy he was, petting his head and loving his wolfish face with that bright smile. "I don't mind being met with enthusiasm."

When I stood up, Dorian was watching with a patient, pleased expression.

"Ready to come in, or do you two need a little more time?" he asked, failing entirely to sound irritated, especially when he had a half-smile pulling at the corner of his mouth.

Straightening to my full height and with chin high, I nodded. "I'm ready if Bear is."

A breathy laugh escaped as he shook his head, then stepped back and gestured for me to enter. Bear blundered past me and trotted inside, and I followed. Dorian shut the door behind me, and I lingered in the entryway, taking in every detail.

Much like the cabin, this appeared to be clean and stylish. I could see beadboard paneling and cool tones in a dining room to the right, but when Dorian murmured, "Just through there," I followed the trail Bear had blazed into an open kitchen and living room.

"This is really nice," I said, enjoying the gray marbled countertops and stainless appliances. There was a deep farmer's sink and a butcherblock kitchen island along with a small bar. I was so flustered that very first night when I'd broken in, I hadn't appreciated how nice everything was. The living room had a warm tone to it, but everything faded when I noticed the stunning setup.

"Have a seat. I thought we'd be informal. It's what I do for the guys, if you don't mind." He waved a hand toward the coffee table where a half-dozen small plates held all manner of tiny, beautiful bites.

"This is amazing," I said, more breathless than I had been when I said hello last night. Because it was beautiful.

And I now knew he was the one who'd been sending food to our book club. And then I remembered the things I'd said about whoever was responsible for that food... Heat burned in my cheeks and I said a silent prayer. *Here's hoping Jo didn't actually tell him what I said all those months ago!*

CHAPTER EIGHTEEN

Dove

Dorian Forrester, giant tree-farming ex-special ops soldier, served me tea in a dainty bone china cup with a fine golden honeycomb pattern and little porcelain bees perched on the arch of the handle.

They were stunning. And completely unexpected.

"I wasn't sure what kind of tea you like, so I went with a classic English breakfast. I also have chamomile if you prefer decaf or something lighter." He arrived with a teapot that matched the delicate cups and all the requisite dishes for cream and sugar.

"This is so lovely. I'm a little embarrassed to say I didn't have any idea this would be so fancy," I said, heat at my cheeks.

"What did you expect?" he asked, holding aloft the teapot in question, then guiding it down low to pour the warm liquid into the cup after I whispered, "Yes, please."

"I'm not sure. I guess a less ornate setup, maybe?"

He huffed softly. "It's gotten fancier over the years."

"Years? You've been doing afternoon tea like this for years?" I lifted mini tongs and selected a perfect sugar cube. The fact that he had cubes made this even more delightful for some reason.

"Kenny started it years ago. When I was struggling, he'd come over and make me try different teas and little treats. He'd pretend he needed my help figuring out what each tea tasted like or whether to order this or that item for a meeting, but it was just an excuse to check on me." His eyes stayed on his cup where he stirred in a drop of milk.

"Check on you," I repeated, not quite a question, but feeling around in the phrase for more information.

He sighed and took a sip of tea, savoring the drink and taking his time with it. I watched his throat work to swallow and enjoyed my own tea while bracing for whatever he'd tell me. Jo and Jess had mentioned something had happened to him, and I'd also wondered.

He adjusted his big body in the seat. His knees were higher than the coffee table. The squat setup was the only thing *not* fancy about it, but somehow, it made him look even larger in this moment when his shoulders had risen toward his ears and his face had gone serious.

Was I making him uneasy? It was the last thing I wanted, to make him uncomfortable, especially in his own home, his sanctuary.

"You don't have to tell me. You've hinted at something in your past and I'd like to know you. If you're not ready for me to know whatever this is about you, that's okay."

I hoped he'd let me in sometime, but it didn't have to be right this second. It felt like I'd stripped naked in front of him more than once lately, between how we first met with me in his bed to me sobbing into his shirt, and yet I didn't feel embarrassed, and I certainly didn't want him to feel pressured.

"I don't mind telling you. It's not something I keep hidden. It's just more..." His gaze shifted around his quaint, cozy living room, then snagged on Bear, whose head had perked up like he could sense a shift in Dorian's mood. "It's more I don't want you to think of me differently, but I don't really know that that's an issue."

"Well, I can't make any promises, but I can say so far, I think of you as a bit of a mystery with serious baking and tea skills. Also, you're an excellent landlord and you appear to be a lovely dog dad and a great friend."

His light brown eyes lingered, the way they settled on mine sending a fresh trill of nerves straight to my toes. I couldn't read his expression but everything in me wished I could. So much hid behind those eyes and that beard.

"Thank you. That's very kind."

I shrugged a shoulder and reached for what I now recognized as one of Dorian's signature items—a tiny lemon tart.

As I took a bite, he spoke again.

"I was always pretty quiet. It's not unusual in the EMU —lots of people are introverts, despite what the stereotype and media depictions might make many think. Anyway, I was quiet, but after my last deployment, I started struggling hard. Things went wrong, and I had some physical therapy to do where I'd gotten injured, but I didn't address the mental health piece."

What had he seen and done? How had he been injured? I wanted every bit of detail, but I wouldn't stop him when he'd just started opening up.

I wouldn't allow myself to cry. It wasn't fair to him to

start blubbering over his moment and put myself in a position to need comforting, but my heart was already aching and I wanted to wrap him up with my whole body like an overgrown koala and just hold him.

"I got depressed and eventually, suicidal. I never attempted, but I came close. Kenny, Beast, Luc, Doc... all the guys, they were there for me."

My breathing had shallowed and I forbade my eyes from leaking out the liquid emotion rising in me. This man... this strong, beautiful man. "I'm so sorry."

He shook those words off. "I am, too. I'm sorry I put them through it, I'm sorry I put me through it. I'm sorry for the people who didn't survive that deployment and how the ripple effect of those events still impact my life and others', even today. But I'm also grateful."

I studied him, aching to understand. So much hurt, yet also so much compassion. It was a dichotomy, one I was realizing made Dorian who he was, a study in contradictions that somehow also made perfect sense. He had been in situations that demanded brutality but he was entirely gentle. He seemed so closed and withdrawn on the outside, but here he was sharing these most intimate truths.

"I struggled with why I survived and three of my teammates didn't. I struggled with how not to hate myself for things I'd done, even though when I did them, they'd been justified and part of the mission. I even started hating things about myself—my face, my chin, my size... I was just misery wrapped in anger shrouded in grief and it all added up to depression that took me years to figure out."

Realizing I'd frozen with my teacup oddly suspended, I set it down with a slight rattle. "You didn't give up."

With a small shake of his head and a grim smile, he continued. "I didn't. But it's not all tidy. I still struggle. I have to be careful with my routines and the things that help me feel good. I go to therapy, and I do what works. And I try not to fear slipping back into that place where even lifting my head to greet a friend felt like a task too great."

My heart cracked open and I stood. He rose, too, his exemplary manners on full display.

"Would it be terribly presumptuous of me to give you a hug?"

His gaze nearly burned into me as though he were looking for a reason I needed to offer him this. He would find no words from me because I didn't have them. I only knew the gut-level demand ruling me said to hug this man this instant.

When he nodded, I stepped right into his space and wrapped my arms around his solid torso, then squeezed.

His scent was pine trees and crisp air and a sweetness like honey or spun sugar and lemon. It was absolutely divine and if I had been any more lost to the moment, I might've nuzzled my face into his chest and huffed him like a scented candle.

"I'm so sorry you've had to go through that," I said into the cool fabric of his dark blue button-down.

His arms loosened, and I took the cue. Focusing on the food and table so I wouldn't tumble over it and ruin the afternoon, I settled back into my seat and thought through what else I could say.

"Still working through mild agoraphobia and ochlophobia with a side of anxiety and depression. So I'm..."

His expression darkened, and my heart stuttered, waiting for what judgment he might settle on himself. I couldn't stand the idea that he'd fault himself for the fallout of a traumatic event, or what was likely multiple events over many years.

"You're amazing. And I'm not saying that because I'm hoping for more treats on my doorstep. I'm saying it because you are. You haven't given up and you're still working toward healing, even when it's hard." My chin wobbled, the jerk, but I pressed my lips together to steady it. "I just think, not everyone keeps working. But here you are, and you've got this whole regimen of things that you know help, so you do them."

"I also live on a tree farm and only see people when I'm willing to," he mumbled, nudging a half-eaten éclair around his plate.

"Well, me, too."

His gaze flicked to mine, and he raised a brow. "Guess that's true."

"See?" I shrugged. "I'm not sure I know anyone without a little cocktail of anxieties and traumas, though I know they don't always affect people the same way. I don't mean to make light of what you've been or are currently going through. More that... you're not alone. Maybe in your unique mix of things you have to deal with, yes. Those are all yours. But in terms of being someone who's just trying to figure out how to handle what's been piled on his plate?" I reached out and touched the back of his hand with the tip of my pinky, then held his gaze with mine. "In that, you're not alone."

CHAPTER NINETEEN

Dorian

Dove's words flapped around me like mangey birds at the beach for the rest of our tea, diving and pecking at me mid-thought.

In that, you're not alone.

Even two years ago, I might've fought her on the idea. Now, there was no refuting it. And *right now*, as she threw her head back and cackled at something I'd just said—*yeah, me*—I couldn't help but acknowledge she made me feel less alone than I'd ever felt.

It was glorious.

It was also awful.

I'd never liked a woman like this—in a soul-deep kind of gnawing way that meant I had to remind myself not to stare at her pretty, heart-shaped face or those pink lips, or her bright blue eyes, and also in the sense that I wanted to gather her up in my arms and shield her from anything that might threaten this sparkle she got when she was being a little silly.

Every second spent in her vicinity was a new bridge formed between my heart and hers. I had no idea if she'd allow passage, but I wanted it.

And yet.

I'd just explained the myriad reasons any bridge-crossing would be foolish at least and cruel at worst. I'd healed enough to recognize that being with someone in a romantic capacity wasn't shackling them to me. I was doing well and knew myself and my diagnoses well enough to manage them. But someone like Dove? Someone so knitted into the fabric of her community, who worked in town and reveled in being near people and wanted to be surrounded on all sides by her family and friends?

Not quite a match made in heaven.

"You went serious on me there, Dorian Q. What's wrong?"

Her voice interrupted my brooding thoughts. "Sorry. My brain waylaid me."

Amusement twitched her lips. "Brains can be jerks sometimes."

I huffed a laugh. "Indeed, they can."

"So listen, can you confirm you're the person who's been sending in food to the Romance Readers Book Club?" Her eyes dipped to her plate, and she fiddled with a remaining piece of her slice of roasted vegetable quiche.

"I am. It wasn't a secret." *Except that you asked Jo not to tell anyone.* "Or I didn't mean for it to feel like one. More just didn't want the pressure of people knowing."

Her gaze narrowed on me, and despite the searching glance, or maybe because of it, my pulse ticked higher.

"Uh, well, yes. Yeah. That's me." Why were my cheeks hot? Why did my heart start pounding with the admission?

When I looked to Dove, her mouth was open slightly and her eyes wide.

"Did Jo happen to... convey any sentiments shared at the first one you did? Or... you know, any of the ones you've done these last few months?"

Was *she* blushing? This made no sense.

"She said everyone really loved everything. Sometimes, she's told me which things disappeared first, but... is that not true? Are people not eating the food?"

She bounced in her seat. "No! No. I mean, yes, they are eating it. *We* are eating it with gusto. I don't think I've had a single thing I didn't like and some of them were truly..." Her plush lips pressed into a thin line.

Curiosity sparked low in my gut. Something about the way she was clearly holding herself back made me feel restless.

"Truly..." I prodded.

She shook her head, finally circling her eyes back to meet mine again. A bolt of connection or familiarity or *something* struck.

"Can't actually say what I was going to say so, uh—" She glanced up to the ceiling like the answer might be written there.

The word *orgasmic* filtered through my mind and I swallowed hard. She wouldn't use that word now, of course. We were both a bit bolder in our letters. But what would she say? And did it make me pathetic for wanting whatever word she might supply? Fortunately, she saved me by speaking again.

"It was all just so good. Are you thinking about starting up a business?"

My turn to shift restlessly. I settled my saucer back on the table and plucked a few apple slices from one of the platters. "No. I don't think I'd enjoy it that way."

She nodded like this made sense. Did it? Was it foolish to go around aggressively baking just for the joy of it? Just because I liked to and other people seemed to like the literal fruits of my labor?

Her phone buzzed loudly and she jumped, then plucked it from a small purse I hadn't noticed and looked at it warily. Her shoulders slumped, and she shoved it back into her bag without answering.

"Do you need to get that?" I asked, not wanting her to miss an important call, though selfishly wanting her time and energy all to myself while she was here.

Brow furrowed, she loaded her plate with more food as she spoke. "No. No, I was afraid it was my brother again, but it wasn't, thank goodness, and anyone else can wait. But really—" She sat up and gave me a stern look. "Really, he should wait, too, right? Like, why would I answer him after what he just did?"

Admittedly, I could be a little slow with things like this. Had I missed something? Should I know who her brother was? Maybe he was some bigwig in Silverton or Salt Lake and other people would understand the reference. My tendency to stay tucked away here often resulted in me being oblivious to the goings-on of town or even society at large.

"Sorry, I'm not sure what you mean." Damn but I hated the ignorance baked into those words and the realities of my life that caused them.

Instead of looking shocked or hurt, she slapped a hand over her mouth. Her eyes flickered around, searching again for an answer, then she sighed heavily, a pained smile behind her hand as she released it.

"You wouldn't. No one would, because I don't talk about my family." She swallowed, fingers knitting together in her lap. "So, you were just so lovely and honest with me, I could reciprocate, right? I mean, you're not going to think I'm a total weirdo—well, you probably already do, so that's no harm done. And beyond that, it's reality. I can't change my past, right? So maybe the way to be honest, the way to really let someone in and deal with my loneliness and everything is to, you know, just let it out there. Right?"

Those bright eyes blinked back at me, and I hoped with everything in me I could give her the right answer. I didn't love that I'd laid out my past at her feet, but she hadn't stomped on it. She hadn't even sneered. If anything, she'd championed me.

I shifted forward, hands on my knees and just shy of touching hers. "I can say I'd like to know the truth about you. And I daresay it won't change my opinion of you."

Her eyes flashed, and for once, I thought I read what she was thinking. She wondered about those last few words —what did I think of her?

I wouldn't dream of telling her right now.

Maybe someday.

The wariness written into the rise and fall of her chest and the tightness in her cheeks and around her eyes made me want to take her hands and press kisses along her knuckles. It made me want to hold her close and promise her she'd be okay and whatever she had to tell me wouldn't change anything.

At this point, nothing could change the path I was on. Some part of me had accepted that the minute she rested her head on my shoulder weeks ago.

"I grew up in New Mexico for the most part. In a little community that had its quirks, you know? Women wore long skirts and after they were married, they covered their heads with bonnets or caps. From the outside, it might've seemed like we were Mennonite or something, except we used basic technology like cars and such. There were a few horses on the property but we had four-wheelers and dirt bikes and stuff."

She flexed her fingers into one another, then spread them wide over the skirt of her dress and a low, bitter chuckle came out as she fingered the hem of the material resting just above her bare knee.

"Guess I wear shorter dresses sometimes just for the *I'm an adult and you can't tell me what to do* flex."

When she lifted her eyes to mine again, I settled in to listen because here it came. Whatever it was, the gravity in her face said this was the crux of what she didn't want to say, but for some reason felt compelled to.

"It wasn't just a community. It was a cult. I didn't really get it because it was all I'd ever known. I thought the way they treated the girls who arrived from somewhere outside our community was normal, that they were different and had to learn to adjust to our culture, thought my mom crying all the time was normal."

She exhaled long and slow, then continued, "That place was raided, and we moved to Idaho. I guess the cult leadership had been involved in some shady dealings and the FBI thought they'd find evidence. Someone tipped us off and we all left overnight. When we settled in Idaho, things got worse."

This time, I did reach out, clasping her hand in mine. I couldn't stand the thought of her living through something like that—being in danger, and ultimately not escaping it even then.

She took hold of me, her grip firm and unrelenting.

"Long story short, my parents passed when I was twelve and my brother was fourteen. He had some issues, and by the time he was free, he was old enough to be on his own. The community kept me close until I finally got through to one of the younger women who notified my only remaining relative. When I was fifteen, I came to live with my grandma here, but by then, my brother had opted out. He's been all over, and I only hear from him every so often. It'd been three years until a few hours ago when he called and told me to stop being a slut."

I jolted at the foul word like I'd been shot, and she held on to my hand tighter.

It'd been a long time since I'd felt this kind of vicious desire to harm someone. I would only need a little information, and I could find him. I could make this, at least, a little better for her.

After a slow, calming breath in, I spoke in a low, rage-roughened voice. "What is his name? Where does he live?"

CHAPTER TWENTY

Dove

Well, hello, angel of darkness Dorian.

Call me a simpleton, but having a man wanting to defend my honor was more than a little hot. Especially with his large, warm hand steadying me and his general existence calling to me more and more.

"His name is Hawk, and while I love that you would ask that, I have no idea. I also don't think it's worth worrying about. He has clearly been drinking some new cult's Kool-Aid and that means I won't be able to reconnect with him."

As much as that set my heart to aching, this had happened before.

"Sometimes, he'll pop up like this and say horrible things. Other times, he'll be penitent, asking for forgiveness and full of regrets. I never know which version of him I'll get, and Nan has helped me work through it a bit. I guess I've accepted I can't change him, at least for the most part."

I still hoped he would change. I couldn't imagine ever giving up on that hope.

"Nan is your grandmother? Was she involved in the cult?"

His posture had relaxed, and Bear, whose head had popped up to surveil the situation when Dorian's low rumble had come out asking for Hawk's name, had snuggled back down to rest on his paws.

"She wasn't. Apparently, she tried to get my mom to leave and one time when my mom and I went to visit her when I was about seven, she'd actually tried to get us out but..." I shook my head.

How Nan had wept when she'd told me about it, ugh. Even the memory of her retelling the events was brutal. I couldn't imagine what it'd been like for her to see her only daughter dragged back to a world where she was mistreated and her children set on a course to face the same.

"I'm sorry, Dove."

I'd noticed Dorian's voice before, but today, something about it was sending a low-level hum through me every time he spoke. Saying my name?

Cue the urge to curl up and roll around in it.

"Thanks. I'm mostly a fully functioning human being. I've figured out how to have friends and live in a normal community. I even went to college and have had a good life, overall. But there are some things I missed, and I just don't know if I'll ever catch up."

"Like what?" he asked, squeezing my hand once and releasing me, then picking up the teapot, waiting for my wordless reply.

Once I nodded, he poured more tea into my tiny beehive cup, and I sipped a drink, nerves rioting in my belly at the thought of telling him.

Like dating. Like falling in love. Like understanding men. Like sex.

No. I could not possibly say those things. Not like that, anyway.

"Well, I've never really dated. I think seeing how relationships went in my early teen years kind of messed me up, not to mention losing my parents." I didn't want to talk about how. "Feels like I have some broken pieces and I'm not sure how they fit back together."

He seemed to sense I didn't want to be more specific, holding up his cup until I joined him. His gaze, a weighty, almost palpably heavy thing, settled on mine.

"To your broken pieces. Every bit of you is beautiful and worthy of love."

He dipped his head and took a sip while I sat frozen, utterly skewered by the toast. After a second, feeling the deluge coming, I sniffled. Who had ever so plainly and fully accepted me? Who had ever been so completely lovely and thoughtful? My friends did, I knew this, but it'd happened bit by bit. It felt like this man had appeared in my life and made it his job to show me what love looked like. Not that he loved me, but just that he knew so clearly how to express the right thing.

I cleared my throat, and guzzled down the still-hot tea, eyes slipping around the room to avoid landing back on his, even though that was where they ended up.

Brow furrowed, he watched me. My lips contorted, pressing together and tucking between my teeth like this had a hope of stopping the tears already lining my eyes. Shaking my head, I closed my eyes, sending tears down my cheeks before I opened again.

"Thank you." It was only a whisper, but I meant it with my whole heart.

Slowly, so, so slowly, he reached out and slipped his roughened palm against my cheek. His thumb arced across my skin, wiping away the tears and their tracks, so much tenderness in his gaze as he did, it almost made me start crying again.

What is happening to me?

I startled when a gust of breath warmed my arm at my elbow, then melted at the sight of Bear at my side, worry scribbled across his brows. Dorian's hand withdrew, and I swiped at my other cheek, then indulged in wrapping my arms around Bear's regal shoulders as he sat next to my legs.

"I think this boy may be the sweetest I've ever met," I said, sliding a hand along his back.

Somehow, he smelled lemony and clean. I wondered how often Dorian bathed him considering he was a farm dog who ran around with his owner in the day-to-day business of the place.

"He's a lover, that's for sure. He's actually my ESA," he said, expression soft as he watched me stroke my fingers over his dog's head.

"Emotional support animal? That's amazing." I pet along the sides of Bear's face. "What a good boy to be so sweet and a helper. You're such a good boy." I'd devolved into my *talks to animals* voice, and Bear's feathery tail waggled with pleasure.

After a big inhale, I dropped a kiss to Bear's head and stood. "Mind if I wash my hands?"

Dorian hustled over, guiding me to the kitchen sink. I admired the tiles and backsplash, the painted cabinets and the overall quaint yet polished feel. We returned to the living room and talked about lighter fare—his favorite things to bake, my favorite book club reads so far this year, and as we piled plates and platters back into the kitchen despite his protests against me helping, what I liked best about Silverton.

"That's easy. First, the people, then the mountains. And these last few years, I'm very grateful to a few strapping lads who decided to open up a new security company and bring in so many amazing people." Good grief, I was a cheeseball, but it was true.

Wilder Saint and Bruce Camden's choice to settle here in Silverton meant they came here, but so did Tristan, who brought Winnie. So did Adam, who'd found Jo and given her another reason to stay. It brought both Jude and Jess, who'd reconnected and had given me an honorary nephew. It brought delightful Kenny Carmichael and his swagger, then helped lock in Elizabeth. It brought Luc, who'd proved to be a wonderful partner to Elise. Heck, in a roundabout way, it'd even brought in Eddie James-Williamson, who towed gorgeous Bri Williamson along with her.

And maybe best of all, it brought this man standing at the sink with rubber gloves and the pinch of a smile at his lips.

He settled a few dishes into the dishwasher and shucked the gloves.

"Can I help?" A sturdy pile still waited for him, and I wanted to prolong our time together.

"No, that's not your job."

I moved past him on an odd whim, sliding my hands into the gloves and diving in. "It's not my job, no, but I want to help. It's the least I can do."

"This isn't right. You're a guest." He shifted beside me, scowling.

I grinned over at him, oddly pleased by the opportunity to ruffle him a little. "Let it happen, good sir. You can wrap up what we didn't eat while I do this."

For the next few minutes, he shuffled around tidying up and I finished washing a few things he clearly hadn't planned on me touching. When I went to remove the gloves, despite their being big enough for his much-larger hand, they stuck.

I tugged at the left one, but before I reached the right, he was there.

"Let me," he said, towering and a little broody as he slowly pulled off the glove.

My breath caught, the slide of rubber over my skin a sensation that should not be sexy in any way, but here it was. Happening in real life just like I told Elise I'd never see outside a historical.

A man is sensually removing one of my gloves!!!

Oh, but the things that could come next! He might brush his thumb over my pulse point—he'd feel the way my blood surged at his nearness. He might take something else off next—another glove? Perhaps unlace a corset and slide his hands under a chemise—

I made a weird sound not unlike a gurgle, and Dorian asked, "You okay?"

"Mmhmm. Yes. I just... really enjoyed you letting me help." I planned to beam at him, all kinds of casual and hiding the internal riot happening, but when I looked up, his honey-brown eyes were so intently focused on me, it stole my breath.

Our gazes stayed like that, locked for a beat, before Bear nudged under my hand and broke the spell.

We wandered toward his front door, sensing it was time for me to go even though I didn't want to. He didn't seem in a rush for that, either, but I didn't want to overstay my welcome.

At the front door, he lingered, not reaching for the

handle. "I'm glad they settled in Silverton, too, by the way. I don't get into town all that often, but I like it."

It shouldn't have made my heart flutter, but it did. "Yeah? What about it do you like here?"

He rubbed a hand over his beard, the bristles against his skin making a fine rasping sound. "Love the trees, especially on this property. Love the mountains." His gaze settled on mine. "Have to say I love the people."

My heart flipped. Obviously, he wasn't confessing his love for me, but those eyes and that voice. The way he towered over me. The way he'd been so tender and support- ive, and how this felt like something more...

Honestly, *the way he just removed my glove!*

"What was Jo supposed to have told me?" he asked, halting the direction of my thoughts.

More like bringing all thought and breath to a screeching halt. Because I couldn't possibly tell him I'd said something about offering him my *maidenhead*, I believe was the term I'd used after a particularly unbroken stint with historical romances.

Cheeks aflame in seconds, I cleared my throat. "Oh, nothing. Just how amazing it was."

One brow raised.

"The food was great. I just... conveyed that with enthusiasm."

I just said, "Tell him I'll trade my maidenhead for a chance to eat this food regularly, how about that?"

A maniacal giggle burst from me, and I reached for the knob. "So, Dorian. Thank you so much for a lovely after- noon tea. I've never done that before, and I loved every second."

He nodded, then whispered, "What'd you say?"

Shocked he wasn't letting it go, I shook my head and skittered out the door. "Thanks, Dorian Q!"

He hollered after me, "What'd you say, Dove L. Jensen, the sixth?"

With another cackle, I jogged across the expanse between our houses and turned back when I reached my own front door. "I'll never tell you!" And then I ducked inside before I could say anything to condemn myself further.

CHAPTER TWENTY-ONE

Dorian

Bear and I spent yesterday wandering around the farm taking care of small tasks to keep busy.

Mostly, we dealt with peculiar issues Pedro and Connor had mentioned, and I suspected maybe they were thanks to our pesky neighbors. Another fence post knocked down where it'd been sturdy for years. A few apple trees on one side of the small orchard picked clean and a few branches broken, almost like kids had hung on them and broken them off. They needed repairing, pruning properly, and cleaned up.

No reportable offenses, but a hassle, for sure. And it kept me busy.

At least, my body spent the day doing that. My mind passed the hours by reliving every second of my time with Dove the day before, playing those last few minutes on repeat.

Her wry smile, the embarrassed flush to her cheeks, and the way she literally ran out of my house laughing... what was she doing to me? Someone had pumped pure adrenaline into my bloodstream based on the way my pulse raced whenever she came to mind.

Also, why had she gotten so intense after washing the dishes? I had a long way to go to fully understand her, but I didn't mind the mystery.

I'd also found a letter this morning when I stepped out on the porch.

Dear Dorian,

Thank you for tea and the delicious food. You are truly a gifted baker and cook. In your last letter you asked if I have any allergies—all clear here. As for aversions, the only thing I don't enjoy is eggplant, and by that I mean the actual vegetable eggplant, not the insinuation an eggplant emoji implies.

I'm off to work or I would start this over, but I'll trust, as you have so generously in the past, that you can pretend I said nothing about eggplant emojis and focus on the food. Eggplant is slimy, tastes gross, and makes my throat feel scratchy. Other than that I love it and would eat it all the time.

I don't expect you to feed me, just to be clear. But I'd also be a fool not to make sure you know I've loved every bite of food you've made that I've had a chance to try, and I have no doubt that'll continue.

Happy Sunday,
Dove

. . .

Stapling my thoughts to the food-centric matters and not her side quest into suggestive emojis, I brainstormed a number of dishes I could make that would be easily shareable and reheatable in case she got home late or at an odd hour, as she often seemed to.

This morning, I'd arrived at Saint Security for the weekly all-hands. I didn't always attend these meetings, but I'd been feeling the itch to show my face and put in some time. Technically, I was on the books with Saint as a part-time employee, but I rarely worked twenty hours a week for them.

This afternoon, I'd need to repair a fence that'd been knocked down on the eastern border of the property so Pedro and Connor wouldn't have to spend any more of their time on it this week. If I pitched in, it'd be done in a few hours.

As Wilder and Bruce wrapped up the meeting and the overseas Saint employees signed off of their virtual teleconference screens, everyone greeted me with enough enthusiasm to make me feel welcome, but not so much I felt the urge to run. Granted, it'd been a long time since I'd felt the desire to truly turn and leave after arriving somewhere, but I appreciated how no one tiptoed around me. They said hi, good to see you, whatever, and then they moved on with their lives.

Except Kenny, of course, who always had an extra little twinkle in his eye. But this morning, Elizabeth had slipped her hand into his and they'd snuggled into chairs side by side and he'd only glanced over at me with a big goofy grin on his face twice.

"Glad to see you've emerged from the castle," Kenny said, patting my back.

"Happy to see you, too."

And I was. They'd been over for tea a few days ago, but Kenny and Liz would be heading out on a honeymoon soon, Luc had a busy assignment coming up, and Beast had largely been tucked away with his family lately. Adam stopped by here and there, but now that I wasn't in dire straits, he tended to text or call.

"Stone, good to have you. Can I pass you an assignments list?" Bruce asked, casual and friendly as always.

Still, my gut clenched. "Of course. First, I have an issue I wanted to bring to your attention."

His brows rose. "An issue?"

Tristan, Wilder, and Doc sidled up right as Kenny, Elizabeth, and Luc joined the growing huddle.

"Possible issue. The commune that shares a property line with my farm is potentially escalating. They've been making overtures, for lack of a better term, and I thought it might be wise to have them on the radar. They weren't involved in the events with Elise, but I'm getting a sense that wouldn't be far off for them anymore."

Some of this had to do with the dumping and other small things we'd noticed around the property. And some of it had to do with a gut feeling.

"Sego Lily Commune? Is law enforcement tracking?" Wilder asked, stern face engaged. He'd grown up in Silverton and would be the last person to jump to a conclusion about the place.

I nodded. "Yes. But I noticed just the other day they have a new sign. It's no longer Sego Lily. It's Patriot Ridge."

Several groans went up around the circle, but Kenny spoke first.

"Why do idiots have to couch their idiocy in patriotism? Like, what does that even mean?" His expression turned so grumpy, it was laughable.

"Easy there. We don't know they're idiots. But it's notable, for sure," Bruce soothed.

"We know they dumped hundreds of pounds of garbage on Stone's land. We also know they've been more aggressive in their interactions, and Cordy and Maybell or whoever the old couple in charge used to be got forced out," Kenny countered.

Doc settled a hand on Kenny's shoulder. "They're definitely worth being aware of. You need anything right now?" he asked me.

"No. Just figured I should mention it. Chief Whitacker and Sheriff Ryan are both tracking as well, so if something heats up, they're aware."

Fortunately, both the Chief of Silverton PD and the Sheriff for Juniper View were decent men who cared about their communities and didn't jump to conclusions. They wouldn't be about to raid a commune, or camp, or whatever it'd become without plausible cause, and right now there was no cause. Just a... feeling.

Once again, my thoughts bounced to Dove and her childhood. Did she know I lived directly next to what might rapidly be developing into a cult? The sweet old folks who'd run Sego Lily Commune had been hippies of the highest order. But their way of life had been dying out, or so Maybell had told me the one time we'd talked before I'd gotten wind a few months ago that they'd "moved on" and someone new had taken over.

They'd been communicative when Elise, Luc's girlfriend, had been abducted and we wanted to confirm they hadn't seen any activity. In the end, the kidnapping had had nothing to do with the people of Patriot Ridge, but all the little nudges into my property, the attitude of the handful of men dirt biking around like it was a threat, the stepping into my orchard... it set me on edge.

The conversation continued for a few minutes, everyone agreeing it would be good to keep an eye out. I promised I'd keep them aware of any issues I had, too, though it wasn't necessary. Whitacker and Ryan were doing their jobs as well as they could and hopefully, it'd simmer down.

"No pressure with the schedule. I know it can be a busy time with the farm," Bruce said, nodding to the schedule still projected on screen and the list of vacancies they needed people to opt in for.

"I'll be here." I'd sign into the scheduling portal after I spoke with Pedro to deconflict a few things. It'd be fine.

Luc and Kenny followed me out as most everyone else dispersed to their offices.

"You know you don't have to sign up for anything. We'll get it covered one way or another." Kenny's tone held a hint of concern.

"I know. I'll find some days. I owe it to Saint to show up from time to time." I jogged down the stairs, oddly anxious to get back to the farm.

Actually, not all that odd since I often felt an itch to be home, even after a nice long stint without a panic attack or major issues plaguing me. Old habits and mental health pathways died hard.

Realizing they weren't behind me, I turned to find Luc with his arms crossed at the bottom of the stairs and Kenny frowning.

"You don't owe Saint," he said, almost like a question.

We weren't getting into this now. We'd been over it before and it would come around again. For now, I wanted to get back home and help with that fence and let Bear run around a bit before we got cleaned up and I could make something good for dinner. I waved a hand and moved toward my truck, not needing to look to know Kenny was rolling his eyes or huffing dramatically, and Luc's face likely hadn't changed.

"'kay, love ya, see ya, bye! Give my best to His Majesty!" Kenny hollered as I loaded into my truck.

I backed out of the parking spot and eased up alongside the stairs, rolling down the driver's side window to pin him in his belligerent face.

"Bye, Kenny and Luc. See you soon. I'll say hi to Bear for you—send my regards to Kit."

Kenny grinned, and Luc sent me a mock salute. They both turned toward the door as I left.

Anyone who'd gotten a hint of my sense of obligation to Saint Security had said it was misplaced—that I didn't owe them anything. They claimed I should do what I wanted, even if it meant *not* working at Saint at all.

But how could I do that? How could I abandon the people who'd literally carried me through the worst times in my life? How could I live here, where they'd all moved for the purpose of being part of Saint, and just... not show up?

It wasn't the kind of man I was, and Kenny could continue to get riled up about it—it wouldn't change my mind.

CHAPTER TWENTY-TWO

Dove

My visit with Nan after work had gone well. For once, I didn't feel the pinching ache around my heart when sitting with her in one of the parlors. I felt happy, especially as I saw different friends stopping by to say hi and fawn over her and me.

She had friends. She had a whole life, and she seemed brighter. I knew very well isolation was one of several major contributing factors to rapid mental decline and correlated with increased incidence of dementia, injury, and all kinds of other issues in the elderly. It was part of the reason we'd decided the move to Silverton Springs made sense.

I simply hadn't realized how small and closed-in her life had become. She occasionally visited friends, did the beauty parlor, as she called it, weekly, but she couldn't simply wander out of her apartment and find a group to chat with.

She didn't have companionship at meals or reinforcements if she needed something when I was away at work.

Breathing in the surprisingly warm evening air, I took a few moments to appreciate how vividly I could see she was thriving. And maybe it meant I was doing a bit better now, too, because I didn't even feel the urge to cry.

Okay, fine, a little tear had snuck out of one eye—just the one!—as I got in my car to head home. But it was a tear of gratitude. Of relief.

Of knowing the person I loved most in the world was settled and in a place where she could be happy, and of course where I could come see her whenever she and I wanted.

Work had been fine, though the familiar itch to do something else, something more, had shimmied its way under my bra strap and stuck like a stray hair. I couldn't stop thinking about how restless I was at work, especially since I'd thought once I sold the house and got Nan settled, I'd feel so relieved and happy, and work would improve, too.

So... where was the old satisfaction in my work now that I wasn't hanging on by my fingernails?

A low *woof* caught my attention, and I looked up to see Bear bounding toward the path I walked that led to the back yards of both my little cabin and Dorian's house.

"Hi, Bear!" I bent to pet his head as he swirled around me, but realized he was wet too late. "Gah! You're soaked!"

He yipped another cheery little bark, eyeing me and then walking toward his house. He stopped, looked back, then started walking again.

"You want me to follow you? Where's your dad?" I asked, as though this clever boy could actually understand me.

He panted, excitement in his every movement, until his ears perked up as a low whistle reached us.

"That must be him. Should we go see him and figure out how you got all wet?"

I couldn't help the grin on my face because he was so joyous in the way he galloped back the way he'd come and slipped around the far side of his house. Dorian must've been working over there, and I'd never actually seen that side of his place.

Because of this ignorance, I wandered around the corner, heedless of what would befall me in the next few seconds.

When I came to the side of the house, what did mine eyes behold? A tall, muscular man standing half-naked under a shower head. Water sluiced down his dark hair and over the tanned, firm architecture of his back and onto stone pavers at the ground. Bear trotted up to the person, and my stomach sank just in time for him to turn and watch his dog zip back toward me.

He froze, the sight of me clearly unanticipated.

And I stopped in place, the vision of Dorian Forrester naked from the waist up and *showering in the waning golden light* not something I'd ever possibly be mentally prepared for.

So much skin. So many, many muscles. Biceps, pectorals, abs, obliques, and a frankly aggressive vee of an Adonis belt shoving my gaze downward to notice a pair of low-slung soaking wet pants.

Who showers with pants?

How tragic and also miraculous he did, or I'd be even less capable of words right now.

He reached for the spigot and turned it to the right until the water trickled, then stopped. After grabbing a towel draped over a metal beam to one side, he scrubbed it over his face, hair, and then around his neck and shoulders.

I *finally* managed to pull my eyes from the absolute insanity in front of me and focused my attention on Bear.

"Dude, that was a total ambush," I told him under my breath.

The dog just panted happily, his smile wide and toothy.

"Hey," Dorian said, now too close to ignore that yes, he was very much still shirtless and despite his efforts, which were weak at best, he was still glistening with water droplets on his shoulders and chest.

I didn't dare look lower, but no doubt his pants, etcetera were still dripping wet.

"Do you shower outside often?" I asked, because there was no chance I could pretend this wasn't happening.

Inscrutable as always, he shrugged. "Not often. Bear got muddy so I gave him a shower out here and by the time we were done, I was covered. Figured I'd do a first pass out here before I go destroy my bathroom with dirt."

Very reasonable. Completely understandable.

Exceedingly attractive.

No! Bad brain! We do not objectify our beautiful mountain man baker friend! No!

"Right. Makes sense. Absolutely."

I turned away, glancing at the cabin, trying to remember why I was even out here. Why had I left my house and entered the perilous wild where I'd stumbled upon this mountain of a man in nearly all of his rather unignorable glory?

"How was your day?" he asked, drawing my attention back to him before I valiantly bounced my eyes away again.

He was just so beautiful, and I hadn't seen a real-life flesh and blood man without his shirt on in, well, ever. At least not one who wasn't a patient, and when I was in work mode, I didn't feel things like whatever was happening right now. No, I'd never seen a man like this.

Especially not one who made me mini pies and liked tea and had the sweetest dog and the most soulful, endless eyes...

Stop it already!

"It was good, actually. Work was fine, and seeing Nan was kind of amazing." I peeked at him, face only. A swoop of attraction made me stumble. *Still a problem.*

He reached out, grabbing my upper arm and steadying me. *And now he's even closer!*

That large, warm hand on my skin felt a little bit like it lit a fire underneath the point of contact. It sizzled out from the touch simultaneously searing me and scorching every brain cell I owned. After a second, I found my feet as he released me and awkwardly chuckled as a way to say, *"I'm totally fine and not literally falling all over myself because you are not only the kindest man I've ever known, but now I can confirm you are the actual hottest and that is not awesome because I was already struggling not to have a gigantic, unmanageable crush on you."*

"What made it amazing?" he asked.

The abs? The pecs? That dusting of dark hair I wanted to press my hand against...

"Oh, uh... the visit? With Nan?" *Get a grip, woman! You're better than this!* "She was just so happy. She's doing so well there. And I'm not hating it here. So it was good to take a moment and let that settle in."

When I dared to look at him, the soft smile on his face threatened to slay me.

I mean, come on! Didn't he realize he was five-alarm fire

hot already and then he hit me with a little smile and a hint of teeth? Did he want to be attacked out here?

If I was a bear, he was a tent with an uncovered fruit tray slathered in honey as I trundled out of my hibernation cave. *Come on, man!*

"Glad to hear it, Dove. That's great."

We shared a smile. Or at least I hoped it looked like a smile because currently, my insides were disintegrating and reforming into shooting stars and rainbows at the same time.

"Mind if I bring you dinner? I was going to do a shepherd's pie and some salad. Nothing fancy. Maybe around seven?" He slung the towel over one shoulder.

I swallowed hard. "Uh. Dinner? Me? Seven?"

He chuckled, but his expression faded into concern. "You okay?"

Finally, my humanity broke through the fog of desire and attraction. More heat joined the already blazing blush on my cheeks and I scrubbed my hands over my eyes.

"Yes. Sorry. I think maybe I need a snack or something." Hypoglycemia brought on by ogling such a magnificent specimen—that was a thing, right? I gave him a sheepish look.

"I have food inside if you need. Or—"

"No, thank you. You're already feeding me dinner, right?"

A pleased look crossed his face. "If you want."

If I want. Hilarious. "Yes, please."

He nodded. "Good. Then I'll see you around seven for the delivery. For now, I better head inside and get cleaned up."

Dear sir, you need not get cleaned up on my *behalf!*

Bear trotted ahead of him.

"Thanks, Dorian."

I did not let my hungry gaze trail after him as he plodded his way toward his house because I was heading to mine. And I would not look back.

Not that I needed to. The image of him was now burned into my brain, and I was not mad about it.

Closing the door behind me, I sank to the ground, still blushing and kind of wanting to scream to let out this wild energy romping through my mind and body. Exhaling, I let my head fall back with the sigh and rolled my eyes at what a mess I was even as I laughed because there was just no other option.

No. *No, I'm not hating it here at all.*

CHAPTER TWENTY-THREE

Dorian

Bear raised a knowing set of furry brows.

"Hush. I'm just making up for earlier." I finger-combed my unruly hair into something decently presentable and eyed my beard. It was still on the overgrown side of things.

Which was fine. Because I wasn't doing anything other than taking her dinner. I'd put it in the oven after my shower and spent some time puttering around the house trying not to acknowledge how antsy I was to see her again.

Also trying not to remember the way her cheeks had gone pink when she rather shamelessly looked at my chest. Heat simmered low in my gut, and as I tried to figure out if anything else could improve my haggard appearance, I marveled at the feeling.

It'd been so long since I'd been attracted to someone.

Even longer since I'd felt excited to be with them. After years of healing, first physically and then emotionally, that little flame Dove had lit was a miracle.

Any effort to pretend I didn't feel the pull between us had evaporated in the unseasonably warm evening air when her clear blue eyes traced the shape of me.

The oven beeped so I gave up on this physical appearance business and focused on the food. She hadn't hated the view this afternoon if her blush and her runaway talking were anything to go by, but was there anything else between us? Or was this simply what friendship with a beautiful neighbor felt like? Was it the natural course of what me coming out of a years-long period of self-imposed celibacy resulted in?

Identifying it as such was a cheap substitute for what it felt like to me, but could I trust my own judgement on the issue? And more than that, if she was interested, could I really offer her anything? She had sacrificed for her family and gone through so many hard things. Like I'd reminded myself before, she loved Silverton, and she was an extrovert. What kind of life could she possibly have with me?

My alarm went off, signaling I had five minutes to wrap up her food and deliver it so I got to work. I'd baked the shepherd's pie in two small dishes so she could have her own. I'd also made some quick rolls, a salad, and an early apple pie. This was a meal that should've been made in October, especially since the day had been so warm, but I'd been craving comfort. Hopefully, she wouldn't mind.

"Are you coming?" I asked Bear as I opened the front door with a bag containing Dove's dinner in one hand.

He perked up from where he'd slumped on the cool kitchen floor and loped down the front steps, then headed straight for Dove's porch. I joined him, and just before I pressed the doorbell, the door swung open..

"Hi. Sorry. I was not trying to be creepy and I definitely wasn't pacing around right here by the door. I just happened to hear Bear and, yeah." She waved a hand with a little chagrined smile. "Hi."

Everything she did felt like a deliberate assault on my admittedly paltry efforts to not fall deeper under her spell. Had she been cool and collected or standoffish, I would never think twice about her. It simply wouldn't appeal, nor would it bust through my innate distrust of my ability to evaluate her level of interest.

But this? This flustered, honest, funny woman was so completely desirable, I could hardly remember why I'd come except to get another look at her before the day came to an end. She had her hair pulled back in a ponytail sitting high at the back of her head with little blonde wisps framing her face like earlier. She'd changed from the shorts and T-shirt into a pair of what looked like sweatpants and a fresh T-shirt that said "Pemberly U" on it.

Bear sat on my foot, which shook me from my Dove-induced stupor. I held up the bag. "Dinner. Should be warm. I hope it's not too heavy. Eggplant-free, I promise."

She giggled with such naked delight as she took the bag, my stomach flipped.

"Thank you. It's just a disgusting vegetable. Who would grow such a thing?" she asked, leaning against one side of her door frame.

"I have a few growing in my garden, but—"

She reached for the door and started closing it. "Well, that's given me all the information I need..."

After a beat, she flung it open again with a wry grin. "Kidding, of course. Unless you do try to feed me eggplant and then we're going to have a tough conversation. Do you understand, Dorian?"

She was playful. Fun. Whatever burdens she'd been shouldering these last few weeks, they were easing, and nothing made me gladder than seeing the proof of it here in front of me.

Well, nothing except maybe the low-level suspicion she was flirting with me just a little.

"I promise I'll never feed you eggplant. I have no doubt I can stick to that promise. I'm reliable."

She tilted her head, eyes skating over me in an assessing sweep. "I'm sure you are."

Bracing my hand against the frame, I leaned in. "I am."

Her lips parted, and her eyes softened as they flickered back and forth between mine. The air grew thick, the dim sounds of crickets disappearing as I took in the arch of her brows and the perfect slope of her nose. Her eyes appeared to be smiling even when she was still staring back as though transfixed.

I knew the feeling.

She reached up with her free hand, moving so slowly I thought it'd never reach me, but eventually, her palm pressed against my cheek and jaw, her fingers settling next to my ear.

Electrified, I leaned closer. Bear still had my foot stapled to the porch, but I didn't want to ruin the moment. Instead, maintaining the connection with her, whatever this was, became my primary objective.

Bear shifted, ears perked, and he let out a bark.

Sadly, this startled Dove, and she pulled her hand back, then her eyes shifted over my shoulder where I turned to see a large white SUV trundling down the drive.

"Is that a police car?" she asked, worry infusing her tone.

"It's Sheriff Ryan. Juniper Creek's sheriff," I explained, hoping it'd set her at ease but feeling a deep sense of foreboding at the sight of the man parking, engine off, and slipping out of his front seat.

"Sorry to disturb, Dorian. Ma'am." He tipped his head, now covered by the cowboy hat he'd settled on his head as soon as he exited the car, at Dove.

"What's going on?" I asked, worry crawling up my shins before I set a hand on Bear, who'd stayed close.

He shook his head. "Not sure it's much of anything, but we had some reports of some issues around Patriot Ridge. Thought I'd come out and see if you'd had any issues on your line. I'm sorry it's so late."

"Not that I saw earlier. We weren't where the trouble's been in the past, but we can ride out there if you think we should check. What kind of issues?"

Dove shifted, and her hand slipped into the one of mine not resting on Bear. My heart warmed as Ryan spoke.

"We ended up arresting two kids who'd started a small fire. Someone saw them run back to the commune borders. They seemed to think they couldn't be questioned or taken in if they crossed the line." He sighed and shook his head. "Jackson Smith, seventeen, and Ransom Petersen, eighteen. A Hawk Jensen and a Cory Smith came and bailed them out. I haven't seen any of these guys around, and I suspect they're part of the new crew who's made the switch from Sego Lily to Patriot."

Dove had gone stiff next to me.

"Did you say—" She cleared her throat of the rasp she'd started with. "Did you say Hawk Jensen?"

Like lightning, the realization struck home. Dove

Jensen... and Hawk must be her brother. She hadn't seen him for years, and he was right here?

"Yes, ma'am. Do you know any of them?" the sheriff asked.

She dropped my hand and now clasped hers together, pressing them close to her body.

"Just Hawk. He's my brother."

CHAPTER TWENTY-FOUR

Dove

I'd slept fitfully and rolled out of bed ready for work and as much distraction as possible. Sheriff Ryan had left not long after I'd told him I did in fact know Hawk Jensen. At least, I used to know him.

What kind of messed-up person is upset that their brother hasn't tried to see them after the only contact they've had with him is him calling her horrible names? I mean really, who does that?

But there it had been at the sound of his name, a bruise deepening with every minute I thought about how close he apparently was and how little he cared to see me.

Dorian could clearly tell how upset I was, but I'd insisted I was fine. He needed to go check his property, and I wanted him to do that—it'd be awful if there was a fire we didn't know about, or any other problems. So I promised him I was going to eat and get to bed early.

What a shift from the moments before the sheriff had arrived, when it'd seemed like we might kiss, to after, when it felt like I was crumbling again.

I was so tired of crumbling.

As I left for work, I found an envelope on my front porch.

Dove,

I'm sorry about your brother. I wish there was something I could do. If you're not too tired after work tonight, knock on my door. Please.

He's a fool to miss out on you. You're a good woman.
Dorian Q
PS. Please knock.

The note stayed with me as I took blood pressures and temperatures and health histories at the clinic, mind numb except the repeating refrain he'd left with me.

He's a fool to miss out on you.

By the time I did knock on Dorian's door, I'd shifted from sad to resigned to accepting, and just as I'd mounted his steps, to angry.

"Glad you—"

I burst past him into his house.

"How dare he, right? I mean what the actual... *Ugh!*" I practically stomped my foot, frustration and anger sending my pulse into a sprint. "How dare he be a deadbeat brother and then call me up like he knows anything about my life and call me names? Meanwhile, he's living in a camp three minutes from my house and fifteen minutes from the town where he darn well knows I've lived for years. And Nan! He could come see her!"

Bear stood watching, on alert, and his perked triangle ears and still tail made me deflate and press my hands over my face. "I'm so sorry. I just barged in here."

Dorian's warm hands gently took my wrists and tugged. "No need to hide. Everything's fine."

"I—" My voice wobbled, and I frowned. "I really don't want to cry about this."

But I already was, and Dorian pulled me into his chest, arms wrapping around me and holding me so perfectly snug and safe, I couldn't manage to cry for long before I was simply hugging him back.

After indulging in his solid warmth for another minute, I pulled myself together and stepped away. "Thank you."

He nodded toward the living room. "Sit. I'll bring tea."

Bear and I shared a look. I imagined him saying something like, *Isn't he so great?* He was such an imposing dog—physically large and his black-and-white coloring was striking. He had a wolfish quality and yet he was such a sweet, friendly dog. Knowing he helped Dorian with his anxiety made him even more special.

The low rumble of an electric kettle sounded after a few seconds in the kitchen, but I took the time to take in the space. Worn couches and a TV on a stand, though not the gigantic eighty-inch monstrosity one might expect from a bachelor's living room. Why didn't I notice this last time? Oh, right, the exquisite tea party setup with the beehive teacups. I'd had eyes only for them and the cakes, and the man who'd baked them. Today, it seemed like I was seeing another aspect of him. Taking it all in, I could confirm Dorian was about as predictable as a summer storm, so I wasn't surprised his space was less traditionally single guy.

"Hope you don't mind chamomile. Figured something herbal might be a good idea." He set down a small tray, one he hadn't used for our fancy tea, and took a seat next to me on the couch.

My heart flipped like a silly little thing. What was it thinking?

He'd taken a different seat before—that was what.

I took the tea and dropped a cube of sugar in. Not super smart, but I decided not to care.

"Those are mini macarons. There's a maple, a pumpkin, and an espresso cream, but don't feel like you need to eat them." His gaze fixed on his own tea as he stirred a small spoon around the edge of the cup.

"Those are almost too pretty to eat," I said, studying the gorgeous little treats, one a saddle brown with lighter filling, one a brilliant orange with a white middle, and the last a café au lait color. They were a gorgeous fall palette and the fact he'd clearly made them himself was simply amazing. "I'm not sure I can eat them."

He huffed. "You can."

Oh my goodness and be still my heart, was this man blushing under that burly beard of his? *Gah!*

I took a bite of the espresso cream and shut my eyes, the texture perfect and not too crumbly and falling everywhere but my mouth like macarons often did, the flavor exploding on my tongue. "I think you're a magician."

When I finally opened my eyes and focused on him, I found him watching me with a pleased expression.

He pointed to himself. "Normal guy."

I giggled and took a bite of the pumpkin one. *Again.* So freaking good. After a sip of tea, the heaviness of the truth about my brother settled in. I didn't want to talk about it and risk crying again, but I also needed to process it.

"Do you think it's a cult? The old Sego Lily place?"

He exhaled, running a hand over Bear's head before notching his chin toward the dog's bed. The good boy obediently moved to his spot and sank down, then sighed.

"Cult is probably a bit strong. So far, they seem like they might be doomsday preppers with a side of extreme nationalism, but who knows. They've messed around, but it sounds like it might be a case of the teens acting out in a situation where they're deprived of other outlets."

I blinked, processing his statement. "That's very generous, considering they've caused you trouble."

He tipped his head side to side. "I'm not sure *trouble* is right, so much as inconvenience. Frustration. Some long days dealing with their nonsense. As a recovered entitled little jerk, I don't want to judge too harshly."

"You were a teenage dirtbag?" It was hard to imagine him as anything but how he was now—giant and gentle and more and more irresistible. Thinking of him as a surly teen with sass made me giggle.

He chuckled low, his baritone voice pleased. "Oh, yes. It was a formative time."

I wanted to know everything about that, but something nagged. "Sheriff Ryan said they started a fire. That's not small."

"True. Fire's a real concern. Kind of a nightmare for a tree farm in a desert climate." He made a distressed face.

An empty laugh tripped out of me. "Yeah." I hated to remember, but he should know my concerns. "I don't want to admit this, but based on what I know of my brother's past, I think you are right to be worried."

His gaze narrowed. "Can you tell me more?"

Even questioning me about my criminal brother's

possibly sketchy new "community" didn't push him into being curt. How had I ever thought of him as grumpy?

I nodded as I chewed the last macaron, the maple flavor a surprisingly delicious morsel I'd be thinking about later. I tended to like fruitier desserts, but these were all fallish and perfect.

"That was so good, thank you," I said, then wiped my fingers on the cocktail napkin he'd brought on the tray. "So, Hawk went to juvenile detention when he was fourteen. That was right after our parents died and he was in a rough place. I stayed on the compound for a few years, then went to live with Nan, and he..." I shook my head at the memory. "He got wrapped up with the people who'd been so influential for our mom and dad."

Dorian waited, listening attentively. He clearly sensed there was more to come, and he was right.

I swallowed hard, then took one last drink of my tea in hopes it might settle the tightness in my throat. "So, my dad killed my mom, then himself. Hawk lost it, started acting out. I retreated in. He burned down a house and the people who were inside only barely survived. He'd had some run-ins with police before that and because of it and the fact that people had been there, he went to juvey. He also called me from jail about four years ago. He was on one of his 'making amends' kicks, which seem to crop up about once every five years."

My chest ached, and I rubbed a hand over my sternum. "One of the aspects of the cult was a lot of talk about purity and obedience. Lots of women 'obeying' but really what that meant was men behaving badly, hurting their wives, and facing no consequences since the leadership wouldn't step in. I'd genuinely hoped Hawk had gotten away from all that crap, but what he said to me the other day makes me think he probably hasn't."

A warm hand slipped over my arm and gently squeezed my wrist. "I'm sorry. That sounds like a hard way to grow up."

I laughed, but there was no lightness in it. "For the most part, I've made my peace with it. But even without Hawk calling, and now finding out he's so close by, I've been thinking a lot about the way I was raised and how it's affected me as an adult. The choices I've made..."

He waited, ever patient. Always listening.

I wasn't sure I wanted to admit everything to him, but as though he sensed I'd hit the end of my ability to be vulnerable, he caught my eye. "As far as I'm concerned, Dove Jensen, you're a miracle."

And just like that, the tears came again.

CHAPTER TWENTY-FIVE

Dorian

Dove wiped under her eyes and blinked up at the ceiling.

"See? I knew I'd cry again, and I don't want to. You being kind shouldn't make me cry. Me thinking about my dufus brother I haven't really known in over half my life shouldn't either. I don't want to grieve a brother who has never once shown he cares about me. Someone who criticizes me as a slut when I have kissed a grand total of two people in my life? When I'm a thirty-year-old virgin? But even if I'd slept with half of Silverton, how is that his business? How does he get a say in anything about my life or partners or anything?"

I froze in place, eyes glued to her, and her breaths heaved for a few seconds, but the sound faded and silence spread out between us. Her hair sprouted out from her temples and framed her face, her blue eyes rimmed with red and mouth tight with emotion.

And me? I couldn't tell what was happening to me, this intimate knowledge a blow to the head and heart and yet also, completely inapplicable to me.

Slowly, she looked up to meet my gaze.

"So that's a pretty personal thing about me I didn't really plan to tell you, but here we are." She took a deep bow with one hand sweeping out to the side. "I had chances, I just didn't. And sometimes, I wonder if it's because of how I was raised, and other times, I think maybe it's because of how I know my heart works. And then I keep going around in a useless circle and give up."

She'd started talking faster, unraveling with the reality that she'd apparently revealed something she never meant to.

So I matched her.

"I get it."

She snorted. "I'm sure you do."

It was probably the least charitable she'd ever been, and I couldn't blame her.

"Of course not all of it. I have no idea what it was like growing up in that environment and I'm sorry you had to. I'm so sorry for what happened with your parents and how your brother turned out." Just the thought of this lovely, bright woman being treated so poorly as a child made my heart squeeze.

She dipped her head, a tiny acknowledgement of my words. I wasn't done, though, and this was where I could relate.

"I get the other choices to some degree, though. I've been celibate for six years."

Her mouth dropped open.

Closed.

Open.

Her lashes fluttered, and her lips closed again.

"This feels like a double standard," I said, enjoying her shock. I'd long since made my peace with this choice and I never regretted it. Not for a second.

She looked like she might burst as her pretty hands fluttered around, stacking her teacup and saucer onto the tray, then dusting a few crumbs into her hand.

"I'm sorry if that made you uncomfortable, I—"

"No. Not at all. I'm sorry I'm acting like an immature weirdo. I'm just trying to figure out why you'd do that—stay celibate—without being a jerk by asking because it seems so invasive, but then it feels like maybe you wouldn't mind, and I can't decide." She looked up through her thick lashes, a wry little smile tucked into one corner of her lovely mouth.

"I got tired of feeling empty," I said, hoping she'd connect the dots.

With her bright blue eyes on me and my heart rate ticking up, everything seemed vivid. Almost the opposite of what happened before a panic attack—heart rate skyrockets but everything gets blurry. This was like an artist had come along and outlined her in bold.

"Six years ago? That was before the injuries and..." she faded out, and I could see she didn't want to say the words.

Depression. Suicidality. "Yes. Before. I never felt like I could commit to someone very well with the schedule our units kept, but I didn't like the lack of connection or significance that came with more casual interactions."

She nodded. "I can see that. I always figured I wouldn't like that either. I mean, I've never actually dated, but the two times I've kissed someone, it was with very little connection and even that, I didn't like."

I nodded, understanding completely. "Exactly. So I decided to take a break from any attempts at being with someone. Then the deployment where everything changed and it just didn't make sense anymore." Clearing my throat, I glanced at Bear. He watched me from his bed, one brow raising like if I gave him the slightest indication, he'd be at my side.

He would be, too, the sweet beast.

"Having sex didn't make sense anymore?" she asked, evidently puzzled by my last words.

"Maybe?" I scratched at my cheek, thinking I should trim up my beard sometime soon. "I guess it just didn't make sense that anyone would want me when I was struggling so much—not for anything other than physical gratification, and even that seemed like a stretch at the time. I didn't want anyone around me as it was. Then, the meds I was on killed any drive I might've had, so I didn't even feel the desire. And as I've gotten better, healed up and found my way again..."

I still don't know if anyone would want me.

Her gaze intensified on me and she licked her lips, but fury shone out of her eyes. "Are you saying you don't think anyone would want you because you have a history of depression?"

It sounded ugly. Awful. I'd never tell anyone else that. I'd never *think* it of someone else. And yet...

I shrugged a shoulder.

Her mouth dropped open and she launched to her feet, walking right between my legs and cupping my face in her hands. She stared down directly into my eyes, just scowling into the depths of me.

And I sat there, hands on my knees and desperate to hold her steady at her waist over her scrubs, maybe feel the warm skin of her belly if the material rolled up. My heart sprinted, the intensity in her expression lighting me on fire as I sat there, her hands on my face, waiting.

"You have to be one of the best men I've ever known, Dorian." Instead of fierce or furious, her voice held a shudder of emotion. "I envy the person you decide is worth your time and effort, if you ever do. And if you don't? That's okay. You get to decide."

"You do, too," I scratched out.

She held my face a little longer, eyes just staring into mine, burrowing down into the deepest parts of me, until Bear nudged his nose over my leg against her thigh. It broke whatever spell she'd been under, some accidental web I'd woven with all my doubts and fears laid bare that garnered the softest response.

We moved silently save a few quiet "thank yous" and "see you soons" after she stepped away and insisted on carrying the tray to the kitchen. I refused her help with the dishes, and she thanked me again as she left, looking back over her shoulder one last time before she went inside her cabin.

It took me a while to close the door on the moment, on her words... on her. I couldn't stop thinking about her *envying* the person I'd eventually decide was worth my time.

Because more and more obviously, I knew exactly who that person was.

CHAPTER TWENTY-SIX

Dove

The next day, I found a perfect petite cake on my door and a note.

Something sweet for you today. Hope it's a day full of good things. —DQ

So simple. So effective.

Two days after that, when I dragged myself home from a long, hard shift, I found dinner neatly packaged, and I cried while I ate it standing at my kitchen counter before pouring myself into bed, because of course I did.

When Dorian left me two more little tea cakes after my hastily scrawled note about how great they were, I took them to my visit with Nan and we ate them together. She kindly ignored the way my cheeks heated when I talked about Dorian, and we avoided discussing Hawk since there was nothing to be done about him. When I'd told her about the call, and that he was living at Patriot Ridge, she just gave me a grim, close-lipped smile and squeezed my hand. Over the years, we'd said about all there was to say and until he showed his face, there wasn't anything more.

On my one day off, I knocked on Dorian's door, but no answer came. To say levels of devastation rolled over me was putting it mildly. I wanted to see him. Part of me felt like I *needed* to. We'd grown closer the last time we'd spent time together.

In a very real sense, Dorian was rapidly becoming my closest friend. I wasn't looking to replace Elise or anyone else, but in real time, we were getting to know each other in small and fundamental ways. My friends were busy people just like me, but along with their work, they were tethered to their partners and now, in Jess's case, their children. Catherine was working even longer and harder hours than I was, and she hadn't been much for socializing even before her cleaning empire began.

It was all a natural part of the process. I got it. Maybe I was making Dorian an unhealthy stand-in, but I didn't think so. What was growing between us felt so entirely and actively healthy, it was kind of scary.

Sometimes, as I was drifting off to sleep, I'd think about that look on his face when he didn't say he wasn't sure if anyone would want him, but he might as well have said it aloud. I could read it so clearly in the resigned set of his shoulders. My heart would squeeze in my chest, filling up with aching for a man who'd served his country and endured unspeakable things, and then had wrestled with the fallout for years. He hadn't given up, and he was such a beautiful person.

I'd kept my crap together, but I'd wanted to shout, "I'd want you!" But there was no hypothetical anymore. It simply boiled down to the fact that I did.

I wanted more of Dorian in any way he'd be willing to give himself, and there'd been moments that made me wonder if maybe he was thinking the same thing.

As I shuffled out to work with a coffee thermos under one arm and my purse slipping off the other shoulder as I tied the knot at the waist of my scrubs, Dorian's voice greeted me.

"Morning, Dove."

I startled, nearly dropping the coffee, but collected myself in time to haul open my car door and settle the mug into a cup holder and dump my purse in the seat. As I turned toward him, all kinds of butterflies took wing in my belly. He stood tall and dark in jeans, boots, and a plaid shirt rolled to his elbows. He had a hat pulled low on his head, and hair curled from under it at his ears and no doubt at his neck. I'd rarely seen him in anything else—well, except that one time when he'd been missing the shirt part of his outfit.

"Morning, Dorian."

Our eyes met, and my breath caught. He looked so handsome in the early glow of morning, and he was holding a paper sack.

"Thought you might like breakfast," he said, holding it out to me.

I took it, hand grazing his as I gripped the folded-down edge. "I will never say no to breakfast."

Seemingly pleased, he nodded. "Good. You need to make sure you're taking care of yourself."

A bubbly warm glow started at the soles of my feet and fizzed its way up through my entire body.

"Thank you. I had yesterday off, actually, but I didn't see you around." Like I'd ever been that casual in my entire life.

"I went into Saint for a shift. Sorry I missed you."

My, my, my. The way he didn't take his eyes from mine might've felt odd in a different situation—like too much. But right now? It simply made me feel like someone had dumped champagne into my blood stream.

"Me, too," was all I could manage to say before my watch beeped, alerting me to the hour. I frowned down at it. "I'm sorry. I need to go."

"Don't be late," he said, and took a step back.

And then, because I was me and couldn't let a chance to be awkward pass me by, I whirled around and lunged for his hand, clasping it for a second, then releasing him. "Thanks for breakfast. See you soon?"

Without waiting for his reply or daring to look back at him, I slammed my car door and turned the engine on, flustered and messy but oddly pleased with myself. As I backed out, I could feel him watching, and when I gave one final wave, he tipped his chin my way.

During my shift, I amazed myself by keeping my focus on my patients and not on the man who was single-handedly keeping me fed. The breakfast burrito he'd made had been absolutely delicious with scrambled eggs, bacon, and sharp cheddar cheese in a toasty flour tortilla. He'd also included a little baggy of apple slices and a square napkin with the words "Have a good day, DQ" scribbled on one side in black ink.

Basically, he was wooing me and he didn't even realize it. In some ways, that was tragic. How could I be falling for someone who didn't even *mean* to make me fall? But it was happening, despite my very real knowledge that he likely wasn't looking for anything with me. He might not want anything with anyone. He didn't sound like anything had changed in terms of what he thought or what he wanted.

I wrote him a letter of thanks and wished I had something to offer him. My culinary skills were serviceable, but I was barely keeping myself fed and only enjoying things he brought so generously. What else did he need? As far as I could tell, he had everything he seemed to want.

By Friday afternoon, I was more than ready for a night out at Craic. I slipped into one of my favorite blue dresses with a flowy skirt and fitted bodice with sleeves. Nothing fancy, but it felt good to be out of scrubs, and I'd have quality time with my sweatpants soon since I didn't have any shifts this weekend.

I knocked on my landlord's door, anxious energy surging through me at the thought of seeing him again. Sure enough, when he opened up, my stomach did backflips.

"Hey, happy Friday," I said, waving as though I wasn't standing directly in front of him. "Um, I was wondering if you were going to happy hour tonight?"

Then I took him in—apron over his clothes and hands covered in flour.

"No, I'm not going."

My hopes sank. "Darn. I was hoping we could hang for a while, maybe have a drink."

His brow furrowed and his eyes shifted past me for a moment before landing back on mine. "It's usually a little much for me there."

I nodded. "Thought that could be a possibility. Totally get it. Just thought I'd ask." *Say it. say it, say it, say itttt.* "So maybe we could, you know, do something? Else? Another time?"

"Yes."

The answer came so quickly, so *instantly*, I beamed. "Okay, great. Let's figure it out tomorrow, if you're around."

"I'm around."

"Great." I bit my lip to try to stifle my ridiculous smile because it was absolutely eating my face, but then I laughed because... well, I was too happy not to. "See you tomorrow."

CHAPTER TWENTY-SEVEN

Dove

Thirty minutes in, I was formulating a plan to change Craic materially enough to accommodate Dorian.

Step one, did they have a party room? If so, maybe the Saint folks and us girls could tuck in there and eliminate some of the cacophony and sheer number of people surrounding us. Step two, if he was comfortable, maybe he'd try some low-key headphones or ear buds if noise levels were a trigger for him. Step three—

"Earth to Dove. Where are you tonight?"

Elise's hand on my arm paired with her words halted my to-do list.

"Sorry. Long week." And also, thinking about my neighbor. What was he baking tonight? Did it make me an awful person if I hoped he'd leave me some?

"How are you doing with everything lately?" Catherine asked, concern knitting her brows.

I'd shared a few updates over the last few weeks. We'd finally have book club again next weekend and I was more than ready, but in between, we had Friday nights when I could swing it with my schedule, and the group chat. I'd told them how great Dorian had been, how much I liked where I lived now even though it was a ways out from town. I'd even told them my brother was at the former commune and had reached out.

What I hadn't shared?

My tiny, itty-bitty, baby of a crush on Dorian Forrester.

And because of that paired with my general inability to be stealthy in any way, my cheeks flamed and I ducked my face into my glass of prosecco.

Jo, Nikki, and Winnie all made exclamations and sounds that were completely ridiculous. Liz smiled, and thank goodness Jess wasn't here or she would've pressured me into telling them everything.

Though, I kind of wanted to.

"It's good. Everything's good." Dang, my entire face had to be beet red. "I may or may not have a small crush."

Jo clapped and said, "I knew it!" while Elise hooked an arm around my shoulders and squeezed. Nikki, Winnie, and Catherine all beamed, and Liz said, "Kenny is going to be absolutely unbearable."

"You can't tell him. Please. I—" How could I explain it to them? This wasn't a normal situation. Dorian was... raw. Quiet. I didn't want Kenny, as much as I loved the guy, to barrel in there and blabber about my crush and risk ruining our friendship.

"I won't. I just mean if... or when you guys get together." Liz raised her pint glass slightly. "I promise on my Silver Ridge Pale Ale."

I chuckled. "Oh, well, that *is* sacred, so okay."

She took a sip right as I heard Kenny's voice. "Are we toasting something?" He elbowed up to the table and dropped a kiss to Liz's jaw.

My eyes widened, begging everyone to stay away from the subject we'd just been discussing.

"A little things toast, right, ladies?" Nikki said, raising her glass. "Want to join us, Barbie?"

He perked up instantly. "Of course. Tell me what to do."

"You listen to everyone share a little thing they're celebrating and share one of your own. Then we toast," Winnie explained.

"Sounds delightful," he said, and nodded like he was ready to start.

Nikki began. "My little thing is that I got to explain an advanced calculus concept to Kiley and she got it super quickly." The woman practically glowed with the memory of helping her boyfriend's little sister with math homework.

"That sounds like a nightmare, but I love that for you guys," Elise said, and everyone chuckled.

"My little thing is that I'm helping Tristan with expanding the self-defense part of Saint and it's been so fun to work together." Her soft smile was so completely sweet and Winnie-like.

Everyone clapped and congratulated her.

"I figured out a way to eliminate really tough limescale without using a storebought cleaner, so I am psyched about that." Catherine grinned, then made a face. "So glamorous."

We all chuckled at that, but celebrated her win. The fact that she was truly living her best life being an expert house cleaner and now cleaning influencer? So dang awesome.

Jo shared about completing her most recent book, and

Liz mentioned the feeling of peace she'd been enjoying since she left the CIA, and Elise shared that business at Glazed was picking up the further into fall we got.

Everyone turned to me, smiles of anticipation on their dear faces.

Emotion hit as I looked at them, these beloved people I'd gotten to know so well the last few years. I'd had a long time without real friends—certainly while growing up, and later while I was working, in school, and trying to be there for Nan. I'd never figured it out, always felt a little too weird, a little too needy, to fit in.

But here, with them...

"I think my small thing is just you guys. And that's not small, but... yeah. I love you all, and I'm grateful for you." My voice wobbled on the last word, and Elise pulled me into a hug.

Kenny cleared his throat. "Okay, you almost got me with that one, Dove Jensen."

I chuckled. "Well, go ahead then, Kenny Carmichael."

He grinned. "I mean, I could also say all of you. My job at Saint. My wife." He swooped in for a kiss. "My cat. My nephew. The leaves starting to change. But I think today I'm going to say, I'm thankful that my friend Dorian isn't out at the farm all alone these days."

His beady little eyes fixed on me as Nikki led the salute.

"Cheers to the small things."

We all repeated the toast, and Kenny's eyes twinkled maniacally. One might not think such a thing could occur but trust me, if anyone could do it, it was Kenny.

After everyone had taken a drink, conversation started back up and Kenny kept his focus on me.

"So. How *is* my dear friend Dorian?"

My eyes darted around, keenly aware that this former

super-secret soldier-type guy could probably read all kinds of truths on my face if I let him.

"He's good. He's a great landlord. Super nice guy. Really glad I've gotten to know him."

He snapped and pointed at me. "Exactly. You're getting to know him."

My face fell a little.

"Hey, I think it's awesome. He's one of the best people I know, and so few people get anywhere close. Those of us who've known him since we served, our partners who are getting to see more of him... other than us and his therapist, no one knows the fabric of the guy."

Absorbing his words, I nodded. "Yeah. He's tucked away."

His gaze searched mine for a second. "He is. And he needs someone who's not afraid to push a little."

Someone? Like... like as a friend? As someone more?

I didn't want to entertain the possibilities, but he wasn't being subtle.

"He also needs someone who's kind. Gentle, like he is. Someone who will cherish him."

When I looked at his face now, it held so much sincerity and a hint of caution.

"Are you warning me away from him?" I asked, as much in confusion as wonder.

"Not at all. If anything, I'm warning you toward him. I think you'd be amazing together, but I also don't want him getting hurt." His face softened. "He's family."

That got me. "Trust me, I have no plans to hurt him. You don't know me all that well, but I can promise, I'm not a danger to him." He should at least know that.

But he surprised me when a sly grin crept over his face and he ducked his head. "Oh, you definitely are."

CHAPTER TWENTY-EIGHT

Dorian

Bear bounded away from me directly at Dove, who was wandering down a trail looking like a fantasy. Cutoff jeans shorts and a long-sleeved T-shirt with a repeating pattern that said "One More Chapter" on it. Two blonde braids hung over her shoulders and rested on top of the shirt. She wore sturdy running shoes on her feet, and the stretch between the hem of her shorts and her socks revealed a glorious expanse of her skin.

"How are you boys this fine morning?" she asked, a bounce in her step I hadn't seen in a while as she practically hopped closer to me, then dropped to one knee to give Bear her full attention.

"He's perfect. I'm better now." Maybe too honest. So be it.

She paused, then restarted her pets, blinking up at me with her long lashes and bright eyes.

My chest pinched.

"That's good to hear," she said, a smile growing on her lovely face.

My god, had she gotten more beautiful since the last time I'd seen her? It'd been fourteen hours—maybe fifteen—since I'd refused to join her at Craic and she'd suggested we spend time together today.

She might have. She'd taken the rays of the fall sunrise, stolen them right out of the sky, and they were shining directly back at me.

"Thought we could have lunch together. A picnic, if you're up for it." I forced my feet to stay put so the antsy energy rising up in me didn't reveal itself through shifting side to side like I wanted to.

She stood, brushing off her knee, and nodded. "That sounds perfect. What time?"

Now? This second?

"Noon? That work?"

"I'll be there. What can I bring?"

"Just yourself. See you then."

I whistled the sound Bear knew meant "come" and he reluctantly pulled away from his seat facing Dove and trotted along with me back to the house. Inside, he plunked his furry butt down and panted at me, tongue lolling just a touch in a way that said, "That wasn't nearly enough outside time, thank you very much."

"We've got work to do right now, but I promise we'll go back out. And you can come on the picnic, too."

Not that I anticipated needing him, but who knew. I wouldn't put it past Dove to send me into a panic attack considering my heart rate shot through the roof every time I got near her lately, and if she got close enough? If she touched me?

I might just need Bear to keep me conscious.

At five to noon, I stepped outside with a backpack full of food to find Dove rocking on one of the chairs on her porch.

"You're early," I said, not quite yelling but louder than I'd normally speak to make sure she heard me across the space separating our homes.

She hopped up, showcasing her new outfit. Gone were the T-shirt and shorts. Now she wore a teal dress in a similar style I'd seen before, almost a fifties flair with a full skirt that ended below the knee and tucked in at her waist, fitted through the bodice, with a marigold sweater covering her arms. On her feet were bright white sneakers, and her hair fell in cascading waves behind her.

Heart-stopping.

"I was too excited." She flashed a bright grin and kept coming, right to the foot of my stairs where we met, nearly toe to toe. "Thank you for this."

"You don't even know what's for lunch."

She shrugged one shoulder. "Doesn't matter."

I utterly failed to hide how she charmed me, my smile likely visible from space. As a devoted home cook, I should be offended she didn't care what I'd made. As a man who wanted nothing more than to sit next to her and feed her and listen to her talk?

Delighted.

"We'll see about that. Mind if Bear comes?" I asked, though I'd already brought him out, so he'd get leashed in the backyard if she preferred he didn't rather than get banished back inside. It was breezy and beautiful today, and his coat hadn't thickened up for winter yet, so he'd be fine.

"I wouldn't have it any other way." She looked at Bear and beamed.

It might've made me a simpleton, but I loved that she liked my dog.

Right now, I ate up anything she did or said. She had me under her spell, and I had a firm suspicion there would be no turning back.

The three of us wandered along the path that would lead to our destination. I asked about her time at Craic and she gave me a recap, not failing to mention more than once how loud and crowded it'd been. I had no regrets about not going, even if it meant I'd missed time with her. In that context, I wouldn't have been able to give her my attention.

This was better. A few persistent crickets chirped and little forest sounds chittered as we walked. Squirrels ran from Bear as he loped along, and Dove went quiet after a few minutes so we ended up walking in silence.

When I glanced at her, hoping I wouldn't find her upset or frustrated by the silence, I found her smiling to herself as she watched Bear's excitement. The dog was hard to miss, big as he was, and he also barked and rushed into the bushes now and then.

"He's not supposed to do that," I said, watching him bolt off the path.

"Seems like normal dog behavior. I just pity the squirrel if he finds him," she joked.

"It's decently normal. He should probably be over here with me, but he needs exercise today and I don't have the heart to call him back." He should be a bit closer so he could sense if something was amiss, but he was also blissful when he got to simply run and be wild for a bit. "Living on the farm lets him run around and get his energy out before it piles up and he becomes restless."

There were long months where I had no energy for him. I had nothing but a scrap of a will to live. Adam and Kenny, Luc when he was in town, and Beast, Tristan... they all tried to get him to go out with them. He'd usually acquiesce to a walk, but if they tried for much more, he'd get antsy and agitated until they brought him back to me.

Thinking about that made my heart squeeze like it was being shoved into a too-small glass jar. It hurt, and it made love for my best boy run over.

"I bet it feels good. You're doing okay, right? I mean, do you need him right now?" Worry tented her brow.

"I'm good." Keeping my eyes straight, I admitted, "Very happy to be with you today."

A few minutes later, we reached the small clearing next to the western tranche of Douglas fir trees. Our view started with the trees and past them, the purply-blue mountains rose with patches of autumnal colors beginning to appear.

We ate and talked—mostly her, but I did some talking, too. She asked questions, and I gave more than one-word answers. Kenny would've been proud. I tried not to revel in the way she devoured the roast chicken, warm potato salad, steamed green beans, homemade baguette, and cheese plate I'd brought. She sipped champagne from a stemless glass and hummed as she finished the drink before leaning back on her elbows so she was nearly fully reclined.

"I think you've spoiled me for all other picnics. The food was perfect, the champagne was perfect, and I'm sorry, but if it doesn't end with a cheese plate, I don't want it." She flicked her hair over a shoulder for emphasis.

My laugh came out low but overtly pleased. "I'll have to think of something to one-up myself next time."

I said it before I could register how it might sound, but Dove didn't let me off the hook. Instead, she tilted her head and asked, "Next time?"

"I'd like it if there was a next time," I admitted.

Bear snoozed in the grass twenty feet or so from the blanket to avoid him attempting to pilfer scraps. He didn't tend to be a beggar, but something told me he might try with Dove. I wondered if he could feel my heart rate tick up, and when I glanced over at him, his head was no longer tucked down at his feet. Head up, ears perked, his attention was on me.

As subtly as possible, I held up one hand to show him I was okay.

"Are we dating, Dorian?" Dove asked, effectively pulling my attention from my dog to her in a snap.

Her cheeks were pink from sun and champagne and maybe a touch of self-consciousness in the wake of asking the question. But she didn't need it.

"Are we, Dove? I have to say, I'd be very happy if the answer was yes, but I don't want you to feel—"

"I say yes. Yes. I would like that, too." She tucked her lips between her teeth. "Sorry to interrupt you, I just didn't want you to give me an out, because I don't need it. I'd be absolutely delighted to be dating you, if that's what you want."

Oh, this woman.

She had no idea how much I wanted.

CHAPTER TWENTY-NINE

Dove

Dorian's whiskey eyes were pinned on me, and despite the cool breeze rustling leaves and the pine scent drifting from the neat lines of Douglas fir trees, I might've spontaneously combusted if he didn't stop.

"That's what I want." His voice was low and sandpapery, gaze still glued to mine.

Did I dare push it? Just a little?

This wouldn't even be *pushing*, though, so much as understanding what this meant for him. Because choosing to be celibate didn't necessarily mean not dating... or did it? I didn't know. And my lack of experience in relationships meant I had little precedent. So in my true fashion, I just said the words hamster-wheeling through my head.

"Can we talk about what that looks like? What you have in mind?"

Years later, I'd remember this moment as the one when

I realized just how close Dorian played his cards. Until now, I couldn't have said whether he found me attractive or purely wanted friendship. Yes, he was overly generous with his food and his notes were adorable and he was kind and thoughtful and sensitive. He'd demonstrated all of that to me, but he did the same for his friends. So how would I know whether he thought of me like that?

Except... this pull between us. This connection we had that'd started weaving together with my tears on the porch or maybe even my misguided screams in his bedroom. *Ugh, that sounded a bit wrong.* Point was, we'd connected in unusual ways, but it hadn't felt like dating.

I couldn't say what it felt like, though, because it was certainly worlds apart from the friendships I had with Bruce or Kenny, or even someone single like Ethan Carter.

He was still quiet, and I wondered if the question was too much. "Sorry, maybe that's pushy? I don't know how this works."

I slumped down, letting my back rest against the blanket and shifting my gaze to the puffy clouds above us.

A warm brush against my arm brought my attention to him. He lay on his side now, his head propped in one hand.

"It's not pushy at all. It makes sense we should talk about it. I'm just not sure of how to answer... Not because I don't know what I want, but because I don't know if it's too much."

"Maybe you should just tell me what you want. Then I'll know, and I can tell you the same."

I was practically breathless, my pulse almost thready at my temple and throat. Lying next to him on the blanket was thrilling enough, but his focus and nearness paired with the conversation was almost dizzying in its influence on me.

He dipped his chin, spearing me with those eyes and

sending a flood of awareness from my head down to the soles of my feet.

"I want to spend time with you."

"Me, too. I mean, I want to spend time with you." I swallowed, almost wild with anticipation for his words.

"I want to support you—be there for you as often as you'll let me."

"Anytime. All the time. You honestly already do," I said, smiling too wide for my own good.

A half smile pulled at one side of his mouth, and he leaned, somehow much closer. He was almost *over* me, body lying alongside mine on the blanket and leaning on one elbow. This giant of a man made me feel deliciously small and yet there was nothing I could want more than to be at his mercy when he looked at me like this.

"Good. And I want—" His heady gaze dropped to my lips, then slowly drifted back up to my eyes. "—to kiss you."

"Yes."

As though nature and all its creatures heard my reply, the sounds and even the breeze seemed to still. Our eyes hooked into one another's, locked, and then he slowly moved his free hand to my head. He cupped my face in his warm, big palm and brushed his thumb over the apple of my cheek.

"You're so beautiful, Dove. Your heart, your mind..."

His intensity was searing a hole straight through me and I couldn't think straight. That must've been why I said, "Just the heart and mind, huh?"

One of those heart-piercing smiles broke across his face, and my heart rate jumped again.

"No, not just those things. But I wanted to make sure you know I don't just want you for your body—I want all of it."

He tucked a stray strand of hair behind my ear in the gentlest, most tender gesture that had my breath catching.

He inched closer, a scant inch from my lips. "Make no mistake, though, Dove. I do want you for your body, too."

My lashes fluttered and I swallowed, chest downright heaving by now, and he still didn't close the distance. Impulse took over, and I reached for the front of his shirt and pulled him in, though it didn't take any force. Only the clear invitation, the consent written in the gesture and my very enthusiastic return.

The second our lips finally touched, I slipped my hands into his hair. I shouldn't have been surprised by this big, quiet, sensitive man kissing in slow, mesmerizing passes, but here he was drugging me with his touch and then retreating all too soon.

My eyes reluctantly opened to find him staring at me with naked wonder on his handsome face.

"Why'd you stop?" I asked, then blushed profusely because I absolutely sounded like a little beggar.

He rewarded me with a light laugh, his gaze tracking where the tips of his fingers traced over the ridge of my collar bone, then slid up to traverse the slope of my shoulder. Eyes half lidded, his feather-light touch had so much tension coiling in me, I didn't know where to go with it. I gripped his shirt again, tempted to tug and see if he'd kiss me again, but then he slipped the strap of my dress back over my shoulder—it must've slid down while I'd been lying here.

"We've got time. I don't want to rush anything with you." But then, he dropped his head and pressed one more kiss so completely gentle and *full*, it brought tears to my eyes.

Silly though it might've sounded, it was like everything

this man did had a purpose and that kiss's was to say, "*You're precious to me.*"

"Alright?" he asked, pulling away to see me attempt to discreetly brush away a tear.

"Haven't you figured out I'm a crier?" I asked, rolling my eyes to escape his focus for a breath.

His fingers on my chin guided my face back to his. "I like that you're not scared to feel."

I like every single thing about you.

I didn't say it out loud, but goodness, it was truer with every passing breath.

"You don't seem like you are either," I said, a raw, tender sensation flooding my chest.

His head tipped to one side. "Used to be. Years of therapy and making friends with a bunch of people who were also working on emotional honesty and mental health was key." He chuckled low. "And having Kenny Carmichael as one of my best friends doesn't hurt either."

I grinned, loving that he could own all of those things.

Bear barked, a more aggressive bark than I'd heard in a while. Dorian sat up in a jolt, then jumped to his feet far faster than a man that large should move. While I sat up bit by bit, he jogged after Bear, who'd stopped at the edge of the pines.

If there was something out there, he had to be seeing or hearing it with dog vision. I couldn't see a thing, but Bear was clearly agitated.

Hesitating for a moment, I jogged over to join them right as they turned back toward me.

"See anything?" I asked.

"No. He's looking toward the property line so maybe someone was wandering around. Could've been a coyote or a mountain lion, but he wouldn't have relaxed so quickly if it had been an animal."

His hand extended to mine, and our fingers laced, palms pressing together. My pulse absolutely rioted.

"Kind of did that backwards, didn't we?" he asked, looking down at our hands.

"Did what?"

He released me, and we began packing up the picnic. "Kissed first, and just now held hands for the first time."

Um, adorable. "Technically, we've already held hands. You held my hand that day I cried on you."

He chuckled. "On me, right. Well, that didn't count. It wasn't romantic."

A sizzly little thrill swept through me. "You want romance?"

He raised his brows. "Only with you."

I made no attempt to hide my sigh, and we worked on cleaning up. I threw a ball for Bear with a little thrower thing that let me launch it super far and also meant I didn't have to touch the slobbery thing while Dorian rolled up the blanket and donned the pack filled with our leftovers.

As we walked back, he offered his hand again, and it brought us right back to the conversation.

"So, are you concerned we've done things out of order?" I asked, hoping it didn't actually bother him, but completely unsure.

He squeezed my hand a little tighter, a reassuring pulse. "No, not at all. I think it just means we need to hold hands *and* kiss as often as possible."

I laughed, delighted. "Oh, is that what it means?"

He stopped right there in the middle of the trail with trees arching over us, their leaves fluttering a chorus. He kept our clasped hands linked and slipped the other to my lower back, drawing me a touch closer. "Yes. That's definitely what it means."

And then, he kissed me again.

CHAPTER THIRTY

Dorian

By the time I heard Dove's car on Sunday afternoon, I'd finished cleaning up from tea with the guys and had read and reread the same paragraph of my book while I relived the dream that was yesterday.

It still felt like I might wake up and find I'd crafted the whole day in my mind. It'd been too perfect, and yet it'd been real. The dream of touching her, kissing her, laughing with her... It'd been so free and right. It was real and replete with the sensation of longing and anticipation, yet satisfaction, too. I never imagined laying bare my desire for her would be so completely welcome and returned.

Talk about coexisting feelings.

I'd been practicing a kind of brutal honesty with myself for a while. By brutal, I didn't mean cruel or purposefully abrupt. The effort and brutality came in the promise that I would be truthful even if it hurt, but that I'd also give myself grace enough to handle it.

This ideology had grown out of a need for reality checks, as my therapist had called them. I'd tended to spiral into depressive negativity and often jumped to the worst possible conclusions. Rebuilding my habits surrounding these thoughts had been some of the hardest work in my life.

When your brain is telling you there is nothing worth living for, that no one will miss you, that no one cares if you're gone, that everyone who does love you will ultimately be better off... This is where the reality-checking began. Well that, and quality therapy, and for me, the help of medication.

The further out from the deepest depression I'd experienced, the more grateful I was to have the distance. It was never a guarantee I wouldn't struggle so deeply again, but I knew the signs, and part of such brutal honesty was interrogating whether there *were* signs I was starting to struggle.

Lately, there had been none. Not a one. I'd had to reality-check the idea that Dove might like me more than once because it'd been so long since I'd wanted a woman's attention, let alone believed she might actually be giving it to me with the same level of interest I had for her. My therapist had challenged me, pushed me pretty hard, actually, when I said I had feelings for her but knew she didn't for me. Dr. Corrigan had asked, "How do you know?"

This was always how it started—this cycle of reality-checking an idea that usually resulted in me discovering I'd jumped to one conclusion or another.

Did I know Dove didn't want me? No, not for certain. She was just so light and lovely and social and fun. Could she possibly want someone who struggled with crowds and sometimes even agoraphobia outside his own space, who had a history like I did, and who hadn't been in a relationship for years?

Dove seemed too good to be true on one hand, but she was blessedly willing to show her imperfections and dash that thought. She was completely untouchable for a man who had literally not touched a woman beyond a handshake in years, and yet...

And yet our kiss had awoken a part of me I'd wondered about. Had my desire for sex disappeared altogether? Had it been the effects of depression, or medication? Had it been the result of the PTSD I'd battled with? Yes, I'd been celibate by choice, but it honestly hadn't been a struggle. It had been the path of least resistance on several levels.

Dove had woken me up in so many ways. She'd drawn out a protective drive, she'd given me an outlet for caring for someone, and she'd certainly set fire to the idea that I wouldn't ever feel attraction or desire again.

Could she want me? The astounding reality, based on her notes and her excitement over spending time together, was yes. It'd taken me a few days to wrap my head around that, and every step of the way I'd caveated the idea she could be interested in more than friendship with a giant asterisk ready to remind me that if she didn't, it was fine, and hopefully we'd still be friends.

Her simply asking what we were doing had disarmed all the fears and hedging I might've been attempting to build up in my head. Yes, I'd struggled with whether I could be good for her knowing I'd likely never be done with depression and it would never be done with me. But one of many things I liked and admired about her was that she would tell me the truth.

Just as I was reliving the kiss and the remarkable

restraint I'd shown, I heard a rough bark and shouts in the driveway and sprinted to the front hallway. Dove had just gotten home, and the odds this didn't have to do with her were very slim.

Flinging open the door, I found Bear standing with his fur bunched and teeth bared, a low growl issued to a man in jeans and a black T-shirt slowly backing away from him and Dove.

My heart sank, pulse hammering at my neck. Some small part of me said I should go back inside, should shut myself away from this stranger on my property. But the man in me, the one who wouldn't stand for anyone to be intimidated or harmed? He said to go handle it.

So I did.

"There was always going to come a time when you'd come back, Dovey. You have to admit that to yourself," the man said, backing up another step.

Dove's hand held on to Bear's collar lightly, not pulling at the neck, but clutching it for safety.

"I'm not a part of that world anymore. It's way past time you accept it," she said, voice trembling, but strong.

I rushed down the stairs. "What's this?" I said, murmuring, "Easy, buddy," to Bear as I passed him to stand next to Dove.

Her frightened, aggrieved gaze met mine. "Dorian, this is my brother, Hawk."

"This your boyfriend? Landlord? What is he? You're screwing him for rent or something, aren't you?"

Dove gasped and covered her mouth, and I didn't even think when I charged forward. Two men jumped out of the back cab of the truck idling a few feet behind him.

"You will not speak to her that way." I continued toward

him, intent on taking him by the collar and leading him back to his car.

His friends had other plans. One swung a baseball bat at my ribs right as Hawk knocked a fist to my face. I turned and grasped the metal bat, ripping it away from the man holding it suddenly enough he stumbled forward and tripped, but I took the punch to the cheekbone.

Ow.

"Stop! Hawk! What are you doing? I'm calling the police right now," Dove yelled, panic in her voice just over my shoulder.

Bear bumped against my leg as I tossed the bat in the back of the truck. "Get off my property and never come back."

Hawk had been shaking his hand, likely having broken a finger or two after throwing a remarkably bad punch, though it had hurt, and I'd be bruised. The other fool had rightly chosen to stay out of it.

"Dove, you know what's true. You know what's right."

With that, Hawk and his goons scampered back into their truck as Bear unleashed his ferocious bark and chased them down the driveway.

Dove was with me before I had a chance to turn to her. "You're hurt. Let's get you some ice. I'm so sorry, Dorian. I never imagined he'd come here. I shouldn't have let him. I didn't realize—"

I folded her into a hug, and she instantly deflated, tears coming, too. "I'm alright. Everything's fine. You can't control another person, honey, and I'm not mad at you."

"I'm so sorry. I'm so sorry," she said over and over again as she let me hold her and she clutched at my shoulders.

We pulled back, and I cupped the nape of her neck,

stroking down the long hair cascading over her back. "Come inside?"

She nodded, then dropped to her knees as Bear trotted back to us, breathing hard. He swerved from me to her.

"Thank you, Bear. Thank you for protecting me." She hugged him around the neck and then stood, the three of us heading toward my house.

My heart still pounded like it might try to break out of my ribcage, but with her hand around my back and Bear at my side, no spiraling fear reared its head.

We were safe. We'd be fine.

And as soon as I could, I'd report this to everyone possible and figure out why the boys of Patriot Ridge felt like they had a right to come onto my property and speak to Dove that way.

CHAPTER THIRTY-ONE

Dove

I dabbed at Dorian's head with a damp paper towel. His skin had split the tiniest bit, but as head wounds tended to do, it'd bled like a drama king. He wouldn't need stitches, though.

"I'm so sorry," I said, hating that this had happened at all.

Stupid Hawk. What did he think I would do when he came here?

"What did he want?" he asked, gaze steady on me.

I couldn't return it. The embarrassment and shame still swirling around in my belly made it hard to look him straight in his clear, forthright eyes.

"He wanted me to go with him. Said it was 'time for me to come back.'" My teeth ground together remembering his words and the expression on his face packed with so much certainty.

"Come back?"

I exhaled through my nose, working to calm the inner turmoil and focus on patching up this sweet hero of a man. After covering the small wound with a bandage, I brushed back the hair that'd fallen onto his forehead and finally let myself make eye contact.

"I left a while after my parents died. I think I told you that—I came to live with Nan but he ended up in juvenile detention, then got out when he was eighteen, so he went back. I'd made him promise me he wouldn't hurt himself and he assured me he wouldn't." With a shake of my head, I sighed. "Clearly, he stayed with a group who maintained the ideology of the cult. I don't know if Patriot Ridge is a cult community now or if he and the people he arrived with brought that in or what, but I can tell you that's what we were raised in. And if they have someone they're following like we did the leader back then, it's bad. The way he showed up like he had a right to me... that tells me he's still in it."

Dorian's gaze turned steely. "No one has a right to you but you."

"I know that. That's why I told him I wasn't going with him." Pressing my lips together, I debated telling him the other part. I didn't want to keep anything from him, and it did involve him since they'd not only come onto his property, but they'd also hurt him. "He said I was acting like a whore and I needed to come home."

There was a pause, a stillness in the air that almost made me tremble before Dorian spoke.

"Any idea why he'd say that?"

I swallowed hard, anxiety notching up at the conclusion I'd come to. "I think he was watching us. At our picnic. I'm guessing that's what Bear was barking at."

My cheeks flamed hot, and I was yet again on the verge of tears. *Ugh.*

His hands reached out to rest on my waist, and even in the context of this conversation, the contact sent a thrill through me.

"Do you regret our picnic?" he asked, no more steely grit in his voice. Only concern now.

"No. Not at all. Even if Hawk was being a creep and spying on us, which—" I shivered, genuinely troubled by the thought. "—I don't regret it." With another breath, I summoned the courage to ask, "Do you?"

He let out a soft laugh. "No, Dove. I could never regret a single moment with you, let alone that day."

Shimmering, glittering, wondering elation bubbled up inside me. "So you really must like me, huh?"

He chuckled, then cupped my cheeks with his delectable hands. "I really do. I'm sorry this happened, but you stood your ground. You told him no, and I think he got the message you've got reinforcements."

I gripped his wrists, holding him in place. "I'm sorry you got hurt."

"Don't apologize for your brother again, Dove. You aren't responsible for him." He slipped his hands from my cheeks down to my shoulders and leaned down, resting his forehead against mine.

My heart ached from the touch. "Thank you."

"I'm glad I was here. And I think we need to call the chief and report this."

We pulled back, and I slumped but nodded. "Yeah. We better. I'd honestly been hoping he'd distanced himself from this kind of thing, but I've had a bad feeling ever since that phone call."

Brothers didn't just go around accusing their sisters of

awful things without some sense of self-righteousness, at the very least. But that feeling came from being a part of a culture that had poisoned him against women and society at large.

If I let myself sink down into the grief and anger this reality caused, I'd probably never get back up. Being here with Dorian helped, though. Facing Hawk with him, not on my own... that helped, too. I hated he'd gotten hurt, but if I'd been at the house I'd lived in with Nan, the house I'd just sold, it was so unlikely anyone would've been there to help, let alone someone I trusted like I did Dorian. And of course, sweet, ferocious Bear had kept me safe, too.

This was the crux of so many of my thoughts lately. I trusted Dorian in ways I'd never trusted any man *ever*.

What this meant, I wasn't sure. But I knew that first kiss, the closeness I felt with him, the desire I held for him that seemed to expand out with every breath I took... I couldn't help but feel it was leading somewhere significant.

While I'd been mulling over these things, Dorian had been making calls. Here again was an example of how much I trusted the man. I was used to being the doer in any given situation. Something's wrong, I'll figure out how to fix it. Someone's sick, I'll figure out what they need. A task needs to be checked off the list? Sign me up.

Caretaking had been bred into me quite literally, but it was one part of the culture I didn't look back on with frustration. I loved how my tendency toward caring for others had led me to a profession I loved—even now when I was in a slump with it.

What I couldn't remember doing for a long, long time was letting someone else take care of me or anything I needed to do. But here I was, sitting on a barstool twiddling my thumbs with deep thoughts while Dorian handled the mess. Bear paced back and forth, brushing by my legs with each pass. I let my hand drag over his back, the soothing sensation of his fur and his warmth easing my rattled nerves.

He hung up his phone and rested his hands on the countertop. "Chief and the sheriff will be over in a few. Since it happened here, this is on Silverton land and Chief will take the statements, but Sheriff Ryan wanted to hear what happened. I thought he should. He's helped me deal with some of the problems I've had with the commune, and this seems important and possibly pertinent. That okay?"

"Makes sense. I'd rather they both know what's going on, especially if there are issues for anyone else. I assume this is just about me since I'm related, but..." I shook my head, not wanting to let my thoughts stray to some of the things that'd gone wrong in New Mexico. I remembered girls, scared and dirty, piled into one small cabin next to the leader's house. I remembered them crying all the time, and my mom refusing to talk about them. She never said it, but I'd sensed relief when the compound had been raided and we'd had to move.

Hawk wouldn't be involved in something like that, would he? Could his mind be so warped by now?

"Do you mind frozen pizza?" he asked, tapping on his oven to preheat it.

"I don't at all. I love a good frozen pizza. Though I am surprised the king of homemade deliciousness would deign to eat frozen pizza." I gave him a playful smile, wanting to distract myself from the upcoming stress of having to recount what'd happened.

Couldn't I just pretend it'd never happened?

No. I couldn't. But I could rib Dorian about eating frozen pizza.

"Do I act like I wouldn't? I might like to cook, but sometimes, a cheap frozen meal hits the spot," he said, his brow furrowed in a way that said he might actually be troubled by the thought that he came off as too fancy for a frozen pie.

Unable to resist, I leaned over and pressed my hand over his where it rested on the counter. "No. You don't act like that. I just can't imagine wanting to eat anything but my own food if everything I cooked and baked was as good as your food."

His slow smile made my stomach swoop low.

"I'll keep that in mind."

By the end of the night, we'd both given our statements to Chief Whitacker of Silverton PD, and Sheriff Ryan of Juniper View had been there to listen and ask a few questions. Both men had been patient, kind, and to the point, but by the time it was done, I was absolutely exhausted. Dorian walked me to the door with our fingers laced and kissed my cheek, then my forehead.

I wanted him to press me into the door and kiss me until my mind fizzled out, but I kind of loved that in the wake of a hugely emotional afternoon, he hadn't pushed for anything. He'd taken some of the burden, what he could anyway, and he had given me comfort.

And even in the midst of all of the drama, I was very close to giving him my heart.

CHAPTER THIRTY-TWO

Dorian

I hadn't seen Dove in two days.

I tried not to pout about it, but I definitely was. Mostly, it was her work schedule, although she'd come home earlier than usual last night but I'd been the one out late. I'd taken a low-key job for Saint—one I'd eyed on the schedule as something I could do without too much anxiety surrounding it.

Kenny, Luc, and Jude knew I was struggling with assignments still, but as far as I knew, everyone else thought I'd overcome all my issues and worked part-time because that was the way I wanted it. And in some ways, it was.

I didn't want to be uninvolved. I didn't want to lose my family at Saint. And there was a real fear that if I let this... itch to step back even further take over, I'd do just that.

A small voice suggested I interrogate that premise. At some point, I'd have to bring it up with Dr. Corrigan and we'd likely look at it from every angle. It'd be painful. It'd probably help.

But sometimes, therapy was like that—painful and helpful. And sometimes, knowing this made it hard to want to do, even knowing the helpful part would ultimately and possibly dramatically improve one's life.

Was I in danger of focusing all my attention and energy on the farm and this new thing with Dove and ignoring those niggling little problems I should be addressing? Yes.

I didn't want to think about that right now, though. I wanted to think about how I hadn't really texted Dove much. I had her number, but we'd not breached the chatting wall, likely because when she was at work, she didn't stay tuned into her phone, and if she wasn't at work, usually she was here. Otherwise, she visited her nan and saw her friends, and she'd mentioned she hated to be glued to her phone in those instances.

I appreciated this, so why would I contribute to the need to be tuned in by texting? *And yet...* I wanted to see her. She worked so hard, and she'd been so worn out by Sunday's events. I'd left her dinner Monday night, but since I'd worked late yesterday, I hadn't gotten to. So tonight, I'd track her down.

She rolled into her usual parking spot at nearly eight-thirty. I didn't want to seem like a puppy waiting at the door for her, though it wouldn't have been an inaccurate description, so I decided to take a lap around the kitchen and then exit the house.

By the time I did so, she was still sitting in the car.

Worry spiked, and I jogged over to her driver's side door, sliding the pastry box onto the roof and yanking the door open.

"Dove, what—"

She looked nearly gray in the dim light, her color so off.

"I don't feel good."

"No, you mustn't. Can I help you inside?"

She looked at her hands where they rested limply on her navy scrub-clad legs. "I was going to go inside. Get some fluids and take some meds. But I can't seem to make me do it."

There was something so adorably simple and innocent about that statement, so plain and sweet, and yet the charm it held soured when I acknowledged how unlike her it was. She was quick to act and get things done. She didn't linger in her car, and she didn't talk as though she had no control over her body.

"Can I help you inside, Dove?" I asked again, hoping she'd give her consent this time, but deciding that even if she didn't, I'd try to coax her out of the car and see if I could get a handle on what was wrong.

"You? You can help me with anything you want. You can get it, Dorian."

Her eyes widened and blinked so innocently, I almost wished it were brighter so I could enjoy the expression.

I coughed, trying not to laugh at a time like now. *Good to know I can get it.* She hadn't hidden her attraction to me by any means, but for a heartbeat, I stayed immobilized by the delight before my logic broke through and restarted my movements.

"Alright. Let's get you unbuckled, and I'll help you in. We'll figure this out."

Her soft "'kay" came in a whisper, but she still didn't move. So, I started narrating my movements.

"I'm unbuckling you now." With a click, the belt released, and I guided it over her inert arm and past her face back to its resting, retracted position. "Now I'm going to take your arm and help you up, okay?"

She nodded, not resisting, but barely helping. With more effort than I'd expected, I maneuvered her out of the car, all while she periodically whispered her apologies.

As I guided her up the stairs holding most of her weight slumped against me with one hand around her back, I took her keys and unlocked her door. "No need to apologize, honey. You're sick."

Heat was absolutely radiating off her, and anywhere I touched was burning. She had to have a fever and based on the way she winced and her lethargy, she'd been feeling bad for a while.

After settling her on the couch, I knelt down so we were eye to eye and took one of her hands. "Dove, can you tell me where your medicine is? Do you have a ther-mometer?"

She blinked back at me like I'd posed a riddle. "I have a fever?"

"You do. I want to see how high it is, and I need to get you some medicine. You might need to go to the hospital." I could get her to the Silverton ER in twenty minutes—maybe even fifteen since it was late enough there wouldn't be traffic.

"I'm not going to the hospital. I work there. I literally work there, Dorian. Dorian." She sighed and her head dropped back. "I like you so much and I hate that you're seeing me like this."

Her voice held tears, and I moved to sit by her, brushing the hair out of her face and cupping her hot-to-the-touch cheek with my palm. "I want to help you feel better. Can I do that for you? I can call one of your friends if you'd rather."

I had no doubt Elise or Jo or any of the women she was so close with would be here in a heartbeat if I asked them to.

Speaking of, I texted Doc. Dove might be a nurse, but she couldn't assess herself. If she didn't want to go to the hospital, I'd have to use what resources I had.

"No. You can do it." Her blue eyes blinked open and took a moment before they focused in on me. "I trust you."

A wild roar of triumph rose up inside me, but I quelled it in favor of stroking her cheek. "Thank you, honey. I'm going to get some supplies and I'll be right back, okay?"

She mumbled her assent, and I moved. She'd mentioned medicine in the car, and if she was anything like Doc and other medical types I'd known over the years, she had a decent supply of over-the-counter options somewhere.

I found a tidy basket of brand-name and generic offerings in the linen closet and rifled through them to find a temporal thermometer and a few different options to address the fever. I'd need to figure out her other symptoms, too.

After a scan, the thermometer showed a solid fever of over a hundred and three.

"I'm going to take your sweatshirt off, okay? We need to let your body cool a bit. Can you tell me what else is wrong?" I asked, sliding her arms out and guiding her forward.

Her brow tented in the middle, and her lips were curved into a frown. "My whole everything hurts. Throat. Body aches. I had chills last night. Been feeling worn down since Sunday, but I thought it was all the stuff with Hawk and then work. Guess it was this plague."

"What's going around? Anything you've been seeing at the clinic?" Might give me a decent clue.

"Lots of seasonal allergies. Had a case of norovirus last

week, a few strep throats and a flu B or two. Nothing major. This time of year doesn't tend to be too awful. It's probably allergies for me, too. I just need to sleep."

She said all of this with her eyes closed, her mouth barely moving enough to form the words. *Yeah.* Definitely just allergies.

"When was the last time you ate?" She'd need food in her belly to at least address the fever. Couldn't do much if it was flu. Maybe Doc could bring a strep test.

"I had the dinner you made me last night. It was so good. Didn't have an appetite this morning... guess that should've tipped me off." She sat up and pulled at her shirt, yanking the scrub top over her head and leaving her in only a thin white tank that hugged her glorious curves. "It's hot."

You're telling me. Unhelpful thought, but there was no denying I found every single part of Dove attractive.

For now, I had a job to do. Get her meds, see what Doc could do, and hopefully avoid a middle of the night trip to the ER if things got worse.

She'd put her trust in me, and I wouldn't fail her.

CHAPTER THIRTY-THREE

Dove

A cool hand brushed over my forehead. I leaned into it and hummed.

"Never stop touching me," I mumbled.

He coughed.

He?

My eyes opened wide, lids heavy, to see Dorian gazing back at me.

Mm. Dorian. He's so nice and hot and nice and hot.

"Thank you. I think you're nice and hot, too."

His deep voice had my mouth dropping open because apparently, my inner monologue was broken.

"You're alright, Dove. Doc's here, and Jo came with him. Can they come in and see you?"

I tried to scoot myself upright, but still felt weak and awful. "What time is it? Yes, they can."

"It's about ten-thirty. You were asleep for about two

hours and your fever came down a little, but not as much as I'd like. Doc was kind enough to come over so we don't have to go into the hospital."

His eyes crinkled so pleasingly around the edges. His face, even behind that bushy beard, was so handsome, so pleasing to me.

"I like you so much," I said, a whine in my voice that somewhere in my foggy, fever-addled mind I recognized would embarrass me when this was over.

"Whoa there, my friend. How about we let Adam check you out and give Stone a break?"

Jo's voice filtered into my ears, and I shifted so I could see her.

"You're so pretty. Thank you for coming. I'm sorry," I babbled.

She chuckled but made a face. "You're really out of it, huh? I thought you said you were maybe coming down with something?"

I vaguely remembered texting the group chat that I was feeling off. Then I'd gone to work and somehow pushed through. The minute I sat down in my car, I'd realized I was too tired to safely drive home so I'd let myself nap, thinking I'd take a twenty-minute snooze and wake up refreshed. Instead, I got worse, and had just wanted to get home to my bed.

And if I was being honest, back to Dorian.

"Mind if I take a look, Dove?" Adam asked, taking a seat next to me as I finally managed to edge myself up against the headboard with Jo's help.

I let him at it. He might not've been a medical doctor, but he had an incredible wealth of training and knowledge. He'd trained in Level I trauma ERs and operating rooms, he'd performed a number of procedures in the field to keep soldiers alive, and I had every faith he could handle evaluating me for whatever garbage was attacking me.

After a quick but thorough exam, he swabbed me for all the things and promised to get the specimens into the hospital right away. Since we had some very rural areas in Silverton and the surrounding counties, we had doctors and nurses who did house calls. Adam had recently gotten certified for this so he could provide the service not only to the Saint staff and families, but to the larger community as well. I, too, occasionally took shifts for community call, as we termed it, but I hadn't in a while thanks to my lack of availability.

"Thank you. Thanks for coming," I said, smiling pitifully.

Adam slipped out to speak to Dorian, and Jo lingered a moment.

"He seems to be taking very good care of you. I didn't realize..."

If I had felt any better than I did right now, I probably would've blushed. "Yeah. I haven't had a chance to update on that but it's turning into something, I think."

Her grin was blinding. Or maybe that was the headache talking.

"I couldn't be happier. And I think he's enjoying getting to take care of you."

I snorted, my best impression of a scoff, and shut my eyes after a failed attempt to roll them because *ow*. "I doubt that. But thanks. Assuming I'm better by next Saturday, I'll be ready to report in."

My feeble attempts to stay upright failed, and I slumped back down. Jo left me with a few more kind words and the promise to check in and let everyone know how I was doing, and I nodded off.

Sometime later, Dorian's strong arm cradled me behind the shoulders. "Come on, honey. Just swallow this and you can go back to sleep."

I blinked my eyes open enough to see his serious face, then felt like I was falling backward into a sea of clouds as he lowered me back down.

The next time I woke must've been hours later. I was sticky and my mouth tasted like an absolute horror show, so I stumbled to the bathroom and into the shower. I didn't manage to deal with my hair, but I scrubbed away the worst of the sweat and grime, brushed my teeth, and poured myself back into bed.

Dorian knocked lightly on the door, which stood ajar a few inches.

"Come in," I said, voice small and tired.

"Glad you could shower. I'm sorry I didn't realize you were going to or I could've helped." He cleared his throat. "I mean, I could've done something."

I couldn't be sure, but it almost looked like he was blushing under his dark beard. If I felt any less like something that'd climbed out of a dumpster, I would've been thrilled by all the possible insinuations. As it was, I only smiled.

"Thank you. I feel a little better, maybe, but I think I want to go right back to sleep."

He nodded, crossing his thick arms. "Understandable. Do you think you could get something down? Toast maybe? Or I can warm up some soup I made earlier. I worry that at this point, you're running on empty and your body won't be happy about continuing to take meds."

After seeing it was nearly noon, I conceded. When he walked in with a tray and set it down on my lap, the tears came.

"No, no, Dove. Don't cry," he said, cupping my face with one of his big, lovely hands and wiping a tear with the pad of his thumb.

"You probably shouldn't touch me if I have the flu or strep or... anything. You're honestly doomed at this point." I sniffled.

His smile was small, but so pleased, I didn't know what'd made him so happy.

"Why is that something to smile about?" I asked, grumpy from sickness, exhaustion, hunger, and the thought that this man's good deed of taking care of me would be paid back with illness.

"Worst case scenario, I get sick. I can handle that. I know it's miserable, but it'll be okay if I do. I don't have much of a day job and Pedro and Connor can handle the farm."

He took the spoon sitting on a neatly folded napkin and set it in the bowl of steaming soup. On a small side plate sat a slice of bread I'd bet money he'd made from scratch slathered with butter, and a small glass of water stood next to something purple.

"That's nonsense. I'll be fine. You shouldn't be exposing yourself to me," I said, tempted to cross my arms with a huff except it sounded hard and the soup actually smelled appetizing. Also, *oops*, even I heard that double entendre.

But he didn't seem fazed because he nudged the spoon toward me.

I leaned over the tray and took a bite. *Heaven.* Of course it tasted great. Salty and smooth, somehow. Noodles, chicken, and maybe a carrot in that spoonful, and it was all wonderful. Granted, I already felt like I didn't want to continue, but that was the illness talking.

"Hey, take some more and I'll tell you why I'm here."

I stared him down for a minute, but I couldn't resist the need to know. I took another bite, then a big chomp of bread, and raised my brows.

"Good girl," he said with a chuckle.

I choked on the bread, coughing with aching ribs as I swallowed. He had no idea... just none whatsoever. And I would not address the matter right now.

But at some point? Yes.

"I'm here because I want to be, Dove. I know I don't have to." His melting dark honey gaze bore into mine. "You take care of everyone all the time. At work, in your personal life, and even in your friendships. But who takes care of you?"

Who takes care of you? It was a ludicrous question and one I had a clear answer to. "No one needs to take care of me. I like taking care of other people."

"And I believe you. But right now, the answer to that question is me."

With that, he changed the subject, talking through what I might be able to eat later, if I had preferences, and when I'd need more meds. I had the flu and it was simply a matter of time before I'd feel better.

I was in my body, but not. Sick, sore, but not lonely. I was hurting and kind of miserable, but I had this warm, serene feeling couching my rough edges right now.

As I drifted off to sleep, the answer to why I wasn't worried or sad or missing the comfort of someone with me and watching over me like I'd only ever had with Nan played through my mind.

The answer to that question is him.

CHAPTER THIRTY-FOUR

Dove

It'd been years since I'd been this sick.

It'd also been a long time since someone had taken care of me. My parents really never had. It wasn't the way they did things. I'd go back to our cabin and sweat out a fever. Usually, the camp doctor would bring ibuprofen or whatever. I thought I got antibiotics once, but I was seven or eight, so I didn't know for sure.

When I'd moved in with Nan and she'd doted on me when I got a bad virus just in time for my eighteenth birthday, I'd almost been confused. I'd gotten so used to being alone when I was sick, I hardly knew how to let someone help me. But she did.

And now, Dorian had taken the job.

Next to me, Bear's collar clinked. Apparently, I'd asked for him in my most fever-delirious state, and Dorian had brought him to me. What if he'd needed him?

What did it say that not only the man did what I asked, but also that I asked him in the first place? I trusted him, yes, but asking him for things? I'd been doing it since practically the day I moved in here, but it still astounded me.

"How are you today?" Dorian asked as he stepped inside the front door with hands full of reusable grocery bags and a small bouquet of fall flowers.

"I'm doing better than I have in a few days. My head is clear, I think, and my body aches are gone." What a relief. I still didn't have energy, based on how exhausted I felt after just a few hours interacting with people, but I didn't feel the need to instantly pass out either.

"Good. Do you need anything?" He settled the bags on the counter and came to sit in the big chair next to where I'd made my place on the couch.

Or rather, where he'd helped me do so. Sometime yesterday, I'd gotten tired of being alone in my bedroom and asked if it was okay if I moved to the living room so I'd have the TV and be near the kitchen and, frankly, nearer to him. Apparently, the novelty of having him here had a grip on me and I wanted to soak up every second.

He'd simply looked at me with those soulful eyes and said, "Anything you want, Dove."

"I'm okay, thank you. Jo and Liz refilled my drinks and fed me lunch. It was great, by the way." No surprise, Dorian's food was delicious.

Oh, and Elise had texted about ten times, but she was in the throes of excitement over the recent engagement and fulfilling some huge donut order, so she couldn't make it. Jess was the same—tons of texts, but I refused to let her feel bad. She should stay far away from me so Baby Will didn't get whatever this was I had.

"Glad you liked it."

He had that lightly pleased look he got whenever I mentioned how good his cooking was, though it'd gotten more and more subtle the last few days as my ability to actually eat had all but disappeared. My appetite had finally reemerged late last night, and I was relieved to find it still in full force today as evidenced by the two bowls of soup and three slices of fresh bread I'd eagerly downed.

The real surprise had been when my friends had come knocking right as he'd been leaving earlier. He'd mentioned having errands to run, and apparently he hadn't wanted to leave me alone, so he'd roped my friends into looking after me while he was away. They'd agreed to risk it and help me out, the dears.

I'd already suspected it, but Dorian Forrester was looking more and more like a mother hen.

"Errands go okay?" I asked, curious to see if he'd say... anything.

Face suddenly curiously impassive, he said, "All good. Let me get the groceries put up."

And then, he got up and scuttled into the kitchen as though he really thought my nan hadn't texted me.

"Are you really not going to tell me what you did?" I pressed.

He froze for a heartbeat. I wouldn't have noticed if I hadn't been looking directly at him, trying to read his body language. *Got him!*

He removed items from bags and shrugged one shoulder. "Grocery, stopped into Bloom, swung by Saint. A few other things."

"Like?" I was pushing it, but seriously? Was he really not going to say anything?

His gaze swung to mine, eyes narrowed. "Things."

I huffed and shoved off the couch in one swift, too-fast

movement. "Are you really not going to admit you went to see Nan?"

But before I reached him, I wobbled, a wave of dizzy, world-tilting vertigo sending me sideways. As though in slow motion, my head swam, and I pitched backward instead of continuing toward him. Somehow, he reached me and steadied me with an arm around my back and one warm palm pressed into mine.

"Whoa there, killer. You're going to need to move a little slower."

I could hear a smile in his voice though I had my eyes crushed closed against the nausea.

I groaned, and my head dropped against his shoulder. We stayed like that, him supporting me, until the world shifted again, and I was in his arms. A brutally short few seconds later, he settled me back on the couch, then scooted back to give me space and sat on the coffee table across from where he'd laid me, one hand pressed to my shin like it might help ground me.

"Ugh, that was so dumb and so dramatic," I moaned, gingerly opening my eyes to test whether the dizziness had faded. When my vision no longer swam and Dorian materialized, his handsome face etched with concern, I let them open all the way.

"Maybe not your best move."

I glared at him. "Maybe not, but I was trying to get you to admit you went to visit Nan and are for some reason not telling me. Why wouldn't you tell me?"

I'd gotten a text that simply said, "Best soup I've ever had." And I knew.

"I wasn't trying to keep it from you. Just didn't want you to worry about it."

"Why would I worry about you seeing Nan?" He didn't make sense.

He squeezed the place on my calf where his hand had been resting, then removed it. *Tragic.* Resting his elbows on his knees, he knitted his fingers together.

"I know it's hard for you to have someone taking care of you. I didn't want it to feel like it was one more thing you need to keep track of."

Oh. Was I that obviously uncomfortable?

"I don't want you to feel bad. I just... I want to thank you properly. I can't believe you went to see my grandma and you've never even met her." Like, who did that?

Who just up and took homemade soup to someone's grandparent?

"You go see her every few days. You have lunch with her at least once a week. I figured she'd be missing you and wanted to let her know you were okay."

His gaze avoided mine as though his choice might've embarrassed him now that I knew.

And me?

I could hardly breathe through the crushing, aching, smothering kind of love exploding out of me for this man.

"That's so ridiculously sweet," I eked out, stapling my mouth shut to avoid blubbering.

He heard it, though. Of course he did, and so did Bear, who edged himself closer to my hips and settled his head on my thigh, brows knit with that dog empathy he brought just by being nearby.

Dorian plucked up one of my hands after I swiped at some tears.

"If I'd known it'd make you cry, I wouldn't have admitted it," he said, looking borderline agonized tracking one tear as it slid down my cheek and caught on my chin.

I chuckled out a messy laugh-cry and ducked my head into my shirt in a most ladylike move. With the help of my shirt, I dried my tears and emerged from my little turtle shell a complete wreck of emotions.

"Why are you crying, Dove?"

His voice was so, so gentle. His expression echoed that careful tone.

"I can't tell you." I couldn't blurt out my feelings for him right here in the middle of my veritable sick bed. I couldn't tell him how much every single thing he'd done for me meant, or how much I admired him, or how often I thought of him.

His gaze didn't waver, didn't leave mine. He stayed focused, studying me and clearly desperate to understand what was going on inside this cuckoo little brain of mine.

"Promise me you'll tell me if I can help, okay?"

I nodded, and eventually, he seemed convinced after I verbally promised. I could say the words with honesty because I had a feeling it wouldn't be long before I had to let the truth come out. I wouldn't be able to resist telling him how I felt, but I had to try not to scare him with the ferocity of my feelings, and letting them fly now would do exactly that.

He'd gotten me medicine and nursed me through an awful fever. He'd loaned me his dog. He'd visited my grandma. He'd arranged for my best friends to keep me company while he was gone. He'd fed me and refilled my water and clucked at me when he worried I wasn't drinking enough.

Maybe it was the illness-induced exhaustion that had me feeling downright nineteenth century about all of this, but right now I was absolutely overwrought.

I'd never felt so much, so viciously, ravenously much, for someone, and I had no idea what to do about it.

CHAPTER THIRTY-FIVE

Dorian

Dove went back to work Friday.

She'd been fever-free since Tuesday night, and by Thursday morning felt mostly better aside from tiredness. Her nan and I would be having a word because she'd clearly informed Dove I'd been to visit, which was not part of the deal.

Dove had seemed a touch withdrawn after Wednesday night when she'd cried and wouldn't tell me what was wrong. Maybe there was nothing to tell—she was coming off days of feeling bad, she was unused to being taken care of or needing to be in the first place, and she tended to cry easily as it was.

Still. Thursday, she'd been closed off. Not short or dismissive, but a little more inside her head. Less chatty, even compared to when she was sick. Unless she was unconscious or about to slip back into sleep, she tended to be talking to me or Bear or whoever had come to visit. Thursday, she was practically silent. She kept movies running all day and took a walk in the afternoon. When she came back in, she mentioned she'd be working Friday.

Great news. Perfect, really, because it was time for me to get back to my life. Wasn't it?

It was.

I hadn't slept much, worrying as I had over her and ill-adjusted to sleeping on her couch the first two nights, then banished back to my house the second two. It would've been weird for me to stay at her house after she'd moved out to the couch. I was fairly certain she had no idea I'd slept in the living room so I could check on her through the night those first two nights, nor did she need to. But all of this added up to an antsy, buzzing feeling under my skin that was nothing like the pleasurable hum of talking to her or touching her or kissing her.

No, this was the acrid buzz of anxiety. Bear sensed it and stuck close, leaning against me whenever he had a chance. I worked outside and got caught up on all the things I'd let lag during the day on Friday and ended up baking until the wee hours Saturday once Dove had said she was fine but passing out to sleep after getting home at the end of the day.

It wasn't that I'd expected anything more. I had no right to, and she was still recovering. She needed sleep.

By the time I did head to sleep on Saturday, I knew it would be a bad night. History had taught me the lesson, and though I'd found great joy in taking care of Dove this past week, I'd failed to take care of myself the last few days. I'd neglected the practices I knew helped keep me together, kept my memories from fracturing into shards and invading when I was most vulnerable.

And that's exactly what happened.

CHAPTER THIRTY-SIX

Dove

I'd been hydrating like it was my part-time job and sleeping as much as humanly possible after work. I'd only worked Friday and a half day Saturday since I knew my stamina would take a while to recover.

But at two a.m. after taking care of the necessaries, something caught my attention. Something felt wrong.

I moved through the darkened house and peeked out the front window. Dorian's car was parked in its spot. The lights were out at his house, only the porch light on, same as mine.

But...

Was that Bear? Barking?

The second I realized it was, the hairs on my neck and arms stood up and a jolt of adrenaline hit my bloodstream. I raced to pull on my shoes, then barreled out the front door.

At Dorian's, I knocked once, twice, then tried the knob and miraculously, it opened.

"Dorian?" I called, entering slowly so I wouldn't startle him or Bear.

By all accounts, this was an absolutely insane choice, but my gut said something was wrong.

Bear arrived at the door at a gallop, then instantly turned and walked a few steps, obviously leading me. I followed.

"Where is he, Bear Bear? What's wrong?" My heart was hammering a mile a minute and I dreaded what awaited me. Was he hurt? Had he gotten sick, too?

Something... worse?

Bear padded through the kitchen with focus, on a mission to lead me to Dorian's bedroom. My heart sank when I entered and found Dorian thrashing in his bed.

Not just thrashing, hands grappling an unseen foe, but crying.

"Please, please. Hold on, Baseline. Hold—" His body went still, only his head shaking back and forth in disbelief or maybe trying to escape, and with it a low groan of pain.

"Dorian," I said, not sure if it was wise to touch him.

Bear took what looked like his posting at Dorian's side, whining, then barking. He must've been trying to wake Dorian all this time.

When the large man fighting an invisible enemy let out a low, keening sob, I moved. I didn't know what kind of horrors, exactly, he was reliving but I couldn't stand here and watch.

Using courage and my boss nurse mode, I grabbed his shoulder with firm, insistent pressure.

"Dorian, you're safe. Wake up."

He jolted, almost choking on the mournful sounds he'd been making, but his head jerked again.

"Dorian, love, you're alright. You're safe in your bed. Bear and I are here. Wake up for me, big man. Wake up, okay?" I kept speaking in a soothing but strong voice, gripping his shoulder firmly, until his energy shifted and his eyes finally opened.

Bear let out a little yip and shoved in past me, needing to do whatever it was he was trained to do.

"Sorry, buddy," Dorian said, blinking and clearly trying to get his bearings.

"I'm here, too, Dorian. It's me, Dove," I announced myself so I wouldn't terrify him. He'd been completely out of it in the dream so I hated the thought I might just be lurking here. I flipped on the lamp, and the low glow let me see him clearly.

He looked absolutely wrecked. His exhausted gaze met mine, and my heart lurched toward him, desperate.

"Oh, Dorian. I'm sorry." I didn't know what else to say or do. My hands fluttered around like useless little bats and I had never wanted to touch someone so desperately. I *needed* to hug him, but I'd already invaded his home and interrupted an incredibly awful moment.

"Dove."

His voice was so... defeated. His eyes cast down to the mess of sheets twisted around his hips. Torso bare, I could see every breath he took by the rising and falling of his chest.

He didn't need to say a word. I could help him be more comfortable, though. I could do this.

"Can I check your pulse?" I asked, not wanting to touch him without permission, but the nurse in me needing to get my hands on him. Or maybe that was the needy, physical touch-starved woman who cared so deeply for this man and ached for him to know he wasn't alone.

His slight chin nod was all I needed. I took his wrist and felt the still-rapid thrum of his pulse. "Fast, but coming down."

His jaw flexed, and he made a small movement to show he'd heard me, his other hand resting against Bear's head.

"I'm sorry," he said, so quietly my ears strained to hear him even in the stillness of his room this time of night.

"You can't be apologizing to me for having a nightmare, can you?" My throat tightened, but now was not the time for pesky tears. "Dorian, what can I do? Please tell me I can do something for you."

If it sounded like I was begging, I was.

His eyes slowly tracked up from Bear to meet my gaze. There were so many feelings caged behind his expression and if he weren't already cracked open and spilling out all over the place, I'd want to dig around and figure him out.

Will he let me help him? Should I just leave?

"Hug?"

The small word shot straight to my heart and I instantly moved to embrace him. He wrapped me up and held me tight. I cradled his head, pressing him to me with every ounce of care I possessed.

"Would you stay? Just for a little while?"

His breath grazed my neck, the coarse hair of his beard brushing against the sensitive skin, too.

"Of course," I said instantly, leaning back. "Where do you want me?"

At another time, that might've been a provocative question, especially with me in my thin tank and shorts and him in nothing but boxers. But I had no worries with him, so when he guided me to the bed, flipped off the lamp, whispered something to Bear, and curled around me, I didn't fret over the implications.

Frankly, I hoped Dorian and I would have many nights sharing a bed in the future, but tonight was a kind of ground zero for us. He'd seen me in the ugliness of grief and loneliness. He'd seen me delirious with fever.

This was my first real glimpse at Dorian laid bare. He'd shared some of his past with me, but tonight, I'd witnessed it. Knowing he'd long felt someone couldn't care for him due to what he'd seen and done and the fallout that came from it moved me to borderline gladness this had happened, save for the reality that it'd brought him pain.

"I'm not scared," I said with nearly no sound, knowing it meant little in the context of what had happened, but needing him to know it.

One arm contracted, holding me tighter, and every point of contact between us seemed to press more closely. My hamstrings and calves brushed against the coarse hairs of his thighs and shins. My bottom was cradled in the curve of his pelvis, his muscular, flat stomach lined up with my back. Shoulders far wider than mine, our heads on a shared pillow.

There was nothing sexual about this nearness. Dorian held on to me in the darkness, the pale moonlight making a narrow dent in the black corner of the room, like I was his anchor.

When he did respond, I couldn't decide what it meant.

"I am," he said, a gruff whisper stirring my hair.

I pressed my palms over his arm banded around my waist, praying he would know I was here with him. That it was okay he was scared.

And I knew without a doubt I was exactly where I was meant to be.

CHAPTER THIRTY-SEVEN

Dorian

I woke with the scent of vanilla in my nose and the soft, supple reality of Dove's sleeping form still nested against me. It was absolute heaven.

It was utter agony.

Extricating myself from the bed had been easier than expected. She hadn't stirred, and I hadn't wanted her to. Whatever wreckage of thoughts and feelings I needed to sort through was best done in the quiet and alone.

After letting Bear out, I welcomed the brooding miasma of emotion brewing in me.

All it'd taken was a few days of failing myself and I'd ended up with a nightmare that'd not only been miserable to experience but had also disturbed *her*. How much longer before I was dragging her down in other ways? How long before she wasn't only losing sleep and peace because of me, but socialization? Friendships? Sacrificing a life she'd fought for?

I hated that these were the thoughts lingering in my head as I begged the routine of moving around the kitchen to shake me from the sour mood. I'd woken up with Dove in my arms and I didn't deserve any part of her. Shouldn't I at least have had the dignity to savor that she'd been so close? That she'd been so willing to offer me comfort?

There was also a decent chance that if she walked out into this kitchen in her pajamas, I would forget all about the reasons I'd just listed for caution, and I hated that, too.

The sizzle of butter in the cast iron pan drew my focus, and I let concentration on the task lull me away from the ragged sensations and memories from last night as I cracked eggs, sauteed onions, sprinkled cheese.

When I turned to the bar with two plates loaded with slices of frittata, a fruit salad, and toast, I startled to see her sitting at the island with a mug of steaming coffee in her hand.

Breath caught in my chest, I slid the plates onto the counter, drinking her in. My god, she was everything beautiful all at once. Soft, strong, gentle, a little sleepy and rumpled still but with hair slipping over her shoulders and down her back.

I loved her hair. I wanted to wrap it in my fists. I wanted her to pin me down and let it fall around us, curtaining off the world and caging us in. I wanted it spread across my pillow, across my chest...

"Morning." Her blue eyes were vibrant in the morning light and lit with a gleam I couldn't quite read.

"Morning. Sorry I didn't hear you. Must've been in my own world," I said, irritated with myself, but not surprised.

I'd needed the solace of cooking, the muscle memory takeover of building a meal.

"I enjoyed watching. You were clearly very focused." She lifted her coffee mug and took a sip, gaze never leaving mine.

I slid a plate toward her. "Hungry?"

She snickered. "Aren't you tired of feeding me?"

"Never."

She froze with the fork in hand, then reanimated, moving to spear a bit of frittata. "Really? Never's a long time." Her gaze slipped to mine, then back to the food.

She couldn't understand how deeply I meant it, but I held her gaze for a beat before repeating, "Never."

We both ate in silence for a few minutes, a comfortable pause to the conversation. Or maybe it wasn't comfortable for her, but I was so used to the quiet I didn't realize it?

Was that something else she'd give up for me, if we continued wherever this was heading? Would she give up comfortable silences or eventually, feeling like she could fill them if she wanted? Would she be compelled to grow quieter, too?

"Can we talk about it? Or would you rather not?"

I turned to her, searching for something like judgement or morbid curiosity. It was an uncharitable thought, and of course I didn't find either. She simply waited, eyes clear and patient.

Did I want to talk about my nightmares? Never, save with Dr. Corrigan. Not with friends, ever. But I owed her that, at least. "Sure."

A smile grew and faded in a heartbeat.

"Don't get too excited." Then her hand settled on my arm. "You don't have to if you don't want to. I don't need anything. It won't change anything."

And that was the first time she lied to me. "Of course it will. Now you've gotten a glimpse of what it can be like. A little taste of PTSD, and that was small."

Her brow tented. "Do you still have other symptoms? Is your therapist concerned?"

"I'm—" I slumped and covered my face for a moment before exhaling. "I'm grumpy and tired. I'm always in a bad mood after something like this. So evaluating how I'm doing right now probably isn't smart."

She nodded. "Makes sense and I completely get that. Do you know what might've triggered the nightmare? Or does it happen randomly?"

Steeling myself for all the ways this could go wrong, I explained. "I got out of my usual routine last week. After you were better, I was catching up on farm stuff and did a bad job sleeping."

Her mouth opened wide, her eyes round. "This is because of me? You took such good care of me, and this is what you got out of it?"

"No, no, Dove. I messed up. I worked too much, expected too much of myself the last few days. It's happened before when I've managed my time poorly, and this is the reality of my life. It happens—"

"Please don't pretend you doing so much for me didn't have something to do with it."

I turned her chin so she'd look at me. "I'd have a nightmare every night for the rest of my life if it meant I got to take care of you, okay? This wasn't your fault, and it is *not* an excuse for you to turn down help in the future."

She reared back, almost as if struck. "Yeah? Well, you having a nightmare isn't a reason to push me away."

My mouth dropped open like I might respond, but no words came.

"Yeah, I can feel it. I feel you in your head, figuring out how to convince me this means you're too broken. Well, bad news, Dorian. I'm a nurse. My business is healing. And I'm not here to fix you, but I'm sure as hell not scared of your broken pieces."

"What happens when my broken pieces cause you pain? Hurt you? Make your life harder?" I asked, voice scraped raw with the agony of saying something like that out loud when I already felt naked.

She stood from the stool and turned to face me, cupping my face in her hands. "Someone once told me, 'Every bit of you is beautiful and worthy of love.'"

I swallowed down gravel, heart aching.

Her eyes shone with tears, but she held them at bay as she spoke again. "If there is one man in all this world I am certain won't hurt me on purpose, it is you. In the months that I've been living here, you've made my life better, easier, and fuller simply by existing next to me, not to mention all the practical things you've done to make it better."

"But—"

Her palm pressed against my lips, physically silencing me along with her, "Shhh."

I blinked back, fairly shocked.

"I need you to hear me. I am not perfect, Dorian. I have piles of baggage. Heaps of it. And you may recall the physical embodiment of said baggage literally got you beat up not even a week ago."

Fair, though she was still not fully understanding my concern.

"If you don't want to be together, or if this has turned into more than you want, or you are realizing you're not quite ready, all of those are valid concerns. But if your primary worry right now is that your nightmare last night is somehow a harbinger of bad things, or that you having a history with mental health concerns is something that disqualifies you from being with me, you must hear me."

She paused, holding my gaze.

"I am not scared. I don't know everything about what this means, but last night didn't scare me away. *You* are worth staying for, and there is nothing I want more than to be here for you, if you want me to."

She pressed a quick, hot kiss to my lips, then stepped back. "I know this has been a lot so I'm going to give you some space to think. I'll be home all day, and when you're ready, if you're ready, please come find me so we can figure out what's best. But I promise you it is not listening to all those what-ifs running around in your head, just like I'm going to shut the ones in my head down, too, okay?"

I nodded. She let Bear in as she left, and I stayed sitting there at the bar, mind churning, long after she'd gone.

CHAPTER THIRTY-EIGHT

Dove

Dorian knocked at two that afternoon.

I'd expected something far later. His arriving within a few hours of my leaving his house seemed like a good sign.

Right?

Probably?

I hoped so.

"Come in. Did you bring Bear?" I asked, looking for his best boy.

He raised a brow. "Would you still want me if I didn't?"

I gave him an unamused look, though didn't quite manage to look him in the eye. Was I a coward? Sure. The title fit right now, and I wouldn't deny it. I was scared to see if he had already decided we shouldn't be together, or that he wasn't ready, or that he didn't really want to give it a try. And I wouldn't blame him for any of it.

But I was still scared to see the answer, so I didn't let myself. I just told him the truth to his answer. "Yes."

He didn't realize it now, but it really was that simple. I wanted him. With or without nightmares. With or without his adorable dog. With or without his baking skills, his military past, his *insert whatever issues here*, I wanted him.

So yeah. I was in a bad way here.

"Let me get us some waters. Have a seat on the couch." Was I being weird? I didn't know.

I'd done a remarkable amount of pacing around this lovely little cabin and I was no closer to knowing how things would go than miles ago when I'd started. But he was here, and I needed something to do with my hands while my pulse rate settled, so I poured two glasses of water, then dumped a bunch of bagged popcorn into a bowl.

After setting one glass in front of Dorian, I placed the bowl and my own water down. "My hospitality skills are a little lacking compared to yours. I'm sorry."

Meeting his eyes again felt like a cardioversion. Someone should've yelled "clear!" before our gazes locked and every shuddering hope and dream I had for the two of us whistled to the surface of my skin.

"You never need to apologize. Ever."

Goodness, the veracity and intensity in his voice poured over me in a thrilling wave, but I laughed, too. "That's nonsense. I'm sure at some point I will. Maybe not about my non-gourmet snacks, though."

He slowly shook his head, and I rolled my eyes.

His large hands pressed together, and he stared them down for a few seconds before reconnecting with me. "I want to be with you in whatever way you'll have me."

My stomach swooped and dived, a bird on the wing of a breeze.

"I'll have you all the ways," I burst out before I could censor myself.

But good thing I didn't, because his smile stretched into that full, devastating grin that could've signaled the sun to rise.

"All the ways, huh?"

His expression bordered on smug, which was saying something for this man. He simply didn't broadcast that kind of energy, but he had a hint of it today.

It filled me with a nervous, thrilling thrum, and I popped up out of my seat on the couch, resuming my pacing since apparently that was what my body wanted to do to cope today.

"I think we should lay out our concerns. Obviously, this is very, very new. We kissed once. But we're close..." I didn't want to have to ask—didn't want to finish the thought with, "*Aren't we?*"

He didn't make me.

"We are. I agree. It feels like a lot more than something casual or new."

Goodness, he was steady and certain now. I wanted insight into why, what'd changed, what paths his mind had taken to get to this point so I could follow.

"So I think we should say them out loud. It's not that it'll keep anything from becoming an issue, but more like it helps us understand one another when things happen."

Things like a quiet freak-out after an awful nightmare. Things like fear and worry after your dufus brother tries to make you join his cult.

If I waited much longer, this fizzing, brimming feeling would spill over and I'd lose my nerve, so I went for it. "I'll go first, okay? I'm scared that I'm too inexperienced for you. I'm scared that my lack of a dating history is a turnoff, or even more so, that I won't know how to be a good girlfriend to you. I'm scared that I'm too weird, that my past is too weird, that my stupid brother and his drama is going to make you not want to bother with me. I'm scared I won't—"

He stood and cut me off halfway around the kitchen island, facing me and placing his hands on either side of the counter so I couldn't pass without ducking under his arms.

"Say it," he said, not touching me, but energy and presence so palpable it almost felt like he was.

I swallowed, huffed out a jumble of nerves, and said, "I'm scared I won't be what you want physically. When the time comes. Since I'm, again, inexperienced."

He knew, but he might not realize the severity of it.

Good grief, what I'd give to read his mind right now, but his expression gave nothing away. He just looked for another few seconds that felt like at least five minutes and then tipped his chin down.

"My turn?"

Heart hammering, I nodded.

"I'm scared I'm not good enough for you. I'm scared I'll drag you down, or that I'll end up struggling with my mental health again and be a burden to you. I'm scared that the quiet, simple life I want isn't enough for you and that I want you too much."

I stepped into his space, just a few inches away. He was gloriously tall and I had to tilt my chin to look at him, but I wanted to be close.

"I don't know what's ahead, but I know if we try, I promise to be honest. I will. And I know it's easy to say those things won't bother me, and in reality, they are hard. Complex. But I will tell you I'm not running, and there's no way you could want me too much."

His hands found my waist and he hoisted me up onto

the counter, then stepped between my legs. The pine and cinnamon scent that clung to his shirt filled my space and I reached for him, locking my hands around his neck as he slid me to the edge of the counter, bodies locked together.

Holy wow, every inch of me was humming with awareness and need. I could hardly breathe, and I could absolutely not stand another second of waiting for whatever he might say.

"You don't have to respond to mine, okay? I don't—"

His big, rough hand covered my mouth just like I'd done to him hours ago.

"My turn."

I nodded.

"You ready?"

Another nod.

"You sure?"

My grin broke out, and he pulled his hand away but ran the pad of his thumb over my lower lip before he did.

Oh. My.

"I'm not worried about your inexperience, Dove, because I might be a quiet man, but I can be a greedy bastard and since the moment I saw you, I wanted you all to myself. I'm no relationship guru either, so we'll have a lot of learning to do. I'm not worried about your ability to be a good girlfriend because you're already an incredible friend and I've seen how you care for the people you value. And honey…" His hand slipped from where it rested on my arm to slide into my hair and grip the back of my head. "There is no part of me that has any doubt I will love every part of you, physically or otherwise."

And then, ladies and gentlemen, I burst into flame.

CHAPTER THIRTY-NINE

Dove

Actually, I remained in a solid, technically uninflamed state.

My lashes fluttered and I was breathing hard. He was just holding me there, held and cherished but also somehow... restrained.

"So, uh, that means you want to continue? Or, you know, see what happens?" I asked, breathless from his proximity and the sheer wanting.

"Yes, Dove. I do. Do you?"

And the second the "yes" left my tongue, his lips were on mine.

This kiss was completely new. It seemed crazy we'd only ever really kissed once, but thanks to my work schedule, then illness, sure enough our first had been our only save a quick peck or two saying goodbye.

Dorian's gentleness was always there, steady and reliable under the surface. But now, there was an insistence, a kind of hunger in the nip and press and pull of his mouth. Our kisses grew deeper, more mesmerizing, and his hand in my hair tightened just like my arms around his neck. My ankles hooked behind his back, and he leaned over, pressing close, closer.

His tongue teased the seam of my lips and I opened to him, welcoming the intensity and thrill of another layer of intimacy unfolding between us.

It all felt so good. So perfectly right.

I could kiss him all night, if he'd let me.

But just as the thought slotted into my brain, he pulled back, running flat hands down my back in a soothing, thrilling caress.

"Let's have dinner."

My brain was still processing the delicious sensations he'd imparted with that mouth, so understanding the words coming out of it took a minute.

"Dinner?"

"Dinner."

"Not more kissing?" It sounded a little pathetic, but I didn't blame myself. Not when this man had been kissing me like that...

"Not right now, Dove." That golden-brown gaze pinned me in place for a beat, then his hands gripped my thighs.

The heat from his palms had me swallowing down an objection to his proposal even as I let my legs unwrap and my arms slide away, untethering him from me.

He huffed. "You have no idea what you do to me."

"Please feel free to tell me," I said, not ready to let this moment go.

He grinned again. My heart flipped and mooned around like a lovesick teen again.

With two fingers, he nudged my chin up, urging me to look at him. I did, knowing the eye contact would do nothing for the need to calm down.

"I would do anything for you, Dove. And right now, what I'm doing is for both of us."

This, I wasn't certain I understood. "Don't tell me you're worried you'll lose control or something? That we'll go too far too soon?"

I'd only seen this kind of thing in books and movies, so I'd never imagined it actually happening.

"It's not a matter of control. At any point, at any time, you can tell me to stop and I'll stop. There's no point at which your consent becomes a given. But I also know that I want you, and it seems like you return the feeling, and we're both coming from a place where it seems like doing everything all at once might not be the way to go if we want to respect each other and whatever we're doing here."

Though the effort failed miserably, I did try to smother the smile working its way to the surface. Ultimately, there was no point in pretending I didn't love every word of what he'd said.

"Fair points, Forrester. Fair points." I gripped the front of his shirt and exhaled long and loud. "Though there are a lot of stops along the way between kissing and sleeping together. It's not like we're about to have sex here on the countertop, right?"

The thoughts sprang out as they had a tendency to do—haphazard and a little thoughtless as to whether I should've censored some of them for people outside the wild west that was my mind.

"Hopefully someday, but no. Not right now."

My gaze snapped up to meet his, eyes wide, and found

him grinning. I shook my head, delighted he could be playful about this.

"Fine then. Let's have an early dinner. But we should maybe head to your house, because I don't have much here."

He gave me a look that said, *Obviously*, and so we made our way across the driveway and into his house. Bear greeted me enthusiastically, and after a few minutes, Dorian had put me to work making a salad while he prepped chicken breasts.

We'd come a long way this afternoon, but I worried maybe it wasn't all settled. Particularly, what had set off the nightmare and whether I could help with that in any way.

"You don't have to talk about this at all. Please hear me say that. But I do want to circle back to what happened last night."

Subtle, Dove. Super subtle. Don't say the word "nightmare" and it totally won't spook him.

The gas stove clicked on and he drizzled oil into a stainless steel pan, then turned to me as he nestled breaded chicken breasts into the pan.

"It was a twist on a recurring nightmare. I'm back at the spot where a mission went wrong. Same place Kenny lost his fingers. He was dealing with the explosive, but Baseline, one of our team, got shot in the neck. I did what I could, but Doc was already working on someone, and I held him while he bled out."

Horror and grief shrouded my mind as I moved toward him. He seemed remarkably calm considering the awful events.

"That's the part I relive. Those last few minutes. The words I said. The look in his eyes. But sometimes, the person dying isn't Baseline. And last night, it wasn't. Or, it was... until it shifted to something new." He swallowed, gaze on the contents of the pan, before he finished. "Last night, it was you."

Tears welled, and I wrapped my arms around him. He turned, accepting the embrace.

"I'm sorry. I shouldn't have said anything," he said, his cheek resting on my head.

I moved so I could see him—so he could see my face and understand me. "No, I wasn't thinking that at all. I'm heartbroken you had to live through that in the first place, let alone dream of it. I'm so sorry, Dorian."

He let me hug him a while longer before he pulled back and moved to the stove, neatly turning the chicken, then gathering me right back into him.

"Sometimes, I feel kind of... foolish for the way I've struggled with that memory. Even now, when I've processed a lot that I simply couldn't for years, I wonder why I've been taken to my knees by that one. Of course it's awful, but it's this gut-level knowledge that death comes for us all that shook me so deeply then."

I stayed quiet, eager to understand what I could.

"So much of what you do in the EMU is based on years of training and rehearsal and preparation. There comes a sense of invincibility, almost an arrogance you have to have to do the job. It's part of compartmentalizing. And when that breaks down..." He squeezed me tight, then released me and stepped back, keeping his hand at my waist. "When it broke down for me, it broke down there. In that moment."

"I can't even begin to imagine what that was like."

He stepped forward, crowding me and brushing hair back from my face. "I don't want you to. This is what a therapist is for. They're trained to take the burdens. And I promise you, I'll talk with my doc about this, okay? I've learned the lesson that letting things fester or convincing myself I've handled them when all I've actually done is shove them down into a hole I think I can ignore has consequences."

"I'm glad. I'm sorry you had to learn that, but I'm proud of you. That said, I don't want you to feel like there are things you can't tell me. Only what you want to, of course. I'm sheltered in a lot of ways, I guess, but I don't want to be kept separate from the hard things. I don't think it'll work that way."

His eyes softened, and he dipped his head, straining to press a kiss to my lips before pulling back and turning to the stove again. "If the same goes for you, I'm in."

And amazingly enough, I was, too.

I hadn't talked about my past much at all. He already knew as much as my friends did. I didn't tend to keep things to myself, but I had no desire to talk about my life growing up in a cult. Maybe it was because I didn't want to look too hard at how it'd shaped me. Lately, it'd been because I'd been so busy with work and stressed about getting Nan settled, so the girl who got to be with her friends didn't want to dwell on how her creepy cult upbringing might've hampered her ability to connect with men or even attempt dating.

Yet, here we were. Shining light on the dark places and clearing them out a little. And even though we'd covered some awfully hard ground, I felt nothing but hopeful for what lay ahead if we kept going.

CHAPTER FORTY

Dorian

Kenny was, as usual, beaming with a toothy white grin as we left the Saint building.

"I love all of this. Every bit of what's happening is just *good*." He patted Cookie on the back.

Beast grumbled his assent. "You're doing good things."

"They're right. Proud of you," I said, hoping my sour mood wouldn't bleed through. I'd been joyful for the surprise engagement he'd ambushed his now-fiancée with, but this morning had knocked some of that from me.

"I'm excited. Happy everyone else is happy," Cookie said, accepting another rough thwack from Beast as we descended into the parking lot.

Prepared to slip into my truck and stew while I booked it back to Bear and my house and eventually Dove, three shadows stretched across the vehicle.

"We going to pretend there's nothing going on here?"

Beast said, crossing his arms and settling into a wide-legged stance.

Cookie raised his brows, and Kenny leaned against the hood, face expectant.

"What's going on?" I asked, well aware they could read me enough to know I was irritable.

Beast blinked back, clearly unimpressed with my feint of confusion. Cookie waited silently.

Barbie broke out into a wild grin. "You're dating Dove Jensen!?"

My heart kicked at the sound of her name, and every anxiety-riddled thought grinding me down in the wake of the day and the close-out meeting evaporated as an image of her face came blazing into my mind.

Beast and Cookie chuckled.

"I love that you didn't say a word but now you're blushing. Your whole angsty energy just changed," Barbie declared.

"Angsty?" Why I asked, I'd never know.

Barbie sauntered toward me and winked. "We'll come back around to the blushing, but yeah. Angsty. Because you feel guilty for not working more, and knowing you, you feel guilty for not having some major Saint expansion project you want to do now that we have our very own resident moneybags," he said, winking at Cookie.

"I'm that easy to read?" I asked, a touch embarrassed I was so transparent.

"Yes," they all said in unison.

More than a little horror struck me. "Do you think Bruce and Wilder know?"

"Yes." Perfectly in sync yet again.

I turned to face the truck, and my head fell against the cool metal of the door frame. How could I explain how terrible that realization felt, or the tiniest flutter of relief that came, too?

"We do need to talk about that, but we've touched on it. I assume you're discussing it with the doc?" He meant my therapist.

"Yes."

I had a little. And after today, I would more. I'd convinced myself it wasn't a pervasive issue, this sense of guilt and obligation, and way down at the heart of it, fear, but clearly, I'd lied to myself.

"Great. Then tell us every little thing about you and Dove," Barbie said, clapping his hands together in front of him.

Beast instantly spoke up. "No. Not every little thing." He sent Barbie a glare.

"Maybe tell us what you want to tell us," Cookie suggested in his reasonable way.

However edgy I felt after the day, these three pestering me about Dove and having every faith I'd handle those challenging feelings about Saint buoyed my mood. It reminded me yet again that I wasn't alone and I didn't need to sink into the disappointment with myself over not having been honest about all of this.

"I'll tell you I'm..." A slow smile spread across my face as I thought about her, the way she'd urged me to share what I'd experienced but didn't push. She hadn't asked for every gory detail, and of course, my tenderhearted love, she'd cried. "I'm really happy."

Barbie burst out laughing, so instantly elated on my behalf, it only made me love him more. Cookie and Beast were grinning like fools, too.

"Now I literally couldn't be happier. I love this for you and her and all of us. Is she coming to the festival at all?"

The Silver Ridge film fest started tomorrow. It'd be a busy time, and I'd agreed to work several days, mostly in the CP. There'd be a flood of tourists, celebrities, and press.

"We haven't talked about it."

Barbie gave me a perturbed look. "Time to get on that. And, if I may very gently suggest, perhaps some tidying up?" He stroked along his clean-shaven face.

Beast chuckled.

"You could use a trim, too, fella," he snapped back. "Everyone with a beard needs to take notes from Cookie because he always looks like a snack."

I chuckled despite myself, and Beast grumbled while Cookie just shook his head.

"Not all of us can look like models," Beast said, then pulled his keys from his pocket. "Gotta get home to the family, but I'll see you tomorrow. Talk to your woman." He pointed at me like I'd have to answer to him if I didn't.

The others followed suit, and I took the chance to go before anyone else popped up ready to chat. It was unlikely, but I wanted to ride this good feeling for a minute and not sink back down into the concerns that'd been tightening around my ribs before we started talking about Dove.

After a stop to pick up some groceries and my holds from the library, I made it home right as Dove was pulling in. Seeing her car was exhilarating in a way that hardly made sense, except that I was in love with her so of course it did.

I... I mean, obviously, I was in love with her.

I could've laughed just from thinking it.

Anything having to do with the woman gave me a burst of happiness.

"Hey there, Dorian Q. How was your day?" she asked, smiling so brightly she practically glowed. She didn't stop coming until her arms were wrapped around me and mine her.

Holding her was heaven. After the riot of feelings, then the swing of joy telling my friends about where we stood, then holding those nagging worries at bay, breathing in her warm, soft scent and feeling her in my arms was like taking my first breath of air after being under water as I kicked to reach the surface.

"I'm glad to see you." The words were so feeble, they sounded ridiculous to my ears. But it was too soon to tell her just how much this moment meant to me.

She pulled back, examining my face. The sun had started setting as I'd left work and now the dusky light made it hard to see her quite as vividly as I'd like.

"Are you okay?" Her hands rose to cup my face, nails scratching against the thick, too-long hairs of my beard.

"I am now." I sighed, loosening a bit more by the second. "But I have to get a haircut for tomorrow."

Her hands stilled. "You do? Why?"

What did it say about me that I liked her response? That instead of, "yeah, you're overdue," she seemed almost dismayed.

"I'm working the film fest. I'm unlikely to do anything public-facing, but it's time. I could look a little more put together." No doubt my cheeks were burning with a blush, but she wouldn't see that very well between the aforementioned beard and the dimming daylight.

"I'm not just saying this because you're my boyfriend. I'm—" She tucked her lips between her teeth and her lashes fluttered.

My grin exploded across my face. "I'm your boyfriend, huh?"

Her hands dropped to my shoulders and she shoved me

away a little. Only enough to rock me back, and I caught her hands and pressed her palms to my heart. "Does that mean you're my girlfriend?"

Her gaze dropped down to her toes, and she kicked at nothing. "Well, I'm not anyone else's, that's for sure."

Gathering her to me, I tilted her chin up, relishing the slightly anxious and yet playful gleam in her eye.

"I'm yours, that's for sure. And as long as you're good with it, you're mine."

"I'm good with it," she whispered, then leaned into me as she rose on her toes and pressed her lips to mine.

I could get lost in her kiss, in the supple feel of her body against mine and the way the ends of her hair brushed my bare wrists where they wrapped around her. I would've lost all sense of time if she hadn't ended the kiss by pulling back and laughing.

"Alright then, that's settled."

I nodded.

"And now, let's eat some dinner and, if you trust me, I can help you with that haircut."

Nuzzling into her neck, a mixture of relief, desire, and something unidentifiable and bittersweet crept into my chest. We'd spend time together—relief. I wanted her as much as I wanted my next breath—desire. And whatever else it was, I didn't want it right now.

"I trust you," I whispered into her skin, amazed and delighted to mean it.

CHAPTER FORTY-ONE

Dove

Dorian had whipped up a delicious dinner while I ran home to change and start a load of laundry. I also grabbed my shears in case he didn't have any. He'd claimed he had clippers, but if he didn't normally cut his own hair, who knew what shape they'd be in. He likely only used them for his beard, and hair could be tricky, especially thick hair like his.

I couldn't have explained why the prospect of cutting his hair thrilled me, but it did. I couldn't do anything fancy, but I knew how to trim, how to reshape, and I'd spent years doing men's hair until the time I left the compound at fifteen, so I certainly had enough experience. I knew it'd come back.

"When was the last time you did this?" he asked from where he stood in the kitchen, loading the dishwasher after having refused my help on the premise that I'd be doing work to cut his hair.

"I've cut two men's hair in the last year—both friends of Nan's. They take people to the salon or bring someone into Silverton Springs, but before she moved in, she offered my services."

She'd been so proud of me for the many skills I possessed, as she often put it, and she wanted me to charge them. While she hadn't been aware of how much money we needed to keep things afloat before we sold the house, she'd known I was working my tail off, and a haircut that took twenty minutes would be a nice boost.

I'd been simultaneously grateful and embarrassed.

"Am I jealous?" he asked, pulling a bar stool out from the counter.

I chuckled and finished setting everything up. "You shouldn't be, no. They were nice, much older men."

His gaze softened. It was one of those looks that would've seemed at odds with his burly, almost wild appearance, but now it fit him so well.

"Do you want to shower, or just want to wash your hair in the sink? It'll be easier to trim when it's wet."

I shouldn't have let my mind flash to what it might be like if I washed his hair *in the shower* but there it was like a lightning strike straight to my temporal lobe. My hands in his hair, his on my waist, the skin of his palms burning into me, water running down over both of us—

"Maybe just the sink. I'll shower after since I need to do my beard, too, and I can make sure I'm not covered."

Thankful I didn't need to speak, I nodded as he disappeared to the bathroom to get shampoo. When he returned, he settled a towel around his shoulders and leaned against the counters. "You okay? I can definitely just do it myself if it makes you uncomfortable."

A weird, borderline hysterical giggle snuck out of me entirely without my permission. "Um, no. Washing your hair will not make me uncomfortable."

He waited for more, but when I didn't give it, he narrowed his eyes. "Can we acknowledge that wasn't a normal response?"

I laughed full out now, appreciating his directness, as always.

"We can." Woo, my cheeks were downright ablaze. "I can say with certainty washing your hair will not make me uncomfortable. I was just, uh, thinking about, um, something else, and it was... not just washing your hair."

Something in his gaze changed. I couldn't have verbalized what, but it was something a little predatory, if I had to name it. A gleam or an air or a *vibe* that shifted and he stepped closer.

"Tell me more. What more was there, if it wasn't all hair washing?"

I swallowed hard. "Well, the location was... not the kitchen."

A tinge of a smile crept into his expression. "Hmm, not the kitchen. Was it in the shower?"

One nod was all I had to give at this point because my heart was pounding and his hand on my waist flexed with a delicious pressure.

"And were you in the shower with me?" he asked, voice dropping low and brushing across my skin.

He was so close and so deliciously focused on me. What would he do if I told him exactly what'd flashed into my mind? What would he think?

When I didn't confirm or deny a thing, his hand slid

around to my lower back and he pressed me close so our bodies were tight against one another. Clearly, the man had a taste for torture.

"Were you with me, Dove?"

If he hadn't anchored me to the spot, I would've expired from the flash of heat that sizzled from my neck where his breath coasted against my skin all the way to my toes.

"Yes."

There. I'd said it.

But instead of saying anything, he exhaled, almost like he was winded, and rocked his forehead into my shoulder for a moment before stepping back.

The gear shift had me a bit confused, and my heart rate hadn't slowed at all. When our gazes met, his eyes were absolutely aflame with heat and promise.

"That's one way to do it," he said, then chuckled and shook his head at himself. "But I think tonight, let's stick with the sink."

Air whooshed out of me in relief and yes, a tiny twinge of disappointment. Not that the next step in our physical relationship was jumping into a shower together for goodness's sake, but I could admit to very much liking the idea of such an event occurring at some point.

Interestingly, I hadn't wanted closeness like this with a man ever before. Not really. I'd liked a guy in my early twenties, right out of college, whom I'd thought might be *the one,* and in that context, I thought I might want him to be my first and then only. But our relationship had fizzled not long after the thought had come, and I'd only ever been glad I hadn't gotten anywhere close with him.

I'd never regretted my choices. I'd never been embarrassed to be where I was in life without having had those experiences because I'd always felt certain I'd enjoy sharing that with my person, whoever they ended up being. Between busy schedules, caring for Nan, and generally preferring the company of fictional men to the rampant disappointment real-life ones so often caused, I'd hardly even been tempted.

But as I ran the water into Dorian's hair and combed through the wet strands, as shampoo bubbled between my fingers and I scratched into his scalp, as his muscular back and strong neck were on display and he patiently waited for me to finish, I recognized the situation for what it was.

I suspected Dorian was it, and that every glance, every kiss, and every touch was leading somewhere.

Of course this would occur to me as I washed his hair. I'd done this for others, most recently Nan, and it'd always been pleasant. A way I could help her. But with Dorian, it felt... intimate. Charged in some way. Maybe that was thanks to his comments, or my wild imagination, or maybe it was simply due to what had always been building between us.

He towel-dried his hair in a way that made his biceps particularly bulgy and attractive, and he looked at me through long, dark lashes as he sat on the stool.

"You're too tall," I said, voice a little raspy after working in the relative silence of the hair wash. He was sitting down but we were basically face to face. I glanced around, noticing a step stool. "Can I use that?"

"Anything you need."

His words sent a thrill through me, and I could've sworn I felt his gaze as I moved to the little stool. It only subsided when I situated it behind him and combed through his hair. He'd already told me what he wanted—a few inches off the top and the sides cleaned up.

In a few minutes, I finished with a final snip.

"Go take a look and make sure it's short enough. I can take more off."

I hoped I hadn't taken too much, but honestly, it looked so good. His rich brown hair was thick and dark and looked really good longer, but seeing it trimmed up like this made me low-key nervous to face him after he'd trimmed his beard.

I'd seen that once before and it'd been dangerous. I already liked the way he looked. I was already pretty much completely in love with the man. I didn't need him shifting from broodingly handsome to downright *hot* in a matter of minutes.

Without a word, he moved to the bathroom and not long after, he emerged. "Thank you." He took the clippers and left again.

I busied myself with sweeping up the hair. I'd wondered if Bear would come investigate but he'd greeted me, ate dinner while we did, and had returned to his bed in the living room.

A few minutes later, he called for me.

"Dove, could you come here?"

I moved instantly, and so did Bear. There wasn't strain in his voice, but there was *something*.

He was standing in front of the sink shirtless, a small animal's worth of hair on the counter, looking at his reflection. His gaze shifted to meet mine when I entered.

He was gorgeous. Literally everything about him was.

He already had been, of course, but now I could see the shape of his jaw more distinctly. He'd trimmed the beard short, only a little longer than Luc's, and he was honestly unfairly handsome. He'd neatened up the line at his neck and it looked downright dashing instead of borderline unruly like it had.

"Is the beard short enough?" he asked, scowling at his reflection with what was no doubt a too-critical eye.

"I think I need to take some of those self-defense classes with Tristan and Bruce," I said, not entirely sure what was coming out of my mouth.

His brow furrowed more than it already had been. "I don't disagree, but why?"

I sighed, walking up to stand next to him and not at all hating how we looked side by side in the mirror. It should've been odd, our height difference and his dark hair and eyes with my blonde locks and lighter features, but instead we just looked... right. Maybe no one else would ever think it, but to me we seemed an awful lot like a quirky but perfectly matched set.

"Because I'm going to have to know how to throw elbows properly when the ladies of Silverton see you."

CHAPTER FORTY-TWO

Dorian

We had twenty minutes left before my shift would end and I couldn't wait. I'd enjoyed my time with Tristan in the CP, but knowing I'd get to see Dove in a matter of minutes meant I was restless.

It could be said I'd been restless since the day she'd cut my hair. Maybe long before that. The memory of her fingers in my hair, the light tugs and quiet between us as she trimmed... I'd had a moment where I'd thought about abandoning all efforts to keep my hands to myself and just take whatever she'd give.

Especially after she'd come into the bathroom when I'd asked her to, thinking I'd see if she thought the beard was short enough and she'd looked dazed. By *me*. As though I wasn't constantly on my heels with her, barely catching my breath for how much I wanted to be near her.

I'd had to berate myself into forgetting her comments

about the shower, too. And cruelly, I'd been working often since then and we'd hardly seen each other. How could we be neighbors and yet barely manage to make eye contact for three days?

Thankfully, she'd gotten a ride to one of the films in the festival with Nikki and Winnie, and I'd get to drive her home.

In ten minutes. Not that I was counting down.

"Everything going well for you?" Tristan asked now that things had settled down.

We were manning the CP—the command post—where we fielded calls and tracked all of our team, their clients, and anyone else we needed an eye on, plus local police channels. This helped give a heads-up to our staff if anything was reported, and was part of the process when managing multiple clients at a major event like this.

Most of the celebrities our team was guarding had slipped into an after-party or called it a night.

Eight minutes.

"Going well. Trees are looking good. Think we'll have a good season this year."

Tristan nodded and offered a smile. He was a quiet man, and I'd always appreciated his ability to speak without words. We had that in common.

"And Dove?"

Of course he knew. The Saint Security gossip mill was likely running full force. Nothing malicious, but these people loved to share the latest and it was second only to the EMU gossip when we were active.

"She's better than I could've imagined."

He smiled in earnest now. "Perfect."

I failed entirely in the mission to look anything other than completely gone for the woman. As a man who had been head over heels for his wife before ever even meeting her in real life, he wouldn't judge.

"Congrats on the expansion." I'd said as much a few days ago when Bruce and Wilder announced some of the changes coming to Saint thanks to Luc's investment, but I hadn't seen him one on one. He'd be building out a new dedicated combatives training space and offering a much larger course catalog. "Sounds like you and Doc will have a lot of fun ahead."

He leaned back in his chair, fully at ease discussing the likely hundreds of hours of work looming. "Should be a good time."

I hated it, but the feeling didn't change the fact that his words made guilt and something like jealousy bubble up in my gut. Shifting against the unsettling sensation, I checked my watch.

Six minutes.

The door swung open and Bruce peered in. "Hey. Dove's here if you want to knock off a minute early. I'll hang with Oak."

Without a thought, I shot out of my seat, thanking him and saying farewell to Tristan as I went to the tune of their low chuckles.

Outside, down the stairs, and with a short jog to my car, I found her laughing with Nikki, Winnie, and Jo.

"Ladies."

I was glad she'd had a good night. She'd mentioned how excited she was to get dressed up and spend time with her friends after such a stressful work schedule. Instead of their usual Friday night happy hour, they'd spent an evening at the festival.

Well, everyone save for Liz and Jess, both of whom were working the event. Jess and Jude were both still only working part part-time, but they both seemed to enjoy taking turns getting out of the house. They'd struck a balance, and Jess had tomorrow night off and would attend book club, which Dove felt was a good compromise.

"You look nice, Stone," Jo said with a bright smile. Winnie and Nikki agreed, and they waved their goodbyes to Dove.

I couldn't have said what they were wearing for all the money in the world. Pathetic given that my job had once hinged on my ability to be observant and take relevant action based on the evidence I'd discovered. Not tonight.

Tonight, in the glittering moonlight with the shadowy mountains behind us, I could only see Dove.

"You're breathtaking." I pressed a hand over my heart like it might help this rush of intensity taking place. She was so beautiful, and it wasn't the way she'd done her hair or makeup. It wasn't the deep blue dress clinging to her stunning, mouthwatering curves.

It was her. That beaming smile I'd seen when I walked up and the way she'd hugged each of her friends while I'd just swallowed down the image of her in front of me after waiting all day for it. It was the soft expression that flooded her face and how she stepped forward and reached for my hand, tucking it close to her heart like maybe she'd missed me as much as I'd missed her.

"You're not so bad yourself." She made a show of looking me over head to toe, then bit her lip.

White-hot wanting burst in my chest and zipped out to every limb. "Ready to go?" My thumb brushed across the back of her hand.

"Yes."

Inside the car, she talked about the movie. There were famous names involved with the acting and she'd seen all the stars there. She didn't seem particularly awed by them, but in a town where major movie stars and celebrities often visited and sometimes settled down, the locals didn't tend to be wowed by fame.

"Did you like it?" I asked as we pulled onto the farm property. A few more minutes and we'd be home.

"I... didn't hate it? But it's not something I'd ever want to watch again." She huffed a little. "Actually maybe I did hate it? It was a lot of mopey shots of handsome men looking wistful and slightly angry because the world had wronged them. The only women in the story were either elderly or flighty love interests. It felt out of date, and honestly, I'm pretty tired of women being depicted as accessories or enemies. Give me strong women with strong friendships and healthy interactions with men who've done the work to deal with their issues instead of blaming the world for problems everyone else also has."

Her heated words rang between us and I waited for more. It felt like words were lingering, not quite verbalized. When we parked, I nudged her. "And?"

She sighed. "Honestly, I think it reminded me of my brother and probably the way my dad was. I mean, nothing to do with a cult, but enough of that put-upon ideology that makes men into monsters, frankly. It's self-indulgent in a way that makes me feel sick. Not the fun, 'treat yo'self' version from *Parks and Rec*." She scowled out the window toward her cabin.

"So you're saying you loved it."

She tsked and smiled. "Yes. Can't wait to see it again when it's on streaming."

I slipped out of the car and jogged around to get her door right as she opened it.

"Oh, thank you." She bit her lip again, almost like she knew it drove me wild.

"I'm sorry you didn't like the movie," I said, linking our fingers and walking slowly toward her door. I didn't expect an invite in after we'd both worked and it'd gotten late. But I didn't want to rush these last few minutes together by racing to the doorstep.

"It was still fun to go. I'm just glad it wasn't Jack or Jenna because I don't know if I would've been able to pretend to like it."

"Would you pretend?" I asked, curious to know whether she really would lie about liking the movie for the sake of people who were connected to her friends.

She shrugged one lovely bare shoulder, drawing my attention to the smooth line of her skin. I wanted to press my lips there, at her shoulder, the base of her neck, the line of her collar bone.

An audible exhale had me glancing up to see her shaking her head. "You can't keep looking at me like that."

I stepped closer, drawn in as always. "I don't know how to stop."

She turned on the step and gripped the lapels of my jacket. "One of us better figure it out or we're in trouble."

CHAPTER FORTY-THREE

Dove

One week after the film fest, Dorian and I had shared dinner several times, he'd brought me breakfast every day he hadn't had to work early, and my brain was absolutely obsessed.

Actually, not just my brain. My body was very much attuned to anything and everything he did, and my heart was an absolute sucker for the guy. It was almost impossible to exist for more than a few seconds before one of them was circling back to thoughts, feelings, or desires for him.

And honestly? It felt so good.

I'd always imagined resisting such a feeling, since that so often happened in books. For one reason or another, a heroine would resist the growing desire for someone because of whatever reason rooted in their backstory.

For me?

Maybe I was facile, but I'd always wanted love and

companionship, to feel known by my partner and to have that person want me. Dorian already gave me all of that, and we'd just barely gotten started.

When I'd asked him if he'd be up for going to the latest Josie Wade release party at All Booked Up, he agreed. He'd had a very busy week with working the festival and when we spent time together on Sunday night, he'd been visibly worn down. Working had taken a toll on him in a way the farm work he did never seemed to, but the schedule had been crazy, so that made some sense.

Still, I worried he was stretching himself too thin. Took one to know one, I supposed.

He knocked on my door at exactly six, right when he said he would. That was one of many things I liked about Dorian—he did what he said he'd do. There was no guess-work involved because he wasn't playing games or making a secret of wanting to be around me.

"Hello there, boyfriend. You look handsome."

My, oh my, he really did. He wore dark jeans with dark gray sneakers and a button-down shirt. I liked that he'd made an effort, but still looked comfortable.

His eyes drifted over me, then settled back on mine. "You look beautiful, as always."

I beamed at him, happy he thought so. It wasn't like I was subtle when I got dressed up for non-work events. When you wear scrubs to work, I suspected almost anything else looked close to fancy. I'd worn a cocktail dress to the movie premiere—which honestly was the worst, because who wants to sit in an old-timey movie theater in a strapless dress? Tonight, I'd donned a blue dress with little white books in a pattern all over it. It was quirky and cute and perfect for my dear friend's release.

It also happened to be very flattering. It had a sweetheart neckline and tucked in at my waist but gave me room for the reality that was the softness of my belly and thighs. Why would I want a waistband or a button fly when I could wear a dress?

"Thank you. And thank you for doing this. I know you've been so busy," I said as we descended my steps toward his truck.

"It has been a busy time. Now I don't have much going on again until after Thanksgiving when the season kicks off. I have time to recover." He turned his head, bending to press a kiss to my temple.

These were the sweet things he did so naturally, it seemed laughable he hadn't been a doting boyfriend before. How could someone so gifted in taking care of people live so long without a place to put all of this affection and care?

Hello, pot, meet kettle.

Fair enough, I could've been talking about myself.

We caught up on our days since we'd both been busy and had only traded a few texts and a quick hug last night before he crashed and I did some glamorous adulting like paying bills and making grocery lists. I'd missed him, and it seemed so silly, and it made so much sense.

"I think it goes for about two hours, but just let me know when you're ready to leave," I said as he parked in the Saint Security lot.

"I don't want to rush you. I'm happy to celebrate Jo and the new book."

He slipped out of his seat and rushed around to open my door. I stood on the step runner of the truck and wrapped my arms around him. He was over a full foot taller than me and standing up like this let me look down on him just a little.

"Thank you for being here," I whispered into his lips, then kissed him softly.

His hands settled on my hips, then pulled me toward him with a rough jerk. Heat burst through me in a flashbulb of awareness and he wrapped his arms tightly around my waist, then lifted me from the spot and slowly, so, so slowly, let me slide inch by inch to the ground, holding my gaze the entire time.

"Anything for you, Dove."

Would it be inappropriate to climb him and have my way with him? Inexperienced I may have been, but we'd grown closer in the last few weeks, more kissing and contact, and every bit of it knit us together in ways I simply wanted more of. He couldn't do stuff like that and expect me to just... carry on, could he?

"Oh *hello*, lovebirds!"

Kenny's voice broke through the wanton haze clouding my judgement, and right before I turned to look toward where the sound had come from, I caught Dorian's scowl.

"Hello, there, you two," I said, waving to Kenny and Liz.

Liz grinned at me. She was way too excited, but I was excited, too, and nothing about the way I acted with Dorian was subtle or fooling him into thinking I was only part of the way in this, so why not?

"I didn't realize we'd be seeing you, big guy," Kenny said, clapping a hand on Dorian's shoulder.

"Yeah, you didn't mention it," Luc said, materializing from what felt like nowhere with Elise's hand laced in his.

Two more doors slammed, and I saw Beast rummaging in the back seat of his SUV while Jess downright bounded around the corner with the cheesiest expression I'd ever seen.

So. They'd all seen us. And I had felt like we were alone on the moon.

"I just barely asked him to be my date. I'm not sure he was tracking it was happening until then." I squeezed his hand, grateful for his steady and unflappable energy. I wasn't embarrassed to be seen with him in any way, but I might not've chosen for my friends and their husbands and fiancés to see me absolutely swooning over him in real time.

"Glad you're here, Stone. If you need a break, I'm sure Will and Jude will be your excuse whenever," Jess said, winking at me as she glanced back to see Jude tucking Will into a baby carrier strapped to his chest. The giant of a man ducked his head and pressed a kiss to his son's wispy-haired head. As she turned back to us, her eyes widened and she whispered, "Boom. Pregnant again."

I cackled at that, as did Kenny, Liz, Elise, and Luc. Glancing up at Dorian, I found his eyes already on me, a look I couldn't decipher on his face. My heart flipped, and I cupped my free hand around our joined ones.

"You okay?" I asked as he shut the truck door and locked it, then began our walk across the street to the store.

He nodded, raised our hands to kiss the back of mine, and tugged me along.

I hadn't thought about the fact that this would be the first time my friends, his friends, and anyone else in the community would see us out together. In some ways, we'd been in a wonderful little bubble on his farm. But stepping out hand in hand on the way to support my friend and doing it *together* instead of telling him about it later... it honestly felt a little like a dream come true.

CHAPTER FORTY-FOUR

Dove

Jo signed my book, then stood to hug me again.

"Thank you so much for coming, Dove. Truly. And I'm so happy Stone came, too." She notched her chin up in a very Saint Security dude move and I knew she must be acknowledging my date.

"Me, too," I beamed. "And thanks for writing another book I can devour this weekend."

"You should've seen them when we pulled into the parking lot. Absolute fire." Elise widened her eyes, and Liz nodded from where she sat behind Jo, assisting.

A blush consumed my entire head and neck as Jess chuckled from behind me and Catherine, Winnie, and Nikki grinned at my other side, having gone through the signing line before me.

"Okay, I need to hear more about this stat," Jo said, signing Jess's book and giving her a giant hug. "And I also need to snuggle Willy-baby, if your husband will give me a turn later."

We all turned to see a grinning, proud Jude bending slightly, a portion of the carrier folded down to reveal sweet Will's head, and six giant, muscular, badass men absolutely heart-eyed and cooing at the tiny one. The baby held Bruce's index finger in one hand and Kenny's in his other. Adam was saying something to him, Tristan was brushing one of his wisps of hair from his brow, and Luc and Dorian were simply beaming.

My heart lurched and tears sprang to my eyes. I turned to surreptitiously wipe them away, but found my friends sniffling right along with me.

"Okay, this is ridiculous. Why are we *all* crying?"

Liz shrugged one shoulder. "I'm not crying. But my husband is, so that probably still counts." She cast a loving gaze in Kenny's direction and I couldn't help but follow it to see Kenny dip his head to the side to smudge a tear into his shirt.

"I think it's the way they love each other and love that baby. They're not acting like it has nothing to do with them or like they're ambivalent. It's how we feel about Will, too, because he's Jess's, and we love her. But you just don't see men behave this way as often, and I have to say there's nothing more magnetically masculine and appealing than a man being gentle and loving to a baby or small child."

Leave it to Nikki to bring logic and clarity to the situation.

"Well said. It's incredibly attractive," Winnie said. "Like, kind of on a primal level, I'm pretty sure it makes me want to reproduce."

"Relatable," I quipped, right as Elise said, "Okay, I'm

glad you said it because I literally just thought, 'And I'm ovulating.'"

We all laughed at that, and the person standing behind Jess cleared her throat. Thankfully, Bel Morris was no stranger to the whole "gorgeous man being a sweet dad" situation based on what I'd seen of her and her rock star husband around town.

Liz stayed to assist Jo and the rest of us scooted away, each taking a flute of champagne and enjoying the small bites being passed. It was a super-classy setup and I wished Nan had come, but she'd had other plans on her social calendar.

Radio silence from Hawk had been a blessing, but when I wasn't in my normal routine of work or seeing Nan, I did find myself worrying he might show up and make a scene. Granted, if he had any kind of brain, he'd know showing up here with that group of guys just inside the door was the height of stupidity. Even if he had no idea who the rest of the Saint guys were, he wouldn't be able to miss Dorian's towering form.

I got caught up in chatting with friends for longer than I'd meant to, and when I looked around for Dorian, my heart squeezed when I spotted him. I'd checked on him here and there and he'd seemed to be engaged in whatever conversation at the time, but now, it'd shifted.

He stood with a rigid set to his shoulders slightly farther out of his group of friends. The bookstore had filled now that the formal portion of the signing had begun, and it was pretty packed.

As I watched, Dorian's jaw flexed and his eyes shut while his chest rose on a slow inhale.

"Hey, guys, I'm going to head out. I'll see you for book

club, right?" I accepted hugs and blew a kiss to Jo before beelining to Dorian. "Hey, ready to go?"

"What? We don't have to go." Even his voice held strain.

I wanted to wrap him up and cradle him, he was being so preciously stubborn. "I'm ready."

He scowled. "No, you're not. We've only been here an hour." His arms crossed even more tightly over his chest.

"I am, though. It's been great. Let's go home."

His eyes cast out over the room and finally circled back to me. "I don't want you to leave for my sake."

Oh, this sweet, stubborn man. "Any chance we could talk about this *not* in a jam-packed bookstore? Like, maybe, in your quiet living room with a fire in the fireplace and maybe a cozy blanket we could cuddle up under?"

His expression darkened. "No."

I shrugged one shoulder. "Okay. I'll take a rideshare then," and I walked out.

I got no more than ten feet from the bookstore door when he called my name. By the time I turned around, he'd caught up with me.

"What are you doing?"

With a long exhale, I tried to calm the potentially toxic combination of exasperation and delight. What could I say to disarm him and get him to do what he needed to do, which was very clearly be done with the crowd and noise.

"I want to go. I'm making that clear. Unless you're telling me you actively want to stay, then let's go."

His mouth thinned into a firm line. "I don't want to make you retreat into antisocial farm life. That's not what I want for you."

"But what if what I want is for you to be comfortable and happy? What if I would rather go home where I know you feel good than make you stay in a place where you're clearly miserable? You did a great job showing up and engaging, but I know there's always a point where it gets to be too much, and I think that time has come. So, let's go home."

His shoulders slumped a little, and the stubborn tilt to his jaw relaxed. "I don't want to drag you away if you're having fun. I don't want you to cater to me."

He simply didn't understand. It had to be a holdover from his worries about someone wanting him. I couldn't expect all of those fears to melt in the face of our relationship, just like my concerns about inexperience and my family hadn't evaporated the first time we kissed.

But I didn't want him to worry. I wanted him to understand and to believe me.

Wrapping my arms around his neck, I held his eyes with mine. "I had fun. I'm ready to go. It's been a long week for me, too, and I haven't had enough time with you."

"I get that," he said, voice a low scrape.

My heart fluttered as his hands flexed on my waist.

I bit my lip, loving when his eyes dropped to my mouth.

"Plus, can't a girl get her boyfriend to take her home and have his way with her?"

He grinned and I could tell it was despite himself. Then one big hand slid up and cupped the back of my neck under my hair.

"Anything for you."

CHAPTER FORTY-FIVE

Dorian

Wed ridden home in a comfortable silence. I'd never been more grateful for her ability to recognize when I'd grown edgy.

There was a difference between wanting to leave and needing to. I'd had too many moments in the past where the departure became an imperative, not a choice. Tonight, I could've held out a while longer, and I hated that she might be ending her fun because of me.

This was precisely what I'd feared. I didn't want to hold her back or influence her, and tonight, despite her protests, it felt like I had.

When we pulled into the driveway, she hopped out of the truck and scampered up the stairs to my front door before I even made it out of the car. I guess she'd meant it when she said she wanted to sit on the couch and snuggle and talk.

My heart flipped at the thought of getting to sit close to her, to hold her and touch her, and maybe please her in some way. *Any* way. I suspected she thought it was an exaggeration when I told her, "Anything for you," but it was simply a declaration of reality.

I'd do anything for her.

One hand on her lower back, I unlocked the door. Bear greeted us, eager for company, then rushed to the back door where I let him out.

She excused herself to the bathroom, and I went to the kitchen to wash my hands and get us waters. We'd both had a few bites at the event, so I wasn't sure if she'd want dinner.

Steps in the hallway drew my attention to her and I nearly tripped over my own feet when I saw her. She stood with bare feet and the too-long legs of my black sweatpants pooling around her ankles. Up top, she wore one of my T-shirts tucked in a way that made it look oddly stylish.

"Come sit with me," she said, holding out a hand to me.

"You changed."

She gave me one of her amused smiles.

"I did. Do you want to? Let me take those and I'll let Bear in while you go." She took the glasses from my hands, heart-shaped face serene and completely uninhibited.

Thanks to her composure, I didn't let my nerves get the best of me. I simply went to my room and shoved away the thrill of seeing her shoes and dress draped over the chair in one corner of the bedroom. I pulled on gray sweats and shucked my button-up, leaving me in a white undershirt. If she wanted to have this conversation dressed down, we could.

But why hadn't she simply gone home to change? Wouldn't she be more comfortable?

Here came the reminder that I didn't have experience

with women in this context. I hadn't been in a relationship since my early twenties, and it might as well have been a lifetime ago. More than that, I'd never been in one with Dove. It didn't actually matter what any other woman would do or might want because the only one I wanted to please was Dove.

So get out there and ask her.

Sometimes, the voice in my head sounded far too much like Kenny's for my comfort. Still, with that very basic prompting, I returned to the living room to find her curled up under a blanket, Bear on his bed, and her mind engaged in whatever reverie it'd spun, so much so that she startled when I sat down next to her.

"Sorry. Didn't mean to scare you."

She waved the apology away, her fingers tipped with a pretty light pink color that made her hands look even more delicate than they were. "No, that was all me. I was just thinking."

Then she shifted, sliding into my lap and straddling me. She settled there, her weight a delicious anchor to the couch, and she rested her hands on my shoulders. The second she'd moved, my pulse had begun pounding, and now that she'd stopped, I was in no less danger of losing my mind.

"What were you thinking about?" I asked, my voice sounding a bit strangled as I spoke.

She stroked her hands over my shoulders and partway down my arms, then back up. "I was thinking about how to convince you I want to be here."

My brain was not functioning on all cylinders, considering the way she'd positioned herself and the incredible feeling of her body pressed to mine. "I think I believe you."

She giggled, but cupped my cheeks for a moment to

draw my focus fully to her words. "We need to talk about this."

After a moment of clearing my mind of the rampaging thoughts, I registered the concern knitting her brow and nodded. "You might need to move."

She raised one brow. "Not happening. Gotta keep you pinned down for this one."

Refusing to let my baser instincts run away with things, I nodded. Whatever she needed to say, she had a reason for doing it this way. I wanted to know what it was, and I wanted to do whatever she needed.

"I want to be here with you, Dorian. I worry that nights like tonight make you second-guess that." She tugged at a thread hanging from the sleeve of my undershirt.

The heat and adrenaline pumping through my veins banked. I didn't want to have this conversation. Some part of me had hoped maybe we'd just watch a movie and make out a little. Get distracted from the worries that'd been sneaking their way into my dreams and days bit by bit.

"I know you're saying that and you believe it. That sounds like I think I know what you feel better than you do, and I'm not trying to be like that. But I'm worried I—" I cut off, unsure of how to explain the fear without repeating myself.

She waited, palms resting on my chest.

"What would you have done if I hadn't been there? How long would you have stayed?"

Her brows dropped into a glare. "That doesn't matter."

"Yes, it does."

"It doesn't! Because I was there with you. I *wanted* to be with you."

"Sure. But if I hadn't been there, you would've stayed until the end, wouldn't you? You would've helped clean up and spent more time with your friends. You wouldn't have had to make excuses and leave because I couldn't handle it."

Saying the words aloud made me want to shrink into the couch cushions and hide. I didn't want this nakedness, this inescapable honesty. I'd made peace, for the most part, with the way I needed to function in social settings. I needed as much information ahead of time as possible. I needed to know a bit about what to expect. I typically aimed for a certain amount of time, between a half and full hour, before I planned to leave. And when I planned on it, I didn't feel so bad because it was always my intention to leave at whatever time I arranged. Then I could leave, and walking out of the context always felt like shedding a flak vest.

Dove had been studying me, and she had to have seen some of those feelings. They were ugly and embarrassing, the way I regretted her accommodating me.

"Here's what I need you to understand. If we hadn't gone together, I might've stayed until the end. If we were together and you'd stayed home? I would've wanted to get back to you."

I opened my mouth to explain that this was just another example of why I would end up ruining things for her, but she shook her head in a sharp, singular gesture that halted me before I began.

"If we weren't dating, weren't together, yes. I would've stayed until then end. But we are dating. We are together. Right?" She shook my shoulders, a tiny smile pricking at her cheeks.

When I nodded, she rewarded me with a full grin that made my heart squeeze.

"Part of what that means to me is that I want to be with you. I like you, Dorian, more than a little, and I'm sorry to break this to you, but I want to be around you all the time. I want to be talking to you and touching you and looking at your handsome face as much as possible."

Good grief, this woman. "Same."

Her smile stretched wide, and she leaned in a few inches to touch her lips to mine. Before I could deepen the kiss, she continued.

"I also want you to feel good. And you want that for me, right?"

Her big blue eyes blinking back at me so earnestly as she sat here in my lap felt like some kind of cosmic test. Did she want me to enumerate the many ways I would like to make her feel good? "Yes. Absolutely."

She bit her lush bottom lip to hide a smile—she could absolutely tell my mind had wandered to more physical subjects.

"When you kiss me and touch me, you pay attention. You want to do what I like. You want to *know* I'm enjoying it. The same is true with what you feed me. You notice what I scarf down and what I'm slower to eat."

"Like squash," I supplied, grateful for a reprieve from her discussing me touching her because I was only a man.

She chuckled. "Exactly. Like horrid, offensive, useless, disgusting squash."

I laughed at her declaration and took a moment to pull her to me and wrap my arms around her. Why did every second feel like a reward I hadn't earned? A reality that might be snatched from me at any second?

Leaning back, I saw tears glittering in her eyes, and I just knew. I had to tell her. She was so worried about me, but she needed to understand how I worried about her. She needed to understand this was so much more than attraction or dating.

"I will never feed you squash again."

"Thank God."

One tear tracked down her cheek, and I wiped it away with my thumb, holding her close.

"I'm not trying to be difficult with this. But Dove, you have to know that I love you, and I don't want anything between us to cause you harm. I don't want you to—"

"I love you, too. So much."

Our eyes locked, gazes held for a beat, and then everything building between us ignited.

CHAPTER FORTY-SIX

Dove

To describe a kiss as ravenous might've seemed hyperbolic. Until now.

Now I had experienced the absolute destruction and creation that was a ravenous kiss from Dorian Forrester, and I was unwell.

And by that I meant I was deeply mourning the fact that we couldn't let this kiss unspool into whatever delicious things came next because this man loved me, and I loved him, and we had some important ground to cover before we got down to business.

But holy crap, I was ready for that, too.

"Wait, wait a second," I said, breathless as Dorian's lips kissed a trail along my neck and his hands gripped my hips with what could only be described as possessive intent.

He stopped though, instantly pulling back with a deliciously hazy expression that made me second-guess halting his progress.

"Because I love you, I need you to understand."

His eyes cleared, and he waited.

"I love my friends. I'm a social creature. But I'm also exhausted. I'm working a ton, visiting Nan, and I have regular times I get to see my friends. What I have always wanted was to know I had someone who was *mine*, and who would love me for the weirdo I am."

His hands flexed on my hips and his expression softened. "God help me, I do."

Utter elation exploded in my chest at the grin on his face that was no doubt matched by the one on mine.

"Good. In that same way, I love you. Not some version of you I've made up that hinges on you tolerating social gatherings in some new, magical way thanks to the power of my love or something. I'm not loving you with the intent to fix you. I love you like you are, right now, and I don't want you to worry that being with you will change me, because it will."

His thick brows dropped low. "Why are you saying that like it's a good thing? I don't want you to have to change for me."

"But that's the thing. People do change for their person, at least a little. I am a thirty-year-old woman who's been living with my grandmother since I was fifteen. I just moved out not six full months ago and I am changing. Partly because of that, but also because of you. Because I'm factoring you in, thinking about what you'd want, and that is naturally a change."

"That's not what I mean. I don't want you becoming less social or saying no to things because you know I won't like them. What about travel? What about your dreams?"

I shook my head, willing him to get me as I tried again. "I hate to break this to you, but I have never particularly wanted to travel. I'd love to go a few places, but if you don't, maybe that's a girls' trip situation. And my dreams?" Oh, boy, here came the tears. "Maybe this makes me the lamest, but I think you might be it for me. I think you are quite possibly the embodiment of what I've dreamed of."

He still didn't get what a miracle he was.

Yes, I wanted someone who loved me. But I'd wanted a man who was honorable and gentle. A man who could love me and who I could respect. I didn't need him to be a big personality like Kenny or a charming businessman like Bruce. I didn't need him to be wealthy or impressive on paper. More than anything I'd longed for in this life, I'd wanted someone to be kind and gentle, and to especially, particularly love me.

He'd shown me his devotion and love for weeks, if not months, now, and he simply didn't realize he really was a wonder.

His expression shuttered and he shook his head. "How can that be possible, Dove?"

"Why can't it be?"

He swallowed hard and looked around, eyes searching, before they came back to mine.

"Because you are absolutely mine." He cleared his throat and exhaled roughly before continuing. "I keep feeling like you're better than anything I could've imagined. Not perfect, but so beautiful and full of life and light, it almost hurts to be with you because I love you so much."

He wiped my tears yet again, his expression impossibly soft. "Please don't cry. I'm... I'm not saying this right."

"Maybe you are, though." My voice came out watery, but I sniffled and got it together. "Maybe we are each other's dreams. Maybe the hard things we've both been through... maybe they've led us to each other, and they've made us right for each other. They've made us choose each other."

He brushed the hair that'd fallen into my eyes back and tucked it behind my ear.

"Promise me you'll tell me what you need, okay? I'll do anything I can to make you happy, but I need you to know some things about me aren't changing."

I gripped his shirt and shook. "I don't want them to. I don't need them to. I'm sure we'll have challenges. We're both humans with traumatic garbage in our pasts. I have a brother involved in what is looking more like a cult, and you're finding your way through what you want with work... We've both got stuff. But I want to believe that we can help each other, especially if we can trust ourselves to be honest when things aren't going well."

"I trust you. I've never trusted anyone like I trust you."

His earnest, vulnerable response had me marveling at my matching one. "I feel the same."

Someone on the outside of all this might've been shocked by the conversation if they'd wandered by and overheard somehow. I'd moved in here a little over five months ago. How could I feel so strongly, so certain of this man?

In my heart, I could only hear, *how could I not?* From our very first interaction where I'd screamed at him inside his own house to each instance following it, he'd proven himself to be a man of character. He'd shown his capacity for friendship and then, for love. And as if that weren't enough, he'd fed me incessantly and plied me with pie.

His brown eyes held mine, and a pathway opened wide ahead of me. I would never claim to be clairvoyant or anything like that, but I could practically see us down the line, hand in hand, at the end of our lives.

"Tell me what you need."

His voice was a graveled rumble now, and it'd shifted. His hands dragged me closer, my soft against his hard, and our breaths grew ragged.

"Just you."

My words were a whisper, but he heard them loud and clear. He stood, and I wrapped my legs around his waist to hold me in place. Bear perked up, ID tags clinking, but Dorian's command for him to stay settled him back as we moved down the hallway.

At the threshold of his doorway, he stopped, gaze pinning me. "This doesn't have to be more than what we've done. It doesn't have to be anything."

"I meant what I said at the bookstore." I'd wanted to end up right here, in his arms, heading to his bedroom, and soon into his bed. I hadn't been quite sure we'd end up exactly like this, but I wasn't going to pretend I wasn't happy about it.

"You can always change your mind."

I shifted in his arms so he'd set me down, then walked to the bed and sat on the edge. "I'm not changing my mind. Please don't stop on my account."

He dropped to one knee, tugging at the bottom of one of my pant legs, and gave me an absolutely heart-stopping smile.

"Anything for you."

CHAPTER FORTY-SEVEN

Dorian

Bear leaned his head against my shoulder and made a sound that roused me enough to get my bearings.

"Hey, buddy. I'm good. You need to go out though, don't you?" I spoke quietly, not ready to wake from the dream of the last few days. I was resting on the couch because I hadn't slept much. First, because Dove had... occupied my time and thoughts. And then second because we'd had a series of issues on the farm and I'd been working like crazy.

The doorbell rang then and I realized I must've missed the first ring because Bear jumped and edged toward the door as if to say, "Did you hear it this time? Come *on.*"

"Got it, bud." I slipped my feet back into my sneakers and shuffled to the door. Without looking, I swung the door open, surprised to find three faces peering back at me.

Kenny's face fell the instant he saw me scrubbing at one eye.

"Were you asleep? In the middle of the day?"

The edge of panic in his voice was like a punch to the gut. "I was just tired. We had some issues on the farm and I've been busy."

"You're not sleeping. That's usually not a great sign," Beast grumbled, though concern shone in his eyes.

"Come in and get out of the chill," I said, frustrated that I hadn't communicated with them enough for them to know I was doing okay. This was a rather unstealthy wellness check and though I loved them for it and would never begrudge them the check-in since they'd literally saved my life in the past, I didn't want them worrying over me.

They plodded in, crisp brown leaves swirling in the driveway and up onto the porch as I shut the door behind them. Once everyone had settled and Bear had taken up his post next to his beloved Beast, his most favorite person with the possible exception of Tristan and now, Dove, I braced for the conversation.

"I really am doing well. I haven't gotten much sleep lately. Things with the farm have been busy." I folded my hands, not wanting to come out with everything if I didn't have to.

"Wouldn't you be toast and fall right to sleep? Is it anxiety? Or nightmares?"

Kenny's worry radiated off him. As much as he tended to be an optimist and steady when things were going wrong, I'd learned I was a bit of a soft spot for him.

Remembering this helped me not give in to the frustration flirting at the edges of my mind. "No. Nightmares haven't been a persistent problem. Generally, I think my anxiety is really well-managed. And since I know you'll want to ask, I have been keeping Dr. Corrigan informed."

Kenny visibly relaxed. Luc seemed the calmest, and

Jude ran a hand over Bear's head in gentle strokes, my dog blissed out with the affection.

After a beat, Luc asked, "What about Dove?"

I knew it was coming, but I hadn't guarded against it carefully enough. One hand scrubbed over my beard, but Kenny detected the smile despite my efforts.

"Oh, hell yes! Tell us everything!" He practically bounced out of his seat, the former energy filled with concern shifting to something explosively excited.

"Things are going well."

He leaned forward, and Jude and Luc's attention had intensified.

"And? Come on, do I have to beg? I will. I think we all know I am not above begging to hear how my dear friend is doing with the first woman he's dated in... ever?"

I rolled my eyes, Jude loosed a low chuckle, and Luc nudged him likely in an effort to get him to calm himself a bit.

The only way to actually make that happen would be to ride the approaching wave.

"We've gotten really close," I said, heat hitting my cheeks right as Kenny let out a ridiculous, "Oooo!"

"That might be... part of what's kept me up this week."

Kenny gasped, then cackled. "All right, Stone. Get it."

I scowled, and Luc elbowed him in the ribs while Jude shot him a glare.

"I didn't mean it like that." We'd talked a lot, and since we both worked during the day and being away from each other had been increasingly more difficult, we ended up staying awake far too long into the night.

Granted, I also *did* mean it like that, but he didn't need to be commenting like some kind of immature frat boy.

"Pretty serious, then?" Jude questioned.

They knew we were together, but I'd kept a lot to myself. It hadn't seemed fair to Dove for me to tell these guys how I felt before I talked with her about it, but now that we had, it made sense to share with them.

"I told her I love her."

Kenny fell back into the couch with a hand over his heart.

After a beat, Luc asked, "And?"

I fiddled with a thread on my jeans, but ultimately the blazing smile won out. "Apparently, she feels the same."

The explosion of cheers sent Bear into a barky celebration right along with them. Kenny launched out of his seat and pulled me up into a hug. Luc and Jude joined him, patting my back and grinning with so much genuine happiness for me, it snagged in my chest.

Maybe it was the lack of sleep, or maybe it was that these men had been with me through the worst days of my life and it felt like I'd been living the best ones for a while now. When we all settled back into our seats, I couldn't miss the chance to say as much.

"I've been thinking a lot about how my past with depression and PTSD, and even my current issues, will affect Dove. We've talked about it on and off since pretty early on—first generally in terms of if I were to date someone, and obviously now, specifically regarding how these things might affect her."

They each listened in their own way—Jude with his focus back on Bear, Luc straight on with an unreadable expression, and Kenny with a frown grooved into his face, no doubt ready to defend me against Dove or myself.

"It's reality. And I don't think she's being tricked into

this—I've had some rough moments, and you've seen how great she is in social circumstances." They'd seen us leave early at the book signing last week, and I'd mentioned how kind she'd been at Kenny's wedding months ago, long before we were dating.

"She's a good egg, that's for sure," Kenny said. "I wouldn't have recommended just *anyone* to be your tenant."

We chuckled for a minute at his excellent screening process, then I continued, needing to tell them what sat at the heart of my thoughts lately.

"I've been worried my baggage would harm her—that I'd hold her back or keep her from realizing some big dream she has for herself. And"—I gestured for Kenny to calm when he interrupted, springing to my defense—"she's helped me understand I don't need to worry. It doesn't mean we won't have things to deal with, but that she doesn't feel she's compromising by being with me. She seems to think it's a good deal for her, too."

"It is. You're one of the best people on this planet. If she doesn't realize that, then she's—"

"She does, man. She does. He just told us she gets it," Jude said, calming Kenny's rising energy.

"Exactly, she does. And all of this is good for you to get about our relationship, but I've also been thinking about how I'm only ready now—ready for her—because of you guys." My throat tightened, and all of their faces watched as I cleared my throat to finish. "Beyond the fact that I literally wouldn't be here, you've taught me how to talk through my feelings. You've taught me how to calm down, how to look forward, and honestly, how to love. I don't know how well I did that back in the day, but I think I'm decent at it now. I know a big part of that is because of how well you guys have cared for me when I needed it, both when I knew it and when I didn't."

Kenny's lips pursed dramatically as he jammed the heels of his hands into his eyes and sniffed. Jude cleared his throat and nodded. Luc offered a gentle smile.

"Okay, I didn't have crying on my radar for today, but I have to say I think you might be giving us too much credit. I mean, your therapist helped *a little*." Kenny held his hands up in a pinch.

All of us laughed, knowing full well Dr. Corrigan and my doctors back in North Carolina had played huge roles in my recovery.

"Yeah, maybe. But you guys, and Doc, Oak, Bruce..." I shook my head. "I'm grateful."

Kenny beamed, the little softy's eyes glittering. "Yeah, well, that's what family does."

Jude and Luc agreed, and I did, too. Because that was the reality here. That's what they'd offered me so stoutly and insistently. My own family had never felt like this. The only child of parents who probably shouldn't have had kids, I'd hardly spoken to them save birthdays and holidays in the last twenty years. I'd never had hard feelings about that, especially because when I'd needed help, when I'd needed *hope*, my chosen family had been there.

Whether it was the bonds of war and service that roped us together, or whether it was the grit and engrained stubbornness of us as individuals that did it, I would thank God every day for the rest of my life for these men.

If Dove had shown up in my life five years ago, I wouldn't have even seen her. Even two years ago, I was struggling through learning life here in Silverton. A year ago, I was improving consistently, but still needed to focus on establishing the pattern of my life in a new phase—out of the military, in the wide world.

That we'd come together now would never cease to be a miracle for me. And as I grinned back at my own personal miracle workers, I couldn't wait for more chances for Dove to be a part of this family.

To maybe be a part of this larger one, and make a smaller one of our own.

CHAPTER FORTY-EIGHT

Dove

We focused on the book selection of the month for the first hour. Honestly, it was impressive how engrossed in character arcs and settings and meet-cutes everyone was. We usually did a little more chatting before we dove in, but today, I was down to business.

Now that we'd lapsed into the second hour, I was ready. I'd updated them here and there on things with Dorian, but part of me had been waiting for tonight. Our once-a-month book club was a nonnegotiable outing for me, and I'd been counting the minutes until I could see my friends and squeal over my hot, sweet, amazing boyfriend.

I swigged the remaining drops of my prosecco and set the flute down more aggressively than I'd planned.

"Sorry," I mumbled, eying the small handful of beautiful desserts Dorian had made for our evening that hadn't been eaten yet.

Once I realized everyone had gone quiet and still, I looked up to find every one of their faces smiling back at me expectantly.

"What?"

"Are you kidding? We thought you'd come in here screaming about your man but you haven't made a peep. How much longer can we talk about the theme of this freaking book?" Jess said, tossing her paperback behind her with flair.

I laughed, relief and excitement bubbling up instantly. "Okay, I was going to, but you guys were so into the book! Can we please talk about Dorian?!"

Jo clapped, and Catherine grinned. Nikki and Winnie smiled broadly while Liz filled up my glass with more prosecco and Elise gave praise hands to the heavens saying, "Finally!"

And so, I did. I walked them through every sweet thing he'd done and many of the things he'd said. I told them how he'd confessed his feelings so freely, and I'd told him I loved him too, and how I knew it was fast, but it felt so good, and so right.

"I'm so happy for you. I don't think there always has to be some huge obstacle, you know? You're not perfect, but it sounds like you're so well matched. I loved seeing you together at the signing." Jo looked truly pleased, and I loved her for it.

"It was exciting to make our society debut," I said, affecting a ridiculous British accent.

"Oh, and did you, in fact, pledge him your maidenhead? He has been feeding you quite a bit, hasn't he?" Elise batted her eyelashes like she'd asked a normal question.

Everyone paused.

My face burst into flame.

Everyone squealed or screamed or laughed or buried their face in their hands from second-hand embarrassment or maybe disbelief. No, I would not be sharing details, but now they knew.

"I don't want to speak too soon but I can't imagine not being with him, you know? I've always had this inability to see into the future. Not like, my fortune or something, but like... even dreaming up what's ahead. I know that stems from my childhood and all of that." I waved away the past. It mattered, but that wasn't the point I wanted to make. "It's more like I just didn't have big dreams. I had this feeling like, maybe if I could figure myself out, and figure out what kind of person I might like to be with, then suddenly, everything would unfold."

A thrilling, resounding combination of calm and elation filled me as I looked at my friends' smiling faces. In each of their own ways, they understood this. Nikki's life had been all but over when she moved to Silverton. Winnie's was actively in danger and everything she thought she knew had come to a halt. Jo had been hiding who she truly was, Jess had convinced herself she hated the man she'd in some way always loved, and Liz had been so stone-cold focused on her goals, she hadn't even realized when she lost them. Catherine was still head down, driving toward fulfilling her dreams, but until recently, she hadn't been able to even let herself pursue them, and Elise... Elise had never dreamed of having what she did now.

None of us could've predicted where we ended up. None of us could've written a story like this one. Not even our Josie Wade.

"And now?" Elise asked.

I shook my head, the full force of what felt like miraculous clarity hitting me as I whisked a tear from my eye.

"Now I see it. I don't know exactly, but I can see it there. And it's here with all of you, and it's with Dorian."

After much congratulations and pleas for more details and guesses about how long until we got married—which sent my face back to flaming hot Cheeto territory despite secretly being thrilled they weren't thinking I was crazy for being in love with a man I'd only gotten to know a few months ago—we got back to books.

Granted, none of them had much of a leg to stand on. A few had history, like Winnie and Tristan, Jess and Beast, or even Elizabeth and Kenny, but most of us had met our person and it'd been a fast slide to where we were now.

What a strange, wild turn from a few months ago when I'd felt that gnawing ache of loneliness. It hadn't just been the absence of a love life, but I wasn't ashamed to admit I absolutely delighted in having someone to share my love and physical affection with.

I loved that Dorian had given me a ride here tonight and we'd held hands the whole way. I loved that I'd wake up tomorrow and knock on his door and he'd probably have something mind-blowingly delicious for breakfast. Then we'd spend a day enjoying each other in any way we wanted. Maybe he'd need to wander out on the farm and I'd be lazy and read inside on the couch. Maybe I'd spend the night because I hated to be away from him, and he from me.

Who knew how long we could last like this, as neighbors instead of even more than we were, but I didn't shy away at the thought of the timeline being short.

Everyone shared life updates as we nibbled on the delicious mini pies, tarts, and cakes Dorian had supplied us. Something about sitting here with my dearest friends and eating the delicacies my boyfriend had made had me bursting with happiness. I felt so delightfully full, so hopeful, and like the way ahead was wide open.

It was that feeling I'd mentioned—the one where I saw a future in front of me I wanted to run hard after instead of clinging to the next steps, clawing at the path in hopes of surviving and someday figuring out how to get a few steps ahead.

As Jess shared about Will's latest developments and how ridiculously in love Jude and even Bones were with the baby, all of us beamed with happiness. I thought I saw Winnie press a hand to her belly, but I didn't want to call her out if she wasn't ready to say anything or worse, in case I was imagining things. Nikki's math nerd company, as we lovingly called it, had produced a new app and it would launch next year and she insinuated she was feeling like she might be ready for Bruce to propose soon—he would do it the second she let him know. She hadn't held out arbitrarily —their pasts and what she needed almost demanded time, and his way of loving her well was to give it to her.

Winnie was relieved to be on speaking terms with everyone in her family and mentioned she was taking a small role with Saint Security to help with the expansion of both Adam's mountaineering arm and Tristan's combatives and self-defense leg. Her experience as a farm manager meant she was super organized and thoughtful and this was such a cool, fun surprise. She'd been waiting to find what she wanted, and I loved she'd get to work with Tristan and more of the Saint staff.

Glazed was flourishing already this year, and had been since September, which was earlier than Elise thought it would be. Now that she was engaged to a millionaire, she probably didn't need to worry about the drag of shoulder season, but my stubborn, independent friend wouldn't settle for leaning on Luc just because she could.

Liz mentioned being so happy to be here coming into the holidays because she hadn't been in the US for Thanksgiving in a decade, and Jo was swiping at tears just hearing her say that. Catherine had seen a huge uptick in demand for her cleaning business locally, and her online presence had experienced viral growth, so much so she seemed a bit overwhelmed, but excited.

By the time we were done, we committed to getting together between book club meetings whenever possible, and ramping up our group chat. We messaged at least once every other day, sometimes more, but it ebbed and flowed with the realities of life. Anytime we were together made me want *more* time together, and I loved knowing we all felt this way.

After hugs and some cleanup, everyone went their separate ways. Catherine, who looked exhausted, but very kindly offered to take me home, slumped into her car, and I took the passenger side.

"Are you sure you can take me? I can call a rideshare, or even Dorian could get here in a few." I didn't want her falling asleep at the wheel on the way home—I didn't live all that far away, but this time of night the road that led back into town would be pitch black except for the moonlight.

"I'm good. I was up super early working on content, but I want to hear more about you and Dorian. I feel like I haven't seen you or anyone and..." She scrubbed at her eyes, the dark wisps of hair that'd escaped from her ponytail prettily framing her pale face, then gently slapped her cheek. "I'll sleep very soundly tonight."

She pulled out of the spot a few doors down from All Booked Up and we waved to Jo as she locked the front door to the shop, Adam waiting at her side. He raised a hand, offering a friendly smile before turning back to his fiancée.

"They're so cute," I said, sighing a little dreamily.

"They really are. All of you are giving me hope." She eased away from the stop sign and turned the corner.

"At the risk of sounding like a total jerk, are you doing okay with that? I ask because I was really struggling for a while. And it wasn't only because I wanted someone and it felt like everyone but you and me had someone, but... yeah." I stopped babbling for fear of making it worse.

"I get it. And honestly? I'm fine. I mean, yes, I'd love to find someone, but right now, I finally have the freedom to pursue this business and it's taking so much of my time, I don't know when I'd see someone. I'm barely making it to book—"

Her gasp and slam on the brakes had me grabbing the "oh shit!" bar with my right hand and pressing my feet into the floor like I could stop the car, too.

"What—"

Catherine rolled down the window. "Are you okay?"

My gaze swung to a man standing, slightly hunched over in front of the car. Had she hit him? That didn't make sense.

"I'm so sorry, let me—"

An arm reached into her window, pulled open the door, then tapped the unlock button. The door behind me opened, and something hard pressed into my head.

"Don't move, don't scream, don't speak."

The gruff voice held a commanding edge, and in my gut, I knew what was touching me. I wanted to pull away, but fear of disobeying and being hurt made me freeze.

"I have one gun on your little friend and now one on you. You'll close the door and drive according to my instructions, or I will shoot you both before you even know what's happened." He slammed the driver's side door and slipped into the seat behind it, peripheral movement indicating he'd likely just put a gun to Catherine's head, too.

She whimpered, and I wanted to reach for her hand, but I couldn't move. Couldn't speak.

The figure who'd been hunched in front of the car straightened and walked off.

"You're going to drive now, or I shoot the nurse."

Catherine eased off the brake and drove.

My heart sank through the floorboards.

This was planned.

This wasn't a random carjacking.

They knew I was a nurse, which meant they'd likely known where I'd be tonight. Maybe they'd even known Dorian wasn't with me.

They hadn't grabbed me outside the store because some of the Saint men had been there, but just a few blocks away and...

It was official. We'd just joined the worst club ever.

CHAPTER FORTY-NINE

Dove

It took no more than three minutes to figure out where we were going.

I'd suspected from about minute two, and here we were, twenty minutes after getting abducted at gunpoint, rolling into the compound just a few minutes down the road from my own house.

Great.

The good news was, instead of wanting to shrivel up in a ball and cry, I was getting angry. Not usually my default emotion—I wasn't actually all that familiar with anger. Most of my life, I'd avoided it since it didn't do much for me. What good would being angry with my parents, or the cult leader, or even my brother, do me?

But as they pulled me from the car, hands bound behind my back with what had felt and sounded like some kind of zip tie, and then manhandled Catherine out and immediately tied her hands behind her back, I felt the ore-melting fire of rage burning in me.

Because this had to be thanks to my brother, which meant I was going to murder him.

Well, not murder him.

Definitely do whatever I could to get out of this and then have him arrested, right along with his merry band of misogynist peabrains.

Sure, one might argue I didn't know they hated women, but I'd suggest kidnapping two women at gunpoint hinted strongly at just that, not to mention a few other flaws in one's character.

"You're hurting me," I said, hoping some amount of protest might be heeded. I hadn't dared to speak in the car, but the gun wasn't pressed into my head anymore, and I'd started feeling fairly confident they wouldn't shoot me outright since Hawk would be mad. "Where are you taking her?"

No response, despite my continued questions as we walked. I'd ask Hawk—no, demand he tell me.

Granted, Hawk wasn't a leader here. I knew that like I knew Dorian would be waking up in approximately ten hours and if I didn't show my face soon after, he'd know I was missing.

Clock is ticking, crapheads.

We entered a building with faded sunflowers painted on the outside, no doubt a vestige of the sweet tenants who'd been elbowed out. Inside, the barn appeared to be a meeting space with wooden benches and a stage up front with a microphone and lectern. Behind it was a giant American flag and a chalkboard affixed to the wall with the word *HISTORY* in all caps and the *his* underlined.

Oh. Goody.

The claim that the history of the United States and more likely all of humanity was only valuable when looked at through the white male lens had been a common refrain in my childhood. It looked like Hawk had managed to find a group of people with a nearly identical ideology.

My stomach rolled, and I gritted my teeth against the bite at the hinge of my jaw. If I wasn't careful, I'd end up throwing up. I'd never thought of myself as someone who could be triggered by things. For the most part, I'd made decent peace with my past, especially since I'd had such a good life with Nan. But based on the way I felt physically ill, maybe I wasn't as solid as I thought.

We swerved past the stage and exited the barn out a back door, crossed a dirt expanse, and entered another building. Inside, fluorescent lights cast an eerie glow in the hallway. After one turn, we arrived at a room where the goon shoved me inside to find Hawk sitting at a table.

"Hiya, Dovey."

In another life, I'd Hulk out and rip my hands out of my restraints and slap him silly enough he saw stars. In reality, I strained against the zip ties, the plastic cutting into my skin, and took a breath before speaking.

"Where is my friend?"

He merely blinked.

"You realize this is illegal and you are going to jail for this, right? All of you?" I turned to look at the person who'd taken me, but he'd melted away, back outside the door.

"No need to worry about that. You're here to help, and since you're obligated to do no harm, you're going to do it without me doing anything more than asking." He smirked like he held all the cards.

Maybe he did right now, but in what world would

someone not come for me? Did he really not understand the real world enough to know this ended badly for him?

Clearly, making such an argument wouldn't register, so I didn't waste my breath. "Is someone hurt? Is that why I'm here?"

"Calm down, okay? First, you're going to meet Jeb, and then—"

"Jeb?"

His eyes hardened. "Yes. Jeb. He's in charge here. And when you meet him, you'd be smart to keep your trap shut and show him some respect. You remember how to do that, right?"

Eyes down. Soft voice. Respond when spoken to, otherwise be silent. Don't be tempting. Always be willing to serve.

The mantra from my childhood echoed through my mind, and an involuntary shudder racked my body.

"I'm not getting involved in anything here, Hawk. Let me go."

He sighed and shook his head. "Not an option."

"Let me go now and I won't report it to the police." Total lie, I absolutely would, but it was worth a shot.

His sneer could've sliced me open. "Right. I'll believe that the day I believe you're living a righteous life."

Great. Here we went with the nonsense. "I don't think we have much to discuss. You wanted me to meet someone? Take me to them."

I was not going to listen to him spout on about how I was wrong for living my life—how my long hair was tempting men or my pants were an offense to him and all his brethren. I was not about to listen to someone who'd orchestrated a kidnapping tell *me* about righteousness, especially knowing where we'd come from and all the horrible things that'd come along with the culture.

When you put women in cages, you lost the ability to say anything about righteousness.

"Fine. Come with me."

He grabbed my upper arm in a tight, merciless grasp and began walking. He slowed after a few twists and turns in the hallways and arrived at a larger room where a man with dark hair tied back from his face in a low bun and a neatly trimmed beard stood with his hands pressed together, a pleased expression on his face.

My throat tightened, and my pulse ratcheted up. I didn't know this man, but I'd known one like him. He had that energy that said he was in charge and everything would be fine, that he was loving and charismatic, but if anyone crossed him... good luck.

I wanted to be brave. I wanted to spit in his face and run out of here, get across the property line to Dorian's farm and start screaming. Maybe Bear would hear me, or one of the farm hands might be at work early. Who knew. Anything would be better than this.

Except every muscle in my body had frozen at the sight of this man in his tunic-like shirt and slacks, a wolf in sheep's clothes who embodied everything that'd haunted my nightmares as a teen. It was a man just like this who'd filled my father's head with lies, and a man just like him who'd poisoned my brother.

They'd had their own choices to make, but I would never pretend there weren't some people who had a little extra ability to sway weak-minded people. They were the wolves, and here I was, standing in front of one again.

"Welcome, Ms. Jensen. We're so glad to have you as our guest." His smooth, low voice would've been pleasant if I didn't know any better.

"Do you kidnap and handcuff all your guests? That's not a very kind way to treat people."

Hawk's grasp tightened around my arm, a warning.

But the man shook his head, his face showcasing dismay. "My goodness, my apologies. I was told you'd offered your assistance."

His gaze cut to Hawk's, and my brother's hand instantly loosened. Then in another few seconds, the zip ties were cut.

"I'm Jeb Johnson. Please." He extended his hands to me.

Internally, I recoiled, but externally, I was still frozen. When his hands covered mine, they were soft and warm.

"Take a moment. Do you need anything? Some water?" His solicitous tone made no sense.

I'd had it. "Why am I here?"

"Did your brother not tell you? Hawk, come now." He clucked at Hawk like an old man might, though he couldn't have been much older than me. "One of my friends is in labor. She's been struggling for the better part of a day. We'd like your help, if you're willing. And after that, we've got a few other people who could use your attention."

I blinked, absorbing this. "I'm here to help with medical needs?"

Some part of me relaxed, knowing this was actually something I could do. If the root of all of this drama came down to them needing medical care, I could handle it.

They wouldn't have needed to kidnap me either. It might've taken some convincing, but didn't Hawk know I'd willingly help if I could?

"Yes. What else?" Jeb looked truly troubled.

I shrugged, relief flooding me. "Never mind. Please show me to whoever needs help."

And I would've taken that ease with me if I hadn't seen an odd glint in Jeb's eye as he cast my brother a look that chilled me to the bone just before he set a hand on my back and led me away.

CHAPTER FIFTY

Dorian

I hadn't heard a peep from Dove by nine the next morning.

Not that she'd said when she expected to be up, but she was naturally a fairly early riser. Since I was, too, we both enjoyed the pattern of a touch more sleep on weekends followed by breakfast and a lazy morning together.

I'd made quiche and a loaf of pumpkin chocolate chip bread. I generally preferred the brighter flavors of spring and summer, but the fall pumpkin and spice and richer palates were undeniably cozy.

By ten, I'd gotten restless. When no answer to my text came, I wondered if maybe she'd been out later than I'd realized. I'd passed out from exhaustion around eleven and she hadn't gotten home. Usually, we texted goodnight, and when I woke up and saw she hadn't said anything in response when she arrived, I didn't let it bother me.

Except it did bother me because it was unlike Dove. Granted, if she'd stayed out late or maybe had a little too much champagne with her girls, maybe she was sleeping it off at someone's house. It hadn't happened before, but who knew?

Her friends would, and since I had Jo's number, I messaged her to check in. When she confirmed Dove and Catherine had left All Booked Up around ten, I figured maybe she'd gone to Catherine's. I didn't know her as well, so when I asked Jo if she wouldn't mind making sure they'd made it to Catherine's house okay, she was kind enough to do just that.

But she didn't hear anything.

And when, a half hour later, she called me to say she'd driven by Catherine's place and didn't see her car, I knew something was wrong.

My pulse spiked, and I had to take a seat and breathe through a blast of panic before I grabbed my keys, wallet, and Bear, and we ran to the truck. On the way, I called Kenny and in eleven minutes, I was pulling up in front of Saint right as Bruce's SUV and Luc's car arrived.

"Kenny's almost here, and Adam's already inside," Bruce said, clapping me on the shoulder. "We'll get this figured out."

On the drive, I'd alerted the Silverton PD and called Sheriff Ryan's personal cell to let him know. The obvious threat was Dove's brother and that meant the Patriot Ridge compound.

Inside, Beast ran a trace on Dove's cell to no avail, which meant it was off. Once Doc got Catherine's number, they did the same, and same problem. The last pings on both phones had been downtown Silverton, which gave us no help.

"Call your contact at Patriot Ridge. Whoever you've talked to about farm stuff in the past," Jaws said, his tone taking on full mission-command tenor.

Relief and focus hit. I could do this. I could focus on tasks in front of me instead of sinking into the worry absolutely gutting me as I thought about what might be happening to Dove. She'd been through more than any person should ever have to endure. The fact that her brother might be contributing to her pain, might be making her life harder or scarier or worse in any way, had me gritting my teeth as I connected the call.

"This's Pole."

The clipped tone came through as usual. Polard Smith had been my primary contact since Cordy and Maybell had been forced out of the commune months ago. He wasn't particularly helpful, but the fact that he'd responded and confirmed they didn't have Elise had put him in more favorable light... until now, when they likely had Dove.

"Do you have her?"

A beat of silence. "Who, now?"

"Dove Jensen. I believe you know her brother, Hawk Jensen. Her friend, Catherine Hewitt, was with her. Don't lie to me, Smith." The edge in my voice emerged in a gritty tone.

"Hold up there, bud. I don't know no Dove or Catherine or nobody, and I ain't keen on the way it sounds like you're accusin' me of something I ain't even heard of let 'lone done."

Jaws, and now Barbie, who'd arrived a few minutes ago, modeled taking a deep breath, so I did just that.

"My girlfriend and her friend are missing. I have reason to believe they're at the commune. I understand you probably don't want the police to obtain a warrant to search the premises, but they will begin working on getting one if you can't help me out here."

The ambient noise in the background of the call muted and all of us waited. This was the moment of truth when he'd either double down that he didn't know anything or he'd cave to avoid police involvement. Little did he know, there was going to be police involvement either way.

After an interminable wait, the line crackled and Pole's voice came through. "The nurse is here. They both came willingly. Nobody steps foot on the property or we stand our ground."

The call went dead and more than one person swore.

Jaws spoke into a phone. "That they did, Chief, but they're saying she went willingly."

A few minutes later, his face was a mask of resolve.

"Chief said they can't go without probable cause she was abducted and that he's saying she went willingly complicates matters. He's going to work on a warrant to search the place, but since it's a Sunday, it'll take longer than we want to wait." He blinked, looking at the circle that'd formed around him. Next to me stood Barbie, Cookie, Oak, Eddie, Saint, and Elizabeth. Beast was still working the computers, likely trying to figure out anything else he could to give us intel.

"So, what? Are we going in to get her?" Barbie asked, verbalizing the question I hadn't managed to voice.

Jaws heaved a sigh and gave a nod to Saint, who held his gaze, then turned to me. "If you think she's there under duress, we go. We do it smart, we do it fast, and we do it as aboveboard as we can so they can't prosecute for trespassing even if we get proof they took her."

"Technically illegal." This from Oak.

"It is. But so is kidnapping," Elizabeth said, jaw flexing.

"And frankly, I think they've messed with the wrong women."

"Damn right they have," Eddie said, nodding in agreement.

"Can't say anything but thank you, then. I was going in to get her with or without you guys," I admitted.

Beast slung an arm around my shoulders and squeezed briefly. "No, brother. Not without us. We're with you, no matter what."

CHAPTER FIFTY-ONE

Dove

I'd slept no more than forty minutes since yesterday morning when I'd woken for my Saturday. Now it was Sunday at some time past noon. They'd taken my watch for fear it was connected to my phone, I guessed, and so I only ever knew what time it was when I was seeing a patient in one of the rooms fitted with a clock.

Where are you, Dorian?

Was it pathetic how my heart was crying out for him? I couldn't blame anyone for this but Hawk and his crap friends, but I desperately wanted my *great* friends to be the super soldiers they were and come find me!

They'd done it before. They'd do it again, right?

"Ms. Jensen, we're ready for you."

Jeb's voice called to me from another room, and my skin crawled for the nth time since I'd met him.

I trudged into the room, bracing. I'd started doing that a

dozen patients back, after I'd helped Violet deliver her baby. Thank goodness I'd seen enough births in the ER or I wouldn't have been able to help her, but her baby boy, though a bit on the small side, was healthy.

Should they get to the hospital? Yes. Would they?

Hopefully after the police get here, yes.

Not that I had any illusions Jeb Johnson was a good guy, but when he'd insisted on staying in the room as I worked with Violet, my uh-oh meter had shot off the charts. When I'd nestled the baby into his mama's arms and asked Jeb if he wanted to get the father, he'd given me a quizzical look and said, "He's here."

He was the father of Violet's baby. He hadn't spoken her name or made eye contact with her. He hadn't held her hand or offered her a drink. He'd just stood in the corner, watching.

Now in this makeshift exam room, I found yet another young woman. She was the fourteenth woman between the ages of eighteen and twenty-three I'd seen and she had a similar affect and symptoms as the others. Since Jeb never left me alone with any of them, I never directly asked if they were here by choice, but I knew in my gut.

Those women were not okay. I didn't know whether Jeb planned to make them all his broodmares or what, but the fury was building even after exhaustion had long since started pulling me apart.

At this point, I'd had it. And so after a quick exam which showed similar signs of malnutrition and possible infection I couldn't properly diagnose without testing kits, I tossed my gloves into the trash and saw an opening. Jeb had leaned out of the room, one foot still glued to the floor in the middle of the doorway as though I needed the reminder I couldn't simply leave, and I had to take the chance.

"Are you here by choice?" I asked, voice low and calm. "Do you want to be here?"

Her deep brown eyes flicked to the door, the same nervous energy so many of the girls had exhibited sending my heart rate up.

But she didn't speak, and time was running out. I didn't actually need her to say it for me to know something was very wrong here, but I wanted the confirmation. I wanted one of these young women to give me a sign and I'd figure out how to get them out of here. If Dorian came, I'd get them out. It had taken me speaking out to someone back in the cult for her to start looking for Nan and then getting me out. I could do this—be like that brave young woman who'd helped me—and pay it forward now.

"You can tell me. I can get you out of here."

Her eyes widened, and she swallowed hard. Her mouth opened, but before she spoke, her gaze snapped up to the doorway.

"We all done here?" Jeb's voice cut in.

My hopes plummeted and with them, all my energy seemed to drain away.

"Yeah. Like Jenny and Gina and Jayla and at least three others, I suspect she has strep throat. They'll need antibiotics, especially if you want to stop this from spreading further. It's irresponsible—"

"That's enough." He looked past me to the woman now cowering in the exam chair and jerked his chin to one side.

She instantly got up and left the room without a word.

"These women... why are they here? What are you doing to them?" My voice shook, and I hated the sound of it.

He turned to me in a slow-motion move that sent a chill down my spine.

"What we do here, Ms. Jensen, is none of your concern.

You only need to do the job you came to do, the one you willingly accepted when you slapped on your first pair of gloves."

Sensing any further argument would get me nowhere and also wear me out even more, I nodded, lips glued together and eyes downcast. I wouldn't challenge him now because I couldn't. I didn't have the energy to run through the woods and even though I had to be close to Dorian's, I wasn't sure *how* close. I also hadn't been out of this building since they'd brought me in. While I was potentially doing some good for the people here, I didn't feel right about fleeing despite the gut-level need to get out and away from this slime bucket.

At some point, I'd make a break for it if no one came for me. But first, I needed to rest.

Following him out of the exam room and trailing just behind in the hallway, I dared ask, "Would it be possible for me to have some food and rest? I'm not sure how many more patients I can see without at least an hour or two of sleep."

His movement was so fast, I never had a chance of anticipating it. Before I knew what was happening, his hand was at my throat and I was pinned against the hallway wall.

"You will do as I say when I say it. You will stop asking questions and trying to play gumshoe like anyone is ever going to believe your lying whore mouth. You will cooperate and do it when I tell you. Then and only then will I consider letting you rest. You are nowhere near the point of showing true loyalty."

And there it was.

Not that I hadn't seen enough here to disturb me, but there he showed his hand, no pretty manners or pretense.

He wanted blind loyalty. Somehow, he'd gotten it from my brother and the other idiots surrounding him. He might've even coerced it out of these women, though I suspected that came far more from fear than loyalty.

He wanted it without treating people well, without respecting others... He wanted it at the threat of violence and subjugation.

At this point in my life, I almost laughed in his face—it was so brutally familiar after the childhood I'd endured. Instead, I stayed silent, uninterested in giving him any excuse to show me what a tough guy he was.

Maybe I was delirious with exhaustion or rage, but I'd entered a weird mental space where I'd long ago stopped worrying about leaving. I knew I'd get out of here. I knew Dorian would come and he'd bring Saint Security and probably the Silverton PD and Sheriff Ryan down on this place —it was a matter of time.

For now, I would survive. I'd help as many people as I could, and when the time came, I'd tell anyone who would listen every single thing I'd seen, so the boys of Patriot Ridge would spend a nice long time in jail.

CHAPTER FIFTY-TWO

Dorian

My hands shook as I loaded my sidearm.

"You don't have to take that. Just take the Taser."

Kenny's voice froze my movements for a half second before I continued strapping on gear. "I'm okay."

When he didn't respond after another few seconds, I finished clipping everything into my tactical vest and looked up. The concern on his face was crystal clear.

"You don't have to do this. We'll get her."

I was already shaking my head. "I have to go. I can't just sit around and wait. I've done this a million times."

It wasn't pity on his face, but something that scratched uncomfortably close to a barely closed wound. "You have, but it's been a while. And you've never gone after your person, right? Not someone you loved like Dove."

My throat tightened and eyes watered enough to make

me blink hard in determination to keep it together. "I know that. But we're not using these weapons, right?"

That was the concept and we all knew it. We'd be fools not to go in armed, but it'd be a mess in terms of law enforcement and we'd certainly be better off not escalating that far if we could help it.

He nodded. "That's the goal."

He held my gaze, and I hoped he could see everything there. I didn't want to do this, but I could. I would.

"I'm not being stubborn or foolish. I promise you I wouldn't be going if I didn't think I could handle it. I can follow orders and if we come across any of the guys I've met before, it might be an advantage to have me there. If I feel like I'm losing my grip, I swear to you I'll let you know."

"Deal." He pulled me in for a bracing hug, then shoved me away. "Now let's get focused and get your woman back." He flashed me a smile as he cinched his vest tighter.

"Let's do it."

We moved quickly and silently from my property line. Most of us didn't maintain the same level of fitness we'd had while in the EMU, which demanded we could ruck march forty miles just in case. Instead, each of us had our own regimen and mine had nothing to do with long-distance runs. I did short runs, lifting, and work on the farm, but some weeks, I only managed the farm work.

All of this meant I was counting on the adrenaline cranking through me and the intel we'd gathered thanks to a drone we flew over the compound to grab photos of their setup. We'd be approaching the long way to avoid coming in the main entrance, but it would only be about a mile through oak bramble and woods until we met with buildings. From there, another half mile through the streets, which would be the most likely to blow our cover, and then to the larger buildings we'd determined were most likely places Dove and Catherine might be.

In just over twelve minutes and thanks to the eerily quiet streets of Patriot Ridge, Jaws, Oak, Doc, Barbie, Cookie, Eddie, Elizabeth, and I approached the largest buildings in two four-man teams. We moved at Jaws's and Eddie's direction, funneling through an easily breached entrance thanks to Cookie's CMOE skills.

We hadn't encountered anyone, but the sounds from the chapel-like building suggested most people were in the biggest structure attending whatever version of church these people held. Hopefully, that meant the way to Dove and Catherine would be clear.

Each step we took, my heart pounded, calling out to her. I willed her to know we were coming, that we would save her—them. We'd save both of them from whatever this whole mess was, and the people who'd kidnapped them would face the consequences.

Beast's analysis suggested this would be the most likely place to find the women, and inside one unattended room, we burst in to find Catherine gagged and cuffed to a metal pipe in the dark.

She instantly started crying, and Eddie and Elizabeth went to her.

"You're alright. We're here. We're getting you out," they both assured her while Doc assessed her for illness and injury.

"Where's Dove, Catherine? Can you tell us anything?"

Jaws asked, striking the perfect note of commanding but gentle.

God bless him, because I couldn't speak. My heart was crawling into my throat and all I could think was, *"She's not here. She's not here."*

"We'll find her. This is good. We'll get her," Cookie said, waiting until I met his eyes and staying with me for a beat while I took a breath and calmed enough to think straight.

He was right. Finding Catherine unharmed save for the trauma of being taken and locked up in a room was the best possible news. Next stop, Dove.

Beast radioed to indicate there was more movement at our second target building, so Eddie and Elizabeth stayed with her. I sent a photo of Catherine to Sheriff Ryan and Chief Whitacker, hoping the evidence of her containment would be enough to get them access. Even if we found Dove, we'd either have to sneak her and Catherine back to my property, which was a long way off on a good day for most people, or we'd walk out the front with their protection.

I voted Option B and I voted it happen *now*.

"Move in."

Beast's cue based on his drone footage led to Jaws's hand and arm signal for us to proceed. We moved in three-man teams now, Cookie breaching another door in an almost joyfully quick picking of the lock and rushing down the hall.

Around the first corner, two men appeared. One shouted and the other made to grab his weapon, but Oak and Jaws had them subdued on the ground before they could move. Barbie stepped in with duct tape for their mouths while I zip-tied their hands and Cookie bound their feet.

"So sorry, fellas. Can't have you ruining the surprise," Barbie whispered, clearly amped up on the small victory.

Jaws signaled to move so we did, covering the distance of the next hallway with rapid, silent steps.

Another two men sauntered up and were taken down. Jaws asked them where to find Dove, but they literally spit in his face so Barbie blissfully duct-taped their mouths and we left them.

Adrenaline was thrumming through me and I hadn't worked on controlling it like I used to. Managing the adrenaline dump was essential, but it flooded me now and I prayed it wouldn't stop until we'd found her.

Just then, Jaws held up his fist, the signal for *hold*. We all froze immediately, and a second later, I heard it.

"If you touch her again, I'm going to have to take it personally and then we're going to have an even bigger problem than we already do, okay?"

Dove's voice and no shortage of her energy and determination shining through. *Thank God.*

Then a male voice rang out with a nasty slur and Jaws's hand moved. We moved.

CHAPTER FIFTY-THREE

Dove

Jeb gripped Lucinda's arm in a grasp so hard I could see his fingers bruising her in real time. He sneered after his nasty epithets and got *right* in my face.

"Your pathetic little threats mean nothing, you whiney little—"

Jeb disappeared in a movement so sudden, I gasped and Lucinda screamed. And then I started laughing like a maniac because Dorian was here!

But before I could launch myself into his arms, six goons I'd seen around and Hawk burst in and threw themselves into a fight. Well, six men did, and while Dorian tried to get to me, to shield me and Lucinda, I felt a hand go around my neck and the muzzle of a gun press into my temple.

"Stop! Stop right now or she's done."

Hawk's voice was hard and so cold, I didn't know him.

That was the reality I'd slowly begun to accept as the day went on and I hadn't seen him. He hadn't checked on me. He'd left me to Jeb and whatever sick plans he had for me once I did his bidding, and that meant this person now directly threatening my life wasn't my brother anymore.

He'd been too broken by our childhoods, too twisted by the lies and manipulations of the people around him, and this was the fallout.

He'd lost himself, and he was now threatening to murder his own sister.

"Move the weapon away from your sister, Hawk."

Dorian's voice came out clear, commanding, and almost compassionate. It was remarkable, and at some other time, it might've even been sexy.

"I can't. It's—this isn't how it's supposed to go! He said she'd be safe here and this isn't right. She belongs here and you're not supposed to be here." His grip around me tightened, and the press of his ulna against my throat threatened to cut off my airway.

"Shoot them all!"

Jeb's voice came in a cry that was then muffled with something I couldn't see in the hallway, and Hawk's arm tightened further.

"Just leave! Just leave and she'll be fine," he said, a twinge of hysteria clear in his tone.

Dorian held out his hands showing he was unarmed. "She'll be fine if you move that weapon, right? You don't want anything to happen to her or you, so please, Hawk, just set it down. We'll figure this out. It's going to be okay."

Out of the corner of my eye, I saw someone moving, but I didn't let my gaze track them.

And then everything happened at once. Dorian spoke in that calm, steady voice, Kenny Carmichael moved toward Hawk from the left, and Jeb's voice rang out again with, "Shoot!"

The sound of a shot was near-deafening in the small room, but I heard it and felt it and was shoved to the ground because Hawk had released me. He hadn't shot *me*.

I looked up just in time to see Dorian hunch, hands pressed to his side.

That's when horror struck and chaos ensued.

Somewhere behind me, people were moving, shouting, begging. I didn't know. I didn't care. I couldn't hear or see any of them as I crawled to Dorian where he'd stumbled back against the wall and slid to sit on the floor. I stripped away the heavy-duty Velcro keeping his vest in place, begging anyone who would listen for the shot to have hit Kevlar and not *him*.

A swell of relief so great it almost knocked me over struck when I saw the bullet lodged into the vest. He groaned, and I scrambled up to see his face.

"You okay?" he asked, voice pinched like the wind had been knocked out of him.

"Am I? Dorian, you just got shot!" There was more than a little hysteria churning in my body and leaking into my words.

"I'm okay. Maybe bruised ribs, though."

His hand reached up and cupped my face, and as our gazes locked and held, the chaos roiling around us seemed to still. Of course it hadn't, but my perception narrowed to him and only him as the calloused pads of his fingers brushed my cheek.

"Are you okay, Dove? I'm so sorry."

I pressed my hand over his, savoring his touch. "I'm just fine now. Thank you for coming for me."

His thumb brushed away a tear. "Nothing could've kept me away."

My cheesy smile could've powered the city, and he chuckled, then jerked with a wince.

"Oh, I'm so sorry. You probably need to head to the hospital."

"He definitely does," Adam confirmed, crouching to take a look. "You're going to have a nasty bruise at the very least. Based on the breathing, I'm thinking they might be broken."

Dorian nodded, and my heart pinched. I hated that he'd gotten hurt. I prayed no one else had. Then I remembered. "Did you find Catherine?"

"Yes. She's okay. Shaken up and a bit dehydrated, but she's outside with Eddie and Elizabeth, giving her statement to the police." Adam gave me a small smile, then turned to Dorian. "The bad news is, we've gotta get you up."

Adam and I helped get Dorian on his feet, and the low grunt of pain as we levered him up made me want to scream. By the time he was up, Hawk was face down on the floor, and a Silverton police officer was talking to Kenny.

Dorian's eyes never left mine for long. I wanted to hug him and kiss him and have him wrap me in his arms so I could cry my guts out. I'd kept it together for a remarkably long time, especially for me, and I just knew a big spill was coming.

Adam patted my arm. "I'm sure they'll want your statement before you go to the hospital. We can take him and you can come with the others—"

"I'm not leaving without her."

Dorian's words brooked no argument, and even though his breathing was still shallow to protect his ribs, he was steady.

Adam chuckled low. "Alright, my friend. If you can handle it, and unless something else pops up, we'll wait until after they wrap up with Dove."

The something else could be any number of issues caused by the impact of the bullet to the vest and then his body, or issues with his ribs if they were broken. Pulmonary issues on the heels of rib injury—contusions, lacerations, and even lung collapses—danced at the edges of my brain but I shooed them away. Sometimes, medical knowledge could be a curse, and I needed to focus and get this next part over with so we could get Dorian checked out.

When we finally stepped outside the building where I'd been stuck for over eighteen hours, the November sky was dimming. I inhaled the fresh air and felt tears gathering at the corners of my eyes.

"Give us a minute." Dorian ushered me to the side of the building, some distance from the crowd of police officers, Saint Security people, and onlookers from the compound.

He stopped and wrapped his arms around me. I held on to him lightly, praying I wasn't hurting him, and shut my eyes. The tears fell as I soaked up the warmth of him and the shuddering relief of knowing this horrible ordeal was over.

"I'm sorry," he whispered into my hair.

"No, I'm sorry." I looked up into his beloved face. The one I'd dreamed of coming for me—the one I *knew* would come. "I knew you'd come for me. I knew I'd get out of here. I'm so sorry for all of this."

His hands came to my face, cradling me with that way

of his that sent swirls of lovely sensation all through me. "I love you."

"I love you, too. And I think I might need to talk to someone to work through this delightful experience." My lip trembled because I was exhausted, and now that the adrenaline that'd zipped through my veins when I'd seen Dorian had bled out of me, I was so, so sad my brother had been part of this.

"You probably do. I have a strong recommendation who's local, but if she's not a fit, we'll find you someone great." He dipped, pressing his forehead to mine then dropping a kiss there, before he straightened. "I think this was my last Saint mission."

His expression was clear. Not cagey or wounded or angry or closed. It was like the experience today had solidified it.

He held up his hand to show a small shake. He looked at it, then shook his head in an almost boyish way. "When I realized you were gone, I went straight to Saint. Of course I did, but it wasn't just because they have the ability to help. Then I was terrified coming here, but I knew I could do it. With these people around me, I knew. But I don't think I could've for anyone else, not anymore, and that's my sign. As we were getting ready, I just... I knew. This would be it. And I can't explain why I know this, but I think I know—" His brow furrowed, and he glanced over at the crowd of bodies milling about, taking statements, taking information, sliding handcuffed men into vehicles. "I know they'll still be there for me. Even if I'm not taking jobs."

I pulled him to me as gently as I could. "I know that without any doubt."

"Can we get your statement now, Ms. Jensen?" Sheriff

Ryan stood a few feet away, a patient expression on his handsome face.

I grinned, determined to move forward—today, this week, this year... indefinitely. "Of course, Sheriff. What else would I want to be doing on a lovely fall evening such as this?"

CHAPTER FIFTY-FOUR

Dorian

A full week after Dove's kidnapping, I straightened my tie in the mirror of my bathroom right before the doorbell rang. Bear's nails tapped as he hustled to the front of the house, no doubt knowing exactly who he'd find on our porch.

I was already smiling as I pulled open the door, the ache in my ribs only a little more than a dull thud with some movements. They hadn't been broken, thankfully, and the soreness of the bruising had taken major steps of improvement in the last forty-eight hours.

"You look so handsome! You didn't need to wear a tie." Dove reached for me, stepping over the threshold and into my arms in a heartbeat.

As usual, my heart thrummed with her nearness. We'd spent hours together this week, basking in each other and the excuse for both of us to take time off. Pretty soon, I'd be in the full throes of the Christmas tree season and time off would be hard to come by until at least the week before Christmas. But for now, until Thanksgiving at least, I would give her every bit of time and attention she wanted.

"Wanted to look nice for Nan."

She beamed. "You always look nice."

I chuckled, pleased it didn't cause lightning to shoot up my side anymore. "I'm not sure that's true. I can get pretty gross out on the farm."

Flames flickered to life in her eyes. "That's still nice in my opinion."

With a shake of my head, I bent to kiss her. Sometimes, her sweet mouth was just asking for it, especially when she was flirty like that.

Bear bumped against my leg and I finally, though reluctantly, pulled away. "You ready to go?"

Dove grinned. "Nan is going to be over the moon."

As we loaded up into the truck and eased off the property, I eyed the entrance to the tree farm as we passed it. I'd been debating something and wanted to bring it up, but hadn't managed to make myself say it yet.

"What are you thinking?" she asked, uncannily sensing my thoughts, no doubt.

With a light laugh, I glanced at her. Damn, but she was beautiful. The November temps had dropped enough that she was bundled in jeans, boots, and a bright blue jacket sporting a faux-fur-lined hood. It was adorable on her and made me want to bury my face into her neck.

Or maybe I always wanted to be close to her. Not even maybe. I did. And the further from danger and stress and exhaustion we'd gotten, the more the desire gripped me.

She'd resolved to back off on work because apparently, being kidnapped had given her some major perspective. She wanted to find the joy in her work again, and now that she'd let herself take a break, she already felt it coming back. In a surprising bonus to the ordeal, she'd said how meaningful she'd found helping the women on the compound and planned to go back and visit them... when she was feeling up to it. I'd made her promise not to rush it, and I believed her when she said she wouldn't.

For my part, I'd committed to ending my part-time work with Saint and letting myself focus fully on the farm. Maybe I'd help with admin or something at some point, but while we were heading into the busiest season for the farm, staying focused on the one thing was my plan.

And maybe, this one other idea.

But part of me wondered why we hadn't committed to simply spending at least three days a week naked in bed. *Something to work towards.*

"Dorian?"

I cleared my throat, my imagination running away from me. "Sorry. I have this idea, but I'm not sure how I feel about it."

"You could tell me, if you like." Her hand found my leg and squeezed gently.

I resolved not to look at her to avoid distraction while driving and also because I'd end up pulling over so I could kiss her, and we didn't need that kind of delay.

"I've been wondering about a little stand or maybe even a small building next to the trees. I could bake stuff and it could be open, mostly during the Christmas season, but I think I'd like to try to open the apple orchard for you-pick next year, and—"

"Oh my gosh, I love this so much. Yes, and yes, and yes!"

She started asking questions and making suggestions and generally cheering for me and didn't stop until we walked into Silverton Springs Retirement Community and ran into Bruce as he was exiting. After greeting him, she winked at me and slipped inside to see Nan while I chatted with Bruce.

"Good to see you out in the world," he said, shaking my hand and hauling me into a back-slapping hug.

As he released me, I admitted, "Thanks. Good to be out." And it was. I felt generally less anxious since deciding about Saint, though my pulse ticked up as I pushed forward *now*. "I'd like to talk to you and Wilder this week, if possible."

His eyes narrowed a bit, but his smile didn't dim. "We'd like that. I'm guessing you're going to tell us you're going to focus on the farm?"

I blanched.

He chuckled and patted my back, reassurance in his every move. "I've been expecting it, but not because there's anything wrong." He held my gaze, that steady, open quality disarming as ever. "You've been through it, and I don't envy you the journey. That said, you've climbed that mountain and then some. You deserve rest."

An understanding like nothing else in life save those shared between people who had trained and fought together passed between us. My throat cinched tight, and I clenched my jaw against the gathering mixture of relief and grief.

"We all do."

He nodded. "We do. For me, this *is* rest. For a lot of us,

it is. It's okay if that's not the case for you. I think I've known that for a while, but I wasn't sure how to help."

Clearing my throat, I grasped for the right way to tell him. "I didn't want to leave Saint. I love all of you and I don't want to lose you."

He frowned, visibly pained, and held my gaze. "You can't lose us, Stone. We're family, and we're not going anywhere."

Without my permission, my eyes misted, and I nodded. "I think I finally get that."

He cleared his own throat and grinned, his classic Crest smile on display. "Good. Then get in there with your woman, and we'll talk this week. You come in; we'll make the time."

With that, he gave me another brotherly pat and waved as he walked toward the parking lot. I glanced up at the mountains, towering and dotted with pines, no snow at the top quite yet, though it would be any day now, and felt incredible gratitude.

It didn't replace or cancel out the fact that I still had work to do. I was still responsible for taking care of myself and doing the things that would keep me mentally and physically well. But a huge part of it all was knowing I had them—all of the Saint staff and especially the people I'd served with and who'd seen me through my darkest hours. I had them, and even though I'd known it somewhere in me, maybe down in my gut, I knew it with my head and heart now, too.

With one final breath of the crisp air, I entered the building and found my way to Nan's room. Inside, Dove was showing off the contents of the pastry box.

"There he is. Get in here, you! I want to try these things and I was told we couldn't until you're here to see my reaction." Nan said this as she waved me in from her recliner. "She said apple turnover and what?"

"Cinnamon scones and then there's a pumpkin coffee cake I'm testing out, too."

Nan fell back, a hand on her chest. "My dying wish is to be buried with my grandson's pastries."

My heart stopped.

Dove's mouth dropped open. "First, ew. No. You are not being buried with food and second, don't talk about your dying wish because last I heard from Dr. Daniels, you are healthy and hitting triple digits—"

"Bah," blurted Nan, interrupting Dove's rant.

Hands on her hips, Dove tsked at her nan. "You will! And third—" Her blue eyes flicked to mine and she bit her lip. "You just called Dorian your grandson."

Did she think I'd be bothered? Upset? Awkward? If so, she hadn't gotten the message well enough yet.

"Oh, please. You'll be married before my next birthday!"

Dove blinked, evidently horror-struck.

Holding back a laugh, I asked, "When's your birthday?"

Nan tucked a few strands of her short, silvery hair daintily behind her ear, then ran two fingers sweetly over Bear, who'd clearly found a new love. "March."

Dove covered her mouth.

"Don't you think, Dorian?" Nan asked, no attempt to hide her smile.

Dove rushed to me. "I'm so sorry. This is awkward. She's—"

"I sure hope so," I said, speaking to Nan but eyes locked with Dove's.

Her open mouth snapped shut before opening again. "Wait. You—you hope we'll be married before March?"

"Yes. As long as that's what you want."

She gripped my wrist. "I do. But, wait. Are you serious? Are—are you asking me to marry you?"

Nan cackled.

"Not yet, honey. But very, very soon, if that's alright with you."

Her cheeks flushed crimson, and she beamed. "That is very alright with me."

Dove

Bear frolicked along the path in front of me. I swore he was even happier now that the weather had turned cold.

It'd been a week since Nan had dropped her *married by March* theory and I still hadn't recovered. But would I ever recover from the utter bliss getting to be with Dorian was? Probably not. And honestly, I was embracing it.

Granted, I'd also been a tiny bit on edge, wondering when he planned to ask me. I was a woman of the twenty-first century so yes, I could ask him if I wanted. But he clearly had plans and I wasn't going to pretend I *wanted* to ask him.

For a girl who'd never really had someone choose her except her own grandmother and female friends, the thrill of Dorian choosing me? I didn't know if I'd ever get over it.

I'd tried to relax and forget about the whole thing,

reminding myself it'd happen when it happened. The holidays were coming, and it was about to be a hugely busy time for Dorian and the farm. I'd never wanted a huge wedding, nor did I have the money for it, so we didn't need to have a long engagement, especially if he wanted to be married by March.

Really? March?

A thrill swept through me at the thought, right along with a little pang that Nan would be my only family there, whenever it happened. Not that I would've tried to invite Hawk before the whole kidnapping thing, but I wouldn't now. I still hadn't spoken to him, and honestly? I didn't plan to.

Something had shifted inside me regarding him as I took care of woman after woman, who'd all been there after either being groomed or coerced by various people of Patriot Ridge—I just knew. Only one of them had admitted to being there under duress, though, and that told me far fewer people were in jail now than should've been. That garbage human Jeb Johnson got a pretty minor sentence since he maintained he didn't realize I hadn't come willingly and somehow his lawyer sold that to the judge. *Sure, guy.*

But Hawk? He'd had a hand in abducting me *and* he'd shot Dorian. He'd be gone for a while. And after seeing all those women, clearly downtrodden and maybe all part of Jeb's weird harem? No. Just, no. We had nothing in common except our past and that didn't mean I had to give him any part of my present or future. I'd tried. I'd made a valiant effort at times, even, and I wasn't going to do it anymore.

Nan agreed I didn't owe him anything, and her blessing sealed the deal. I didn't need to hear his cruel words or even bear his silence if I told him how awful he was. I suspected he probably knew it, and if he didn't, nothing from me would change that. I hoped maybe he'd heal someday, somehow, but it wasn't on me to do that for him.

Bear's bark pulled my attention to him where he'd stopped a ways down the lane, then trotted back toward me.

"What'd you find, Bear?" I asked, crunching in the fallen leaves to catch up with him.

He got within ten feet of me, then circled back and trotted along. Maybe I was moving too slowly for him?

But as I rounded the slight bend, my heart leapt, and it clicked. Dorian stood at the edge of a big quilt in the exact spot where we'd had our first picnic months ago. A basket sat on the blanket, and my handsome man shifted from one foot to the other before he froze himself still.

My pulse skyrocketed because in my gut, I knew. *This is it.* That little nervous movement, plus the *major* spoiler alert from Nan...

"Well, hello there, Mr. Forrester," I said, trying to maintain some semblance of calm as I approached.

Bear circled around me, then ran to sit by Dorian. He smiled down at his dog, then back at me as I arrived in front of him.

"Hello, Ms. Jensen." He took my hand and immediately dropped to one knee.

I gasped. "Wow. Right down to it, huh?"

He nodded. "I can't wait anymore. I want to spend the rest of my life with you, Dove. You're the most incredible woman I've ever met and I count every moment with you to be a gift. I know it won't always feel like that, but I want us to choose each other over and over again as we grow old."

I was crying. Just instantly crying.

He chuckled softly. "Your heart is so tender and beautiful. You are generous and loving. I chose this spot because it was here, at our first picnic, I knew I loved you. I'd known from almost our first interaction it was possible. You were just so silly and unabashed."

We laughed together at that, no doubt thinking of my breaking and entering.

"I've been working on myself, on healing, for a while now. I don't know what's ahead, but I can promise you I will not stop working toward health. I realize it's a risk to be with me—no, no, don't worry, let me finish."

About to spring to his defense, I pressed my lips together instead, forcing myself to listen.

His warm, calloused hand squeezed mine. "It's always a risk to commit to someone. We're imperfect, and being together doesn't magically solve all our problems. I'm not whole because of you. You didn't save me from the depths of my despair, and I didn't save you."

A laugh tripped out of me. "Um, you literally did save me."

He chuckled and shook his head. "Okay, maybe in one sense. But you know what I mean, right? We're not suddenly entirely different people because we love each other."

I nodded, appreciating the point.

"The good news is, we also *are* different people. You've changed me and impacted my life in incredible ways and I hope I've brought good to yours."

Tears again. "You absolutely have," I said, voice watery.

"This has gotten away from me, so I just want to ask you..." He swallowed, dropping my hand for a moment and pulling a small box from his pocket. He pulled it open, revealing a classic plain band and gorgeous diamond I couldn't even make sense of. "Dove Jensen, will you marry me?"

I laugh-cried out, "Of course I will. Yes!"

And then he was on his feet hugging me, twirling me around while Bear barked and leaped along with us, then kissing to seal the moment. After laughing and crying a little more, he wiped my tears and we just stood there holding each other, glowing.

Honestly, I wouldn't have been surprised if you could've seen us from space.

"I love you so much. I can't believe this time last year, I hardly knew anything about you and here we are, about to get married," I marveled.

He brushed some hair out of my face and gazed down at me. *Ugh.* His expression was all tenderness and heat and definitely meant we were not going to be here long enough to enjoy the picnic.

"We don't have to get married before March. She was joking, and though I'm very happy with that timeline, there's no rush. We do have a lot of things to talk about and I don't want you to feel anything but happy and excited about it."

I sighed, loving his consideration. "I won't feel rushed. I'd marry you tomorrow if I had a dress and all my friends could come."

He chuckled and grinned at me, joy so clearly sketched on his face, I had to kiss him again.

"I do have one more important question," he said, his face sober.

"Oh. Sure. 'I'm quite at my leisure,' as they say." I winked.

His brows raised, a twinge of skepticism before he said, "I lost a bet this last week with Pedro. He usually plays

Santa for the 'Weekends with Santa,' but... it's on me this year."

I blinked, then cackled. "Oh my gosh, I cannot *wait*."

He tipped his head side to side. "Well, here's the thing. I thought maybe, you could be my Mrs. Claus."

I giggled, the thought of me and Dorian in white wigs and him with a giant belly and beard hitting me just right.

"It's funny because I never knew I wanted such a thing, but now that you say it, I can't think of anything better than that."

His eyes glittered back at me, a smile pulling his lips on that handsome face. "I can't imagine anything better than you."

I shook my head once, knowing the truth. "Than us."

And turned out, I was right.

Thank you for reading Anything For You. I hope you loved it! Read on for a bonus epilogue to wrap up the whole series!

BONUS EPILOGUE

A few years later

Bruce

Leo snuck up to me, dark curls springing from his head since he'd been refusing a haircut, and peered into my arms.

"You see your little sister, buddy?" I asked my strapping little toddler. He was three and a half, and so gigantic, people sometimes mistook him for older. Almost a preschooler, but they often thought he was kindergarten or more.

Well, unless he was standing next to Will Rawlins, in which case he looked normal-sized since Will already looked about seven at nearly five years old. No one was surprised Beast's child had turned out to be a giant just like his dad.

"She's nappin'," Leo said, his personal lilt making him sound a bit like a tiny Southern gentleman, and it killed me every time.

"She is. You can play with her later, after school, okay?"

I hooked an arm around his waist and hauled him in for a hug. He pressed a kiss to my cheek, then blew one to "RoRo," as we'd all ended up calling Kiley Rose, and ruffled her auburn wisps of hair. I released him, and he bolted across the space back to the little child gate where Nikki waited.

My heart leapt and my stomach clutched low. It'd been a busy few weeks and we hadn't had nearly enough time together. But soon. I had some time off coming up, and she was taking it, too, so we could all just relax. Kiley would come home for the break between semesters, and I'd breathe easy with all my people under my roof.

Though times like these—visiting the daycare for "Afternoon Snuggle Time"—felt pretty damn perfect, too.

Nik winked and gave a little nod. She mouthed "I love you," and I just grinned at her, the ridiculous reality of my love for her causing her cheeks to flame.

"Oh, for crap's sake, will you guys never get over each other?"

My head snapped in the other direction to see Kenny snuggling his twins, one in each arm, in a rocking chair in the corner. Their IVF had finally worked and there'd never been a happier human being than Kenny Carmichael the day those babies were born. Except maybe every day after, since that was just him.

"Like you've gotten over Elizabeth?" Adam asked, changing his youngest's diaper on the other side of the room.

Tristan peeked in where Nikki had just been standing. "Is he really hassling you? This from the man who tears up anytime he so much as *looks* at his wife these days?"

Kenny scowled back at Tristan. "You're one to talk."

Tristan remained unmoved. "I'll cry as much as I want

to when I look at the woman who just carried my child for nine months." Then he dropped to one knee, his boy Tommy just behind him with energy absolutely vibrating off his little frame. "You want to say hi to the Uncs before we go?"

Tristan stepped out of the way so Tommy, the same age as Leo, could say hi to the men he affectionately called "the Uncs."

We'd all done it, this natural thing that when any of us had kids, we called each other aunts and uncles instead of Mr. or Mrs. It just fit in the context of being people who had chosen to function as family, and as our kids grew, we saw the value more and more.

"Hi! Unc Barbie, tell the babies I love them, and Unc Doc, you're doing great. And Unc Jaws, she's really cute and I'm gonna marry her when we're both big, and now I'm going to Unc Beast's to play with Will, bye!"

He darted away down the hall, and Tristan shook his head. "He was recently devastated to learn he can't marry Winnie."

We all chuckled, familiar with Tommy's lover boy nature.

"She doing okay?" I asked, glad to see my friend after he'd been out for the first part of his parental leave.

He beamed. "Amazing. She's in the car—wanted to get out of the house, so we're taking Ally for a drive after we drop Tommy with Jess and Will." A screech and then a cackle had my calm, steady friend's head snapping to look down the hall, then he hollered, "Gotta go!" and jogged after his son.

We all shared a look, enjoying the chaos for our friend. One wild part of parenting alongside friends was our different methods for caring for our kids, but also the varied personalities. Since Tommy and Leo were nearly the same age, we often saw the intense divergence between them.

Apparently, Tommy had gotten Tristan's mom's fire, and Leo seemed to have a huge amount of Nikki's quiet, thoughtful nature. She claimed he was more like me, but whatever mix he was, I loved him. And I couldn't wait to see what this little spitfire in my arms turned out to be. At just shy of twelve months, she was a mini boss and I suspected we were going to understand Tristan and Winnie's lives with Tommy a bit more.

"Hey." Beast stepped through the door, Cookie behind him, and extended his arms to Kenny. "Gimme."

Barbie scrunched his nose, but happily handed over one of his babies, right as Cookie held out his hands for the other.

The daycare and preschool we'd built not long after Will was born and two other Saint employees became pregnant had become one of the best parts of the business. Nestled on a corner of the property in a separate building, there was a huge outdoor play area with a ridiculous series of playgrounds geared toward different ages that Cookie spared no expense on. As the kids got older, we'd added a preschool, which had been hugely popular, especially due to the ever-present need for quality childcare. Now we had about half community families and half Saint families using the facility.

But this? Snuggle time? It'd been Kenny's idea, and it was maybe the best thing we'd ever done. Any afternoon parents were welcome to come in and snuggle their babies. Of course, anyone could do this anytime. But to someone who'd never had this closeness, never had doting parents or even the chance to be near his sibling until far too late, it embodied how sweet our lives in Silverton were.

As Beast and Cookie settled into their seats and tucked their given Malcom-Carmichael twin into their arms, I sighed.

"I think coordinated snuggle times is a real triumph," Kenny said, leaning back and tucking his hands behind his head, eyes closed.

"So you can nap while your friends hold your babies?" Cookie asked, no malice in his tone.

He and Beast came to our weekly scheduled time to get their baby fix, as Beast had once explained. Jess's pregnancy had been miserable enough they'd decided one was the perfect number, and Cookie and Elise had recently started fostering to adopt two amazing kids who were in elementary school.

Barbie snorted. "Let's not pretend you don't love it even more than I do, Sir Beast-a-lot. We both know you're obsessed with the twins."

Beast grumbled but then traced one of the baby's eyebrows with an expression so protective and reverent, there was no arguing Barbie's point.

"I don't pretend I don't love it," Cookie said, smiling down at the twin he was holding. Honestly, when they were bundled, I had no hope of telling them apart.

"Where's Stone?" Adam asked, settling into his chair with his tiniest little person, Darcy Jane.

"Right here, sorry."

Stone showed up in the doorway, bending to unlock the gate while his gaze remained on the eighteen-month-old in his arms.

Barbie popped up and jogged to the gate, unlocking it so our friend could get in.

"Daddy late. But Daddy here." Sweet little Lila snuffled and repeated herself. Her hair sprouted from two dark little pigtails on either side of her head and her bright blue eyes were even more startling than usual thanks to the tears tracking down her full, red cheeks.

Dorian hustled in, dropping a bag and settling into the sofa next to me.

"I'm so sorry, little one. Daddy's car broke down, so I was late. I didn't mean to make you worry." He clutched her to him, snuggling his tearful daughter, before pulling back. "I'll try my best not to be late again."

Those big, bright eyes blinked and she said, "Bear help you."

We all chuckled, and Dorian did, too. It was possible his little angel of a child loved his dog even more than she loved her parents. No doubt she'd love the new little baby who'd arrive in a few months ferociously, too.

Apparently, her faith in Bear couldn't be shaken, even if her faith in her dad temporarily was.

He grabbed a book from the basket set on the low coffee table in front of us and showed her. She beamed, and after wiping the lingering tears from her face, she turned to me.

"Oh hi, Unc Bwooss." Her little voice was so precious. "Babies are sleeping." Though it sounded more like *sweeping*.

"Yeah, the babies are tired. Are you?"

She yawned but shook her head. "No, I not."

I grinned at her right as Dorian did, and then he started reading.

I took a beat like I tried to every time we did this, stepping back from the hassles and harried schedule of work and life and obligations to soak in this moment. Wilder, no longer a daycare daddy now that his youngest had reached kindergarten, held the fort at Saint Security in such moments. These men had been my family for years now.

We'd been through untold challenges while active duty and an incredible adventure since.

Sitting in this peaceful space with the chatter of kids and a baby crying somewhere down the hall, for a moment I could hardly breathe past the enormity of it all. We'd all made it out, made the transition to the civilian world, and we'd all found what we'd been looking for. Purpose, family, home, community.

Here we were. In the throes of wiping noses and changing diapers and teething babies and figuring out what it looked like to parent, we were doing it together.

"Love you guys."

Barbie's words came, putting my thoughts into words. A chorus of "you, too" rang out, even from Beast, and then Lila's little voice came again. "You, too, Unc Barbie." *Bahhby.*

Stone's hand ran over Lila's head in a gentle caress, tucking her closer as her blinks grew heavier.

We exchanged glances, somehow connected in this moment of surreal peace and gratitude.

We were the veterans of Silver Ridge, the men of Saint Security, and we were home.

Bruce Camden

Saint Security 10-Year Anniversary Celebration

I took the stage after a quick kiss from Nik, the spotlight shining down on me and making the audience disappear.

For the ten-year anniversary of Saint Security's founding, we'd decided to do a big fundraiser celebration and invite anyone who'd ever worked for Saint plus all the "friends of Saint," as we liked to call them.

As a company deeply invested in the community, we shouldn't have been surprised by how many people had bought tickets, but seeing the grand ballroom at the Silver Ridge Resort packed to the gills made the nerves for tonight increase a touch.

Standing at this podium like I was some superstar where I couldn't see the people listening? No.

"Could we drop the spotlight, please? I feel like Bri up here, and that's not going to work."

Everyone chuckled as the spot dropped away. Many glanced around to find where Bri Williamson, still as handsome as ever and world-famous, sat with his wife and Saint mainstay, Eddie. Bri waved gamely.

I relaxed now that I could see Nik sitting at head the table with Wilder and Sarah, Oak and Winnie, Doc and Jo, and Barbie and Elizabeth. The table next to them held Beast and Pop, Cookie and Elise, Stone and Dove, Eddie and Bri, Hijack and his husband, Joseph.

We had two more tables of local Silverton office Saint employees and four more for the other stateside offices. The expansion we'd undergone in ten years was mind-boggling when I saw it laid out like this.

We had tables full of Silverton PD, and Sheriff Ryan and his wife had come from Juniper View. The Washingtons hosted a table for our Europe office, and everyone in the community, from our original investor, Julian Grenier, to the local celebrities like the Morrison family, to the actual celebrities like Calla Rice-Saint, Maddie Reynolds, and Jenna Halter, dotted the room.

Then there was the military support, some of whom had retired since this all started, and a handful who were still active. The Cardinals had all showed with their spouses, and Wave had come with his wife. Our old JAG pal Justice came, and so many others it was hard to name.

It was overwhelming, standing here, and a surge of emotion hit me as I took it all in.

"Speech!" Kenny shouted, because of course he did.

The chuckles filled the space and it was enough to help me get a grip.

"He's right, time to get on with it, huh?" I smiled, and everyone laughed generously. I fiddled with the notecards I'd sketched my remarks on, then dove in. After thanking everyone for being there on my behalf and cracking a joke about also doing the speech for Wilder, because everyone knew he wasn't about to get up in front of the room and give a speech—killed, by the way—I launched into the heart of it.

"When we left active duty, I think most of us experienced something similar. There's some freedom, a great deal of relief, and there's also this rather daunting wide-open future. No one's telling you what to do. No one's telling you where to live, or when to show up to work, or even what clothes to wear. When you spend most or all of twenty years or more of your formative years adhering to military principles and demands and expectations, and you have a job you can easily convince yourself matters not only to yourself because of the paycheck, but to your neighbors and family and even the nation, because of the mission? That's different than leaving some other things, I dare say. And when you leave that? Well, first there's this moment of, 'thank God!' And then, not long after that, you think, 'now what?'"

Light laughter rippled through the audience. They were

with me, and I hoped most especially my fellow Saint staff were.

"Wilder and I had a vision and we were incredibly lucky, or blessed, or mathematically likely" —I paused and grinned at Nikki, who gave me a regal and sexy little nod while people who knew her chuckled— "to find people who saw something in it. And we couldn't have set up in a better town."

I led the applause for Silverton and made a point to make eye contact with the mayor and city council members, then the police chief and anyone else I could. Might as well grease the wheels, even now, especially since it was true.

"But the magic of Saint isn't in the fact that we hire the best of the best from the most elite units and agencies the world over, and do top-tier work with incredible resources in less time than any of our competitors in cities ten times as large," I said, a grin on my face as people whistled and applauded.

"Okay, well maybe it's not *just* that." I laughed along with everyone else, relieved they were playing along and letting me have breaks so I didn't speed-talk through this too quickly.

"In truth, the magic is in our bond. Some of us arrived here having forged a bond in battle. Some of us developed it working together. And I know I speak for Wilder, too, when I say it's the thing we're most proud of. We're a company who values its people first."

I could feel the moment getting the better of me, the reflection on years past and plans ahead, and I wanted to get through this so we could get on to the main events. "We've got chances to see what's in store for Saint Security going forward, but I want to say this: thank you. Thank you to every person who put their faith in Saint and made the leap of moving to this small town to work for us. Thank you for letting us pave the way to the next part of your life. Thank you to the family and friends who've supported them as they've made that transition from other realms to this one, and thank you to those who've hired us, because without you, we wouldn't get to do what we do."

I flipped to the last card.

"In ten years, we've accomplished more than I could've imagined when we set out—and I'll admit it, once I got out of the overwhelm when I first moved here, I started dreaming big. I never imagined we'd have two international divisions, two other city-level expansions, and so many offerings here in Silverton." Applause followed so I waited for it to die down.

"I wouldn't have imagined we'd have so many amazing people finding their partners and settling into a life where they love their work and they have time to love their families and live their lives. Where they have struck a balance and pursue what they want to. Where they can grow and change, and maybe that means stepping back"—I looked at Dorian—"or maybe it means stepping up." I winked at Kiley, who rolled her eyes but beamed back at me.

"This is too long already, so let me just say, with every bit of me, thank you. Thank you for letting this dream come alive and become a home to so many amazing people and thank you for the brilliant things you'll all do in the days and years to come." With one last nod, I slipped off the stage to the sound of raucous applause and, embarrassingly, a standing ovation.

In the minutes that followed, each of the team greeted me with hugs and thanks. Some had tears and some just smiled, and all of it gave me so much joy.

I'd arrived in Silverton the guardian of my little sister

with no hope of really living my life until she left high school. I'd figured I'd work hard and wait it out. Nikki taught me I didn't have to delay my life and it was probably the most valuable lesson I could've learned.

It helped me realize I needed to be encouraging each of my people to do the same. In many cases, like me, they'd waited until the end of their military career to pursue their own interests or even their own happiness.

Shaking hands and hugging each of these people, so many of whom had found their partners and started families... there was nothing better.

"To Saint Security," Kenny said, voice rising above the din and raising a glass of champagne higher.

"To Saint Security." The voices of hundreds of people, the wonderful people of this community and the surrounding area that had become our home, rose around us.

I'd always wanted a place that felt like mine. It was the story of so many of us who'd been transient for years, or who'd been all too aware that our military careers would only last so long.

Now?

I've proudly and emphatically found home in Silver Ridge.

Thank you so much for reading Dove and Dorian's story, and if you've been through it all with the team, the entire Veterans of Silver Ridge Series!

If you haven't read from the start, get to know Bruce's story in Made For You.

If you're wondering about Sheriff Ryan, well... he's getting his own book, fear not. Get to know him and his small town of Juniper View.

And if you want to see where it all started in Silver Ridge, check out the Silver Ridge Resort series where you can learn about the Morrison family, their rockstar son Jamie Morris, and how the small town expanded into a world-class resort destination under the tutelage of a grumpy half-German man besotted with the Morrison family's only daughter.

Finally, get the latest release news and bonus content by subscribing to Claire's newsletter: http://www.clairecainwriter.com/newsletter

AUTHOR'S NOTE AND
ACKNOWLEDGMENTS

I have... feelings.

Completing this book marks the end of my third small town series and my fifth series over all. Sometimes I feel still "young" in this business, and in many ways, I am. In others I feel downright crusty and jaded. What I come back to with each book is the utter delight I feel that I get to write books about people falling in love for my job.

This book in particular is one I've been looking forward to... and low key stressing. Any time I get to the end of a series, I feel major pressure to wrap up all the threads and make both the couple *and* the series have a happy ending. But this book is one I've *felt* coming since the moment Dorian popped up on the page. I knew he'd been through some hard stuff, and I knew he deserved a happily ever after with someone who would love him just exactly as he is— enter Dove. I have to say I'm not sure I've ever had more fun or shed more tears while writing a book. It was truly a wonderful time watching this soft, sweet story unfold. And gosh, writing the epilogues back in Bruce's POV was emotional! But I hope you enjoyed it and I hope you know that yes, of course we'll see these folks down the line in the Claire Cain world. Promise.

It's wild that I was writing the first book of this series before my littlest turned three and now she's graduated pre- school and heads off to kindergarten in the fall. My biggest kid just turned thirteen—what? All three of my kiddos bring me so much joy and are the best cheerleaders. Of course my husband is the key here—he's the one who encourages me at every step and does super hot real life romance things like demanding I get the label printer because I deserve it—love you so.

Thanks to my moral support and the best neighbor ever, Brianna Goodwin. The miles walked and talked have kept me sane and filled with joy—thank you, dear friend!

Huge thanks, as usual, to Genny Carrick for her thoughtful and effusive comments. This book may end up being written for just you and me, and I'm perfectly fine with that.

Thanks to Amanda K for your thoughtful insights here.

Thank you to Jess Mastorakos for yet another amazing cover and for your time spent making Bear look just right.

Zee Monodee, I appreciate you so much! Your enthusiasm and help in this book and the series as a whole has been invaluable and every book we get to work on together drives home how grateful I am for you!

Huge thanks Theresa Schultz of Marginalia Editing for your careful proofread of the final version.

There are so many amazing readers who've given their support to this series. Bookstagrammers and readers who've sent me messages and hyped the series as it has come out, or those who've discovered it along the way. There is **nothing** better than hearing from you and knowing this series has meant something to you.

So this is just to say thank you to all of you who've been here long before the Veterans of Silver Ridge series and to those who've discovered Silver Ridge through it. Thanks for being here, thanks for sharing about this series, and thank you for reading. It's because of you I get to do this, and I'm truly grateful.

I'm sad to say goodbye to the series, but you've already met some of the players in the next series, and I suspect this won't be the last book set in Silver Ridge I write. So, like we say in the military when it's time to move on, it's not goodbye... it's *see you later*, Silver Ridge.

ABOUT THE AUTHOR

Claire Cain lives to eat and drink her way around the globe with her traveling soldier and three kids, but is perhaps even happier hunkered down at home in a pair of sweatpants and slippers using any free moment she has to read and cook. Or talk—she really likes to talk. She has become an expert at packing too many dishes in too few cabinets and making houses into homes from Utah to Germany and many places in between. She's a proud Army wife and is frankly just really happy to be here.

You can also join Claire's facebook reader group for exclusive content and fun: https://www.facebook.com/groups/clairecain/

Website: http://www.clairecainwriter.com

E-mail: Claire@ClaireCainWriter.com

Newsletter sign-up for new releases, exclusives, and freebies, including a free book:

http://www.clairecainwriter.com/newsletter

amazon.com/author/clairecain

bookbub.com/authors/claire-cain

instagram.com/clairecainwriter

facebook.com/clairecainwriter

goodreads.com/clairecainwriter

pinterest.com/clairecainwriter

tiktok.com/@clairecainwriter